D1508864

A SCANDALOUS AFFAIR

"Leave this house—or me?" she softly challenged. A trickle of sweat ran slowly down her spine.

Chad stood, then deliberately moved toward her. His index finger extended and traced her damp hairline. He stepped closer, the hard peaks of her swollen nipples grazing erotically against the white ribs of his T-shirt. "What if I said both?"

"Then I'd tell you there was no reason for you to leave."

She could feel the race of his heart pounding against the walls of his chest. Its exaggerated rhythm matched the rapid beats of her own. She stood perfectly still. It was up to him. He would make the first move and then she would surrender to him, to his advances, to his caresses.

"Sam." His voice came from somewhere deep in his gut. "Being here." His eyes roamed across her face. "These weeks have been heaven and hell."

He took her hand and placed it on his heart, and she felt the racing beat of it. She couldn't breathe. Words danced without meaning in her head, tumbling from her lips in a soft puff of moans and tender whimpers.

"I wanted to wait," he murmured, brushing soft titillating kisses along the supple column of her neck, while his free hand found the dip of her waist, his thumb caressing her ribs, then the sensitive underside of her breast. "But I can't."

A
SCANDALOUS
AFFAIR

DONNA HILL

BET Publications, LLC

ARABESQUE BOOKS are published by

BET Publications, LLC
c/o BET BOOKS
One BET Plaza
1900 W Place NE
Washington, D.C. 20018-1211

All Kensington Titles, Imprints, and Distributed Lines are available at special quality discounts for bulk purchases for sales promotions, premiums, fund-raising, educational, or institutional use. Special book excerpts or customized printings can also be created to fit specific needs. For details, write or phone the office of the Kensington special sales manager: Kensington Publishing Corp., 850 Third Avenue, New York, NY 10022, attn. Special Sales Department, Phone: 1-800-221-2647.

ISBN 0-7394-1591-3

Printed in the United States of America

CHAPTER ONE

Associated Press—*In a massive march staged to protest the alleged shooting death of African American Roderick Fields by four white police officers, more than 200 angry residents filled the streets last night in front of Washington, D.C.'s police headquarters at 300 Independence Avenue N.W. The protest was led by civil rights activist Samantha Montgomery, daughter of noted legal defense attorney Justin Montgomery and Congresswoman Vaughn Hamilton-Montgomery (D-Va.), working in unison with several local organizations and unions. Montgomery, who has been extremely vocal concerning police abuses, later said in a statement: "The police in this city have declared open warfare on the African American. This is the sixth gangland-style shooting death by police against 'alleged' suspects of the African American persuasion*

in eight months," Montgomery *vehemently stated under the
white heat of camera lights and photographers' flashbulbs.
"It is painfully obvious that DWB, or driving while black,
is a crime punishable by death in this city—and it will
stop."*

*Roderick Fields, an eighteen-year-old African American,
was gunned down in a hail of bullets during an alleged
routine stop and search on Eighteenth Street N.W. around
midnight on Monday. His two male companions were also
hurt. One youth is listed in grave condition with a gunshot
to the head, while the other is described as seriously critical
with a bullet lodged in his spine.*

*In a hurriedly announced late-night press conference, a
police spokesman identified the four officers involved in the
alleged shooting as Detectives Alan Montana, Josh Hamlick,
Lawrence Stavinsky, and Vincent Dorsey. None of the officers
have made statements to the media, but according to their
lawyers, they were acting in self-defense.*

*Montgomery's stepsister, City Councilwoman Simone
Montgomery, has been equally assertive in her cry for sweeping police reform and a federal probe into recent abuses
during her ongoing campaign for the Assembly seat in her
district. The councilwoman was unavailable for comment
on this latest incident, according to her spokesman, Adam
Parsons.*

*Although tensions were high, there were no injuries or
arrests during last night's protest. A date for a hearing for
the officers has not been set but a preliminary meeting with
law enforcement officials to discuss procedures used in the
fatal incident is slated for this week, according to a police*

statement. The mayor's office has not issued any comment on the march.

Laying *The Washington Post* on the seat next to him, Chad Rushmore closed his eyes and clenched his teeth in seething disgust. *Nothing ever changes,* he thought.

He turned his gaze, unseeing, out of the 747's window, the clouds floating by in a silent stream. He'd spent the last four years touring third-world countries, analyzing international and civil rights laws. He'd seen atrocities that haunted him at night, broke him into cold sweats during his dreams. To return home to a country that prides itself in justice for all, only to see affirmative action overturned, the Voting Rights Act under review, black men hunted like animals and gunned down in streets across the country by police, was to him worse than anything he'd witnessed abroad.

He folded the newspaper in half and stuck it inside the pocket of the seat in front of him. He adjusted his seat and leaned back, finally shutting his eyes to rest. The plane was due to land at Ronald Reagan International Airport in two hours.

It would be good to be back home again. See everyone again. Inwardly, he smiled—Simone and Samantha. They made a formidable team. And he would need all of their skills, all of their energy and resources for what he had in mind.

* * *

Justin Montgomery paced, panther-like across the polished hardwood floors of his artfully designed office. His wife Vaughn's distinctive touch was everywhere, from the placement of the original artwork by Basquiat, Catlett, and Biggers, to the crystal glasses and decanters that glistened like diamonds in the small wet bar on the far side of the spacious but comfortable office. He had to put his foot down when it came to his desk, however. She wanted him to have something contemporary; he insisted on something customary and impressive. So they settled for a rectangular oak desk with a cherry lacquer finish. Women, they had totally taken over his life, he mused not unkindly. And now his daughter Samantha was at it again, and he didn't know if he wanted to burst with pride or turn her over his knee and give her a good spanking.

He turned toward her, his expression a mixture of anger and frustration. His brows drew together. "Did you read this?" he barked, barely containing his ire, not so much at the comments that his headstrong daughter made—once again—but at what could have happened to her as a result of them.

Samantha crossed her long legs and stared at her father head-on. "Are you going to tell me that I'm wrong?" she challenged, loving to duel with the razor-sharp mind of her father. In court, she watched him run circles around the prosecution, hypnotize juries, and simply charm the media. He embodied everything she looked for and respected in a man: integrity, brilliance, a generosity of spirit, loving, funny and handsome. Any man coming into her life would have large shoes to fill.

Justin halted his pacing. "Sam, we've been through this a million times. Spouting incendiary comments in the middle of a high-tension situation is not only dangerous, it's foolish! What if a riot had broken out? You could have been hurt," he added, "or arrested—again."

Samantha bit back a smile, not wanting to incite him any further. She released a sigh, then stood. "Dad," she said as she walked across the room to stand in front of him. She slid her arms around his waist. "You worry too much. I'm a big girl. And you should know me well enough by now to know that I'm going to speak my mind and if it upsets a few people, well . . ." She shrugged her shoulders. "I get my name in print," she added, teasing him with a smile.

"This isn't a joke, Samantha," he returned, trying to keep a straight face. But the truth was his daughter had the uncanny ability to wrap him around her finger with a simple smile. He knew he overindulged Samantha, but it was only because he'd missed so many years of her life when his ex-wife, Janice, her mother, disappeared with her. He'd been so devastated by the loss of his daughter that he'd single-handedly launched Child-Find, an organization dedicated to finding abducted children and reuniting families who'd been separated. But it was Samantha's determined spirit that brought them together. The same defiant spirit that kept her name and provocative actions on the front page of the newspapers.

Ironically, it was Child-Find that reunited his stepdaughter, Simone, with her mother, Vaughn. His and Vaughn's marriage had not only united them as man and wife, but made sisters of Samantha and Simone—the two most willful, stubborn, single-minded young women he'd ever run across, barring his beautiful wife, of course. He was surrounded by them, and if he didn't stand his ground, they'd likely railroad him into anything, with their sweet smiles and sparkling eyes. And he loved them all, madly. He hoped that, with Chad returning to the States and back at the law firm, the two of them could manage to level the playing field just a bit. Chad did have a way of keeping Simone on simmer. Samantha, however, was a different story.

Justin kept his poker face, eased away from Sam's embrace, strolled toward his desk, and sat down in the leather chair he'd spent years getting to conform perfectly to his body. Vaughn begged him to get rid of "that ratty old chair," but it was the one concession he would not budge on. A man had to have something. Besides, it felt too good, especially after a grueling day in court.

He swiveled his chair so that he faced his daughter. He stroked his smooth brown chin. "What are you planning to do, Sam? You have everyone all charged up about this case. Now what?"

Samantha Montgomery pressed her lips together, thoughtful for a moment—her even, dark golden features the perfect landscape for incredible gray-green eyes, just like her mother Janice's—and settled into that expression that boldly faced the cameras. She crossed her arms.

"I intend to take this as far as it will go, Dad. All the way to the Supreme Court if necessary. I'll rally the people together, we'll march on Capitol Hill, outside the precincts, we'll have all-night vigils—I'll do it by myself if I have to, but I will be heard. These people will be heard. I won't sit back twiddling my thumbs when there's open warfare on the minorities of this country. I can't. And I don't think you expect me to."

Justin stared at his daughter, and he knew by the fire in her eyes and voice that she meant every word of it. And nothing in heaven or on earth would stop her.

He breathed deeply, afraid for her and incredibly proud at the same time. He and Vaughn had their hands full with their two fiery daughters. Samantha and Simone's relationship was phenomenal. They were closer than many blood sisters, sharing every-thing from clothes to opinions. Nothing came between them. They fed off each other, fueled the energy that kept them both in the limelight. Now, with this latest incident, Samantha was campaigning in the street and Simone was active on the legal front, pressuring the Attorney General to launch an investi-gation. This was just the beginning, and he knew it. Thank heavens they were both grown and living in their own apartments. Three of them in the same

house would be more than any man should be compelled to endure.

"What can I do to help?" he finally asked.

A half smile inched up the side of Samantha's
mouth. She tipped her auburn head of shoulder-
length dreadlocks to the side. "Keep some money in
reserve—just in case I get arrested again."

CHAPTER TWO

Simone maneuvered her midnight blue Mazda 626 expertly around the snakelike traffic on Pennsylvania Avenue. It was nearly six-thirty, and rush hour—truly a misnomer—continued in earnest.

A copy of *The Washington Post* lay folded on the passenger seat. The high school graduation picture of shooting victim Roderick Fields smiled back at her, full of hope and possibility. She could feel the anger tug at her insides and burn her throat. She'd spent the better part of her morning talking with his distraught parents and the families of the two surviving victims. It was a painful process, made more so by the senselessness of it all. Yet even more frightening was that the Roderick Fields case was not an isolated incident.

The number of unwarranted police shootings of unarmed black men was making a steady and terrifying rise across the country.

Sighing, Simone tried to push the events of the day behind. She would meet with her staff in the days and weeks to come to discuss a plan of action as well as how best to incorporate her ideas of police reform into her campaign for the Assembly seat.

Right now, what she wanted was to concentrate on the visit to her parents' home.

Simone checked the time on the dashboard. If traffic held steady at its snail's pace, she'd probably arrive at the Arlington town house in about forty-five minutes.

A slow smile of unforgotten memories slid across her polished lips. In forty-five minutes, she'd see him again. *Chad.*

Four years. It felt like a lifetime since the last night she'd spent with him. They'd been together that entire evening, speaking in low, intimate tones, laughing softly, touching often, the way lovers do, even though they'd never crossed that invisible line.

It was perfect. Too perfect almost, Simone recalled; from the gourmet food and exquisite wine, the balmy spring air, perfect starlit sky and most of all, the way they connected that night. It was as if they could read each other's thoughts, anticipate every need before a word was spoken. A kind of telepathy of the hearts.

She'd had "a thing" for Chad since her early days as a young intern at her stepfather's law firm. Even then, Chad Rushmore exuded an aura of assurance and total male sensuality that could not be ignored. Combined with his brilliance, good looks and warm personality, Chad was a dream come true for many women.

But their relationship didn't leap off the pages with the intensity of a romance novel. Rather, they began as friends, he being her support and confidant when she'd discovered the real identity of her mother and the circumstances of her birth. And their relationship remained that way until the eve of his departure that took him out of the States for four years.

The high-arching passion in which they'd found themselves that night stunned them both. Perhaps it was the wine, Simone often thought, the incredible atmosphere, conversation and the knowledge that the moment may never come again.

They'd just finished an incredible dinner in a swank eatery in fashionable Georgetown and were driving aimlessly around town, listening to WHUR. "I know a great place just outside of D.C.," Chad had said in that rich baritone that caused shudders to run along her spine.

Simone turned to glance at him. He kept his eyes on the road. "Where?" she asked, almost too eager to prolong their time together, she realized.

"It's called Harvest House . . . a small bed and breakfast."

Her heart thumped, then settled into a more reasonable rhythm.

Chad turned to her, his dark eyes roamed over her face. "Only if you want to," he said gently. "We can have separate rooms. Whatever. No pressure. No strings. I just want to spend some more time with you."

She thought about it for a moment, contemplated the possibilities—and the consequences. "Sure. Why not?" she answered, simple and direct, the way she was about everything.

When they arrived, Simone was instantly captivated by the Old World charm of the rambling building, which looked to be a converted mansion snatched from the pages of a Civil War history book.

Chad held her hand and led her to the front desk.

"Do you have any rooms available?" he asked the desk clerk.

The middle-aged woman with slightly graying hair smiled brightly and opened an oversized, leather-bound register. "Name?"

"Rushmore, Chad. I . . . uh, don't have a reservation," he added.

The woman frowned for a moment, then her expression cleared like a cloud passing over the hillside. "Well, Mr. Rushmore, you're in luck. My reserved clients aren't due until the weekend. I have three rooms to choose from: one facing the garden, one along the side—but very private, and one on the ground floor, which gives you easy access to all of our amenities."

"We'll need two rooms."

"One," Simone piped in, and squeezed Chad's hand.

He looked down into her eyes, saw her intentions

reflected there. "Are you sure?" he asked quietly under his breath.

Simone nodded.

"One room, please," he uttered, his voice low and personal, his gaze fixed on Simone's face.

After checking in and exploring the accommodations, Simone and Chad took a tour of the grounds, then sat for a while in the cozy den, talking about his impending trip and looking into the flames that pulsed in the fireplace.

But the inevitable, the underlying reason for their being there arrived, no longer held back by time and circumstance. And almost as if by tacit agreement, they left the room with the fire and danced to one of their own making.

There was no hesitation, no fumbling moments of embarrassment. It was as if they, this time between them, had always been, only waiting for the perfect moment to expose itself.

Chad walked toward Simone as she stood framed in the moonlit window. Watching him come to her, she imagined him as the dark knight, the virile seducer. Her mouth curved into a smile of invitation.

His right hand, smooth for a man, reached out and tenderly stroked her cheek, cupping her chin, easing her face closer.

A warm breath was all that stood between them and their first kiss, as Simone raised her mouth to taste his. Sweet, shocking sensation rippled through her limbs, the energy, the heat of it pooling in her center. A lightness of being, that's what she thought through the waves of euphoria.

Chad pressed the full length of his body against her. Every line, every curve, every dip was defined, one fitting within the other. She felt the distinctive pulse of his erection swell against her stomach. She wanted him lower, needed to feel him between the heat of her thighs. But she couldn't rush this. Tonight was to be taken slow, savored and sipped like a fine wine.

So they toyed with each other, from tender nibbles on exposed necks, to long deep kisses lavished over yearning mouths, to hungry fingers seeking warm flesh. They taunted and played, laughed, sighed and groaned, danced against the moonlight, their beautiful naked bodies gleaming like polished wood sculpture in its glow.

When Chad cradled her body against him and gazed down into her eyes, Simone was certain, at that instant, he had more than entered her body, he'd penetrated her soul, the only thing separating them was the thin sheath of latex.

The exquisite shock of it set her entire being ablaze. She became sensation, gratefully submitting to the push and pull of him. But Chad wouldn't give himself over that easily.

He slowed his dance inside her until he barely moved at all. The thrust was almost indiscernible, which made it all the more maddening. She felt her walls clamp around the length and breadth of him, demanding that he fill her, complete her, satisfy her.

In turn, she raised and lowered her hips in a slow, sensual spiral and reveled in her power when he groaned in sublime agony, trapped within the deep, wet hollow that made him shudder, advance and retreat, and urge in a hot whisper to give him more of the same.

But still Chad refused to succumb to the temptation that writhed beneath him. Her hot passion spurred him on. He wanted to hear her moans, her sighs, the sound of his name on her lips. And he made it happen over and over again as he dipped deep and long into the honey, then pulled away until only the tip touched her throbbing outer flesh.

Her body trembled, heated. Tighter she gripped her thighs around his waist to capture the pleasure that rose at a blinding speed within her.

"Let go," he whispered in her ear. "Let go and come to me." He cupped her breasts completely, capturing her peaked nipples between his fingers. And the heat began, starting at her toes, winding its way along the lines of her strong legs, settling for a moment in her hips, rising to the pit of her stomach, then returning to that hot, dark, damp place where she held him, exploding in a torrent of white light and pulsing, shuddering release.

Chad held her there, suspended, wouldn't let her go, turned up the heat with a deeper thrust, pulled her closer, sealed their bodies, letting his empty completely into hers.

For several moments they lay there, locked together

in the final throes of aftershock, the tiny tremors continuing, their breath pushed out in deep, hot riffs.

And they kissed, touched, slept, still connected.

The blare of a car horn jerked Simone out of her daydream. Blinking quickly and shaking her head to clear the vision, she eased across the intersection.

Her heart was racing and she could feel a distinct wetness between her legs.

Chad.

Sure, there'd been other men in the four years since that single night. Some momentarily took her mind away from him, but generally not for long.

Chad.

Tonight would be the first time she'd seen him since she watched him board the plane to Uganda. *Four years.* Things changed. People changed. Had he? Had they?

No strings, remember?

CHAPTER THREE

Vaughn wearily changed out of her fitted navy blue suit and hung it among the rows of other tailored suits and dresses that filled her walk-in closet. She pulled in a long breath. Somehow, she'd have to ease into the next gear and raise her energy level if she expected to play hostess.

Her day at her congressional office had been grueling at best. The phone ran nonstop from seven-thirty that morning with calls from reporters, her constituents, and colleagues, all wanting to know how she felt about the latest instance of police shootings—and most of all, her feelings about her stepdaughter Samantha's caustic statements.

Her head throbbed as she padded barefoot to the

bathroom and popped two extra-strength Tylenols without water.

She gazed intently at her reflection in the gold-framed mirror. An attractive, deep brown face confronted her. She could see the fatigue in the subtle puffiness around her almond-shaped eyes and the tension that drew a deepening furrow between her tapered brows. Vaughn slowly turned away at the sound of the bedroom door opening, then closing.

A sudden, familiar warmth inched its way through her body and a smile eased across her full mouth.

She stepped out of the bathroom. The expectation and excitement she felt the first night she'd met Justin Montgomery still made her heart race five years later.

The instant he saw her, all the tension melted from his body and he remembered all over again why he'd married her. Vaughn was everything he'd wanted in a woman. She was intelligent, sensitive, determined, beautiful and the most incredible lover. Even in her forties, Vaughn Hamilton-Montgomery could give these young girls a run for their money.

"Hey, baby," he crooned, quickly wishing that the rest of the night would be theirs and not shared with the arrivals of their daughters and Chad. But that was selfish. Unfortunately, when it came to Vaughn, that was the way he felt.

Vaughn crossed the carpeted floor and became enveloped in Justin's strong embrace. Instinctively, his long fingers gently kneaded the taut muscles of her back, then her neck.

Languidly, she lifted her chin, her rich mouth eagerly awaiting to be baptized by his.

The kiss was slow and sweet, the tenderness born from years of knowing each other flowed through them.

Marriage was bliss, Vaughn thought, feeling her body warm to a sizzle, and she wouldn't change a thing—except the loss of their baby. For that she would always blame herself—her drive and her ambition—the catalysts for her miscarriage. She'd known how much Justin wanted a child between them, and she'd deprived him as surely as if she'd told him no. And now it was too late, she was sure. They'd made love without protection for all the years of their marriage—and nothing.

She held him tighter, lingered over the kiss a bit longer. Every day, for the rest of their life together, she would make it up to him. That was a promise she had no intention of breaking.

Justin, with a groan deep in his throat, reluctantly moved away. He gazed down into her eyes.

"You look tired, babe." He brushed her shoulder-length hair away from her face, tucking it behind her ear. "Rough day, huh?"

Vaughn released a heavy sigh. "That's putting it mildly. It was totally draining." She took a seat at her dressing table, crossed her ankles and swiveled the chair to face Justin. "There's going to be trouble, Justin."

He slowly nodded and lowered his muscular frame onto the edge of the bed. "I know. And it looks as if our daughters are going to be right in the front of the line."

Vaughn pressed her lips together. "You know they're both right. Things have gotten totally out of control. Not just here, but across the country." She wrapped her arms around her waist and shivered. "It's terrifying, especially for black males."

"Believe me, I agree one hundred percent. But I guess I'm just like every other parent: why my children?" He chuckled derisively.

"I know. But I'm proud of both of them. They have the kind of values and vision that's been lost these past generations. After the sixties, we became complacent, Justin, simply because we could drink at water fountains, sit where we wanted on a bus or in a diner, and move into neighborhoods we'd been banned from."

"Legally mandated integration was just a Band-Aid for what really ails this country. Racism," Justin added. "The Band-Aid covered the sore for a while, but now the decay is oozing out of the sides. The hate is still festering underneath."

"I'm willing to do whatever is needed to support them on the congressional floor, or in the street," Vaughn said, the fire underscoring her words.

"And so am I."

They held each other with just a look, their commitment to themselves and their children needing no more words.

Justin pushed out a breath, and slapped his palms on his thighs. "So—what time is this shindig?"

"Nine."

Justin checked his watch. "I promised Chad I'd pick him up at the airport. His plane lands at seven."

Vaughn rose and gently kissed his lips. "Go take a quick shower and change. You don't want to rush."

Justin grinned. "Yes, dear."

She playfully swatted his arm. "I'll go see what Dottie planned for dinner, while you're in the bath."

Dorothy Beamer had been hired during Vaughn's abbreviated pregnancy to help around the house and look after Vaughn. Dottie was more than just hired help, she was her friend. When Vaughn lost the baby, Dottie insisted on staying, and on nights like this one, Vaughn was glad for Dottie's comforting presence.

Moments later she heard the rush of the shower as she made her way downstairs. She had a good life, she mused upon entering the high-tech kitchen. She had a great career, a fabulous husband, wonderful children and enduring friendships. Yet she couldn't help but feel that the foundation of it all was shifting somehow, about to change. Possibly forever.

CHAPTER FOUR

Samantha pulled her candy-apple red Mustang convertible behind her sister's Mazda just as Simone was cutting her engine. She picked up her purse and briefcase from the passenger seat and slid out of the car in concert with Simone.

The locks on both vehicles beeped simultaneously, sounding in an uncanny harmony, and the two striking-looking young women laughed in unison.

"Hey, sis," Samantha greeted, her wide mouth blooming into a smile. She strutted toward her sister, her sneakered feet moving soundlessly across the pavement.

Simone took in her stepsister's carefree attire and casual attitude, both more than adequately camouflaging the keen mind and dancer's body. Samantha Montgomery was probably one of the most powerful women in the post-civil rights movement era. At first glance, the unknowing would mistake her ingenue appearance for the actions and mannerisms of a young college coed. That was the first mistake, to underestimate her, to misjudge her by her look. Simone always believed that her cunning sister should have gone into politics herself—made a run for public office. But Samantha insisted she'd rather fight in the trenches than from the air where you couldn't make out your target.

"Hey, girl," Simone greeted in return, planting a kiss on Samantha's cheek.

"I thought I'd see your name smeared all over the papers today along with mine," Samantha teased, slipping her arm around Simone's slender waist as they walked toward the house. Samantha truly admired her sister and her ability to contend with all the bureaucratic bullshit and still get the job done despite the odds against her. She definitely had her mother's warrior spirit, Samantha mused. When it came to dealing the political deck of cards, Vaughn and Simone were at the top of their game.

"I got honorable mention," Simone joked. "I'm sure they'll get to me before the week is over."

Samantha tipped her head toward her sister. "Not to change the subject, but isn't that Dad's car?"

"Yeah, so?"

"So he must have already picked Chad up from the airport. Wasn't his flight due in at seven?"

Simone's pulse began to throb at her temple. Her throat was suddenly dry. She swallowed. "Yeah, I think so," she finally uttered, trying to stay calm.

Samantha beamed. "I can't wait to see him." She walked faster toward the front door, nearly dragging Simone in the process.

Suddenly, what Simone really wanted to do was run back to her car, turn on the engine and speed away. For weeks, right up until a few minutes ago, she'd been living for this moment, acting it out in her head, rehearsing what she would say, how she would smile and respond when he kissed her cheek.

Samantha stuck her spare key in the door and turned the knob. Simone froze. Samantha turned her head toward her and frowned. "What's wrong?"

Simone blinked. Her smile flickered like a fading light bulb around the edges of her mouth. She shook her head briskly, the sleek, blunt-cut hairstyle rippling past her cheeks. "Thought I forgot something," she lied smoothly and wished she hadn't. Instead, she wished she could tell Sam about the butterflies that were rampaging around in her stomach, or the hot and cold flashes that had taken over her body. But she didn't. She couldn't. In all this time, she'd never said a word to anyone about that night. Not a word. It was all she had left of him after his plane soared away—her dream and her fantasy—and she hadn't wanted to share it with anyone, not even with her sister.

So, here she was, locked in place in front of her parents' house, her heart racing, her palms sweating, and the best explanation she could come up with was she thought she forgot something.

Simone put on her best smile, slipped her arm through her sister's and crossed the threshold. Hey, this was the millennium. No promises. No strings.

Justin rose from his relaxed position on the couch when Simone and Samantha entered the living room.

"There you two are."

Simone's eyes quickly took in the very classy decor of her parents' home, with its gleaming hardwood floors, stylish high-arching ceilings, working fireplace and perfect combination of carefully selected antique furniture. Chad was nowhere among the splendor.

"Hi, Dad." Samantha kissed his cheek and went straight to the bar, mixed herself a short screwdriver and took a quick sip before Simone left Justin's embrace.

"Where is our guest of honor?" Simone dared ask.

"In the spare room, changing. He should be out in a minute."

Samantha sauntered over with her drink and took a seat on the paisley-patterned chaise lounge. "Ahhh, that feels good," she sighed, stretching out her long legs. She shut her eyes. "Any more heat from the other night, Dad?" she asked, referring to possible fallout from the protest.

"You need to talk to your mother about that. Her office was bombarded with calls all day."

Simone and Samantha groaned in harmony. Hearing their father blast them out was one thing, but their mother was a different story. She was merciless. When angry, she was not one to pull her punches.

"You two should groan," Vaughn said, whisking into the room with the same vitality that captivated her constituents. Gone was the woman who was bone-tired and deeply worried about her daughters. In her place was a charming, charismatic hostess who looked poised, relaxed and revived, as if she'd just gotten up from a nap.

Vaughn crossed the room, greeting each daughter with a warm kiss and a hug. "But we'll put all of that aside for the time being and just enjoy the evening. Dottie fixed a great meal and my goal tonight is to relax with my family."

"Sounds good to me," Samantha said with relief.

"I'm going to see if Dottie wants me to bring anything out," Simone offered, pushing herself up from the couch.

Justin turned on the stereo and the sweet serenade of Sarah Vaughan singing "My Man" followed her down the foyer to the kitchen.

When she entered, everything seemed to stand still. He had his back turned to her, unaware of her presence as he was wrapped in animated conversation with Dottie.

"You sure 'ave been missed," Dottie was saying in her lilting Jamaican accent.

Chad laughed lightly. "It feels good to be back, Dottie, it really does," he uttered in earnest. He clapped his palms on the countertop and pushed up from the stool. "I guess I'd better join my welcome-home party."

"Good to see ya, dahlin'," she said, patting his cheek in her customary motherly fashion. "Ahhh, Simone, come take this tray to the folks," she said, noticing her standing in the archway.

Chad slowly turned toward her and his easy, inviting smile spread across his full mouth—one that Simone would never forget. His lids, fanned by curling lashes, rose, revealing the stomach-tumbling sparkle in his eyes.

Simone's breath rushed from her lungs, then caught and held in her throat before releasing in a nervous giggle.

Chad walked toward her, arms outstretched as he gathered her close to his body in a tight, welcoming embrace.

For an instant, Simone pressed her head against his chest, shut her eyes and listened to the steady beat of his heart. She could have stood there forever, inhaling the scent of him, comforted by the strength of him, but of course that was a silly daydream of a one-time fantasy.

Simone stepped back, praying that her smile wasn't as shaky as she felt. She blew out a breath. "Well, look at you. Traveling suits you."

He bowed modestly. "Thank you, ma'am. You look great yourself."

An awkward moment of silence floated between them as they each took an instant to revisit the past.

They stood there stiffly, quietly trying to force down the uneasy surge of memories.

"I, uh, guess we can catch up later. I'd better get this food out there to the starving masses," Simone quipped, needing something to fill the blank space between them.

Chad nodded and stepped aside. "We definitely will," he said quietly as he watched her take the tray from Dottie and hurry back out front.

She looked good, Chad thought as he took his time entering the front room. He wondered how often, if ever, she thought about that night between them. He did. Often. It was one thing that kept him grounded as he traveled from one country to the next, sleeping in countless hotels and hamlets he'd sooner forget.

Why hadn't they stayed in touch during the past four years? he wondered. Many times he'd considered writing to her, just to let her know she was in his thoughts. But he hadn't and neither had she. And as the days turned to months and then years, the reasons for doing so grew dim. After all, he reasoned over and over again, they'd made no promises, had no commitments to each other. And from her reaction at seeing him again, perhaps it was just as well.

He put on his game face and joined the party.

CHAPTER FIVE

Dinner was a robust affair with flowing conversation, laughter and numerous trips down memory lane, and enough food to feed an army. Stuffed with good will and a solid meal, they collapsed into respective spots of comfort in the living room. Soft music flowed from the high-tech stereo system, adding another layer of relaxation onto the group.

Vaughn half sat, half reclined in Justin's arms, her lids growing heavy with each passing moment, even as Justin and Chad carried on an invigorating conversation about new evidence that could totally exonerate the defamed O.J. Simpson.

"From what I've heard, there was suppressed evidence of a phone conversation between Nicole and her mother after the time she was supposed to be dead," Justin stated.

"You know as well as I do that they'll never let that brother rest in peace," Chad responded. "It's bad enough that they couldn't convict him of murder. Folks are still ticked off about that."

"You're right about that," Samantha chimed in. "But imagine if it could be proved he was on a plane to Chicago and she was still alive chatting with her mother? The fallout from that would be worth the price of admission and then some."

Everyone nodded and mumbled in agreement.

"Believe me, if there really was evidence to clear him, they'd bury it until the man was six feet under."

"The restitution, not to mention the total loss of political credibility, isn't something they'd risk."

"But how often have we seen this happen?" Samantha asked, her dark eyes polling the occupants of the room. "It's going on right now, even as we speak. The black man is always assumed guilty until proven innocent. If they're not killed first."

Chad edged forward on the couch and clasped his hands in front of him. He looked pointedly from one to the other, making sure he had their attention. "There were several reasons why I decided to come back when I did," he began in deep, measured tones. "One, of course, is that I missed everything and everyone." For a breath of an instant, his gaze focused on Simone's face, then moved away. "The other, and even more important, is that I think it's time—past time—that we took measures into our own hands."

Justin stiffened and Vaughn quickly put a halting hand on his arm.

"What are you saying, Chad?" Samantha asked. "We turn the clock back to the sixties and get out in the street—in force? Because if it is, I'm with you one hundred percent." She made sure not to catch her father's eyes, but she knew he was glaring at her.

"I was thinking about something that will provoke national attention, with no physical risk to anyone," Chad offered.

The room fell silent, quiet enough to hear each chord of the keyboard played by Herbie Hancock on a track from his latest CD. He almost sounded like the Herbie of old, the young wizard on the ivories with Miles, stretching an old standard to its creative limits.

It was Chad who broke the spell of the music as he spoke solemnly to the others. "I want to launch a class action suit against the D.C. police department on behalf of all victims and families of victims who have been killed, beaten, and unjustly jailed by police. I want it to set a precedent so that the same lawsuit can be brought in every state across the country. I want to bring all of those families together in one massive action against the Justice Department of the United States. It may not be possible to get everyone on board, but it's worth a try."

The silence deepened as the mammoth ramifications of Chad's daring proposal took root. Carefully, he gauged one expression after the other, measuring their reaction. Justin looked stern and contemplative,

Vaughn awed. He could see the wheels spinning in the eyes of Samantha and an awakening on the face of Simone.

"It can be done," he added. "People engage in class action suits all the time for poor or dangerous products, illness resulting from improper medication. You name it. But no one has yet to take on the entire law enforcement apparatus, the vicious national policy of police brutality as a whole, the entire machine and mentality that oils them—the Justice Department."

"It would be unprecedented," Samantha finally said, fully grasping the enormity of it.

"But a massive undertaking," Simone added, also thinking of the legal and political maneuvering involved.

"That's why I need your help." He looked with a plea in his eyes from Simone to Samantha. "Simone, you have a strong foothold in the community. You're gaining a political edge and it would give your platform for the Assembly seat that much more bite and focus."

Simone thought about it and knew it was true. This could very well be the key to seal her election run— or destroy it. Any action taken on a federal level was always risky.

"And Sam, you're the fire. You're out there every day, in the trenches. The press knows you, the people know you. And not just here in D.C. Your name gets noticed in the media across the country. You could easily represent the national voice of the people."

Simone glanced briefly at her sister, who looked mesmerized by the possibility, seduced by the beam of notoriety. And in that instant, a twinge of something unnamed lurked and found a dark refuge in the corner of her mind. Her gaze trailed to Chad and the same determined look as Samantha's lit his face. That thing burrowed a bit deeper.

"Are you really prepared—legally—to pursue something like this?" Justin cut in, breaking the trance, scattering the thing deeper into hiding.

"Yes, I am," Chad stated emphatically. "I've been preparing for months. And I'd like you to work with me on the legal end."

Justin looked at his wife.

"You realize that once this process begins and the wheels are in motion, the momentum will be too powerful to stop," Vaughn said, imagining the ripple effect on the Hill, the sides that would be taken on both sides of the aisle—and most of all the toll it would take on her family. She studied the eager and determined expressions of her children, of Chad, who was like a son, and looked across at her husband, whom she trusted beyond measure. She spoke only to him. "Whatever you decide to do, I'm behind you."

Justin squeezed her hand and nodded, both of them knowing his decision.

Chad sighed audibly, then slowly smiled. "We can do this," he said in an almost hushed reverence. "And when we do—everything will change."

*   *   *

Simone helped Vaughn gather up the dishes and load the dishwasher while surreptitiously stealing glances at Samantha and Chad, who were locked in animated conversation, peppered with musical notes of laughter and light touches on a hand or arm.

Her stomach bobbed up and down like a buoy on rough seas, and the tightness in her throat was the only thing that kept her from screaming.

But at what? she wondered, frowning as she turned the dials and the machine churned to life. She had no hold on Chad, no claim on his heart. He was a free man. Free to do as he chose, as was she. So was Samantha. All unclaimed. Then why did it feel as if that weren't true?

Chad was spending his first night in Justin and Vaughn's guest room, both of them adamantly refusing to let him spend the night in a hotel.

Samantha and Simone said their good-byes, giving their parents the ritualistic kiss, hug and promise to call.

Simone stood aside as Chad embraced Samantha, lightly kissing her cheek and conveying something she could not hear. She glanced away.

"We'll talk," Simone suddenly heard close to her ear as her sister sped away. She turned and Chad was at her side, gazing at her in that familiar way of his.

Simone looked up. "Sure."

He leaned down and kissed her cheek. His lips stayed pressed against her flesh for a moment too long and the old sensations roared to the surface. Did he feel it, too? Her heart pumped faster. "It was good seeing you again, Simone," his voice caressed. "You're more beautiful than I remember." His finger stroked her cheek and it took all her will power not to tremble.

"Maybe we could get together—for lunch or dinner."

"I'm really busy, Chad . . ."

He held up his hand. "Hey, no explanations needed. I understand. Maybe some other time." He opened the car door and held it until Simone was behind the wheel.

She stuck her key in the ignition and the engine purred to life. She pressed a button and the window lowered halfway.

Chad leaned down. "Get home safely."

"Thanks," she mumbled and backed out of the driveway.

Chad watched the car until it turned out of the drive and tore off down the smooth, black-tarred road.

Slowly, he turned back toward the house and quietly shut the door behind him.

That night, lying in bed, Chad stared through the sheer curtains that billowed with the light spring breeze and out onto the seamless blue blanket, sprinkled with star dust. He was home, among those who loved him, and it felt good. Very good.

It all seemed so quiet, so perfect, as if all was right with the world. How deceptive a quiet night could be. Behind closed doors, strategies were devised, lies constructed, papers read, televisions watched and lovers loved. He and Simone were perfect examples of a quiet night, both projecting a picture of cool control, an emotional distance, while still maintaining a tangible warmth. He turned on his side, his thoughts still turbulent.

She'd changed. That was obvious. There was a toughening of her edges, a new aloofness that he didn't remember being a part of who she was. Perhaps it was the work, the things she'd seen and had to find a way to deal with. There was no way she could successfully coexist in the world of politics without developing a tough exterior. A shell to ward off the blindside attacks and sudden assaults of the opposition. Beltway politics at its meanest.

Had Simone become hardened inside as well? She wasn't the woman he'd left four years ago. But neither was he the same man. His journey into the abject misery of the Third World, with its many plagues of hunger, disease and war, had awakened something deep inside him. He saw everything around him now with new eyes, saw beyond the obvious to the essentials of things. Yes, Simone had changed. And it was apparent from her response to him that she'd moved on and had no intention of revisiting the past. How did he feel about that?

Truthfully, it was a mixture of regret and relief. Regret that there wasn't a special someone waiting for him, that she was not what he'd imagined during his time away, and relief that he wouldn't be called upon to live up to or recreate what had once been. The memory was always more perfect than the reality. The mind always played tricks with time and emotion.

Maybe it was just as well. He came back for one major reason—to make a difference. That was what he would concentrate on.

Samantha stepped out of the shower and walked nude to her bedroom. She'd completed a full hour of aerobics, light weights and stretches upon returning from her parents' home.

Her smooth, brown, heavenly sculpted body glided by the full-length mirror. The long, sinewy legs, tight thighs—and just the right amount of curve and lift to her behind to make a man holler—moved in perfect motion about the room. She hadn't reached a point yet where gravity had gotten a lock on her, dragging everything toward the ground. Her 36B breasts were still high and firm and she worked hard at keeping them that way for as long as possible.

Samantha sat on the side of the bed, took a cloth band from the night table, grabbed a handful of her locks and fastened a ponytail at the nape of her neck. She checked her bedside clock and disconnected the alarm. Tomorrow she planned to sleep late—at least until eight and not her usual six.

She switched off her bedside light and slid beneath the cool, mint green sheets that matched perfectly with the patterned borders of her off-white walls. Even in the brutal heat of the D.C. summers, stepping into her room always reminded her of an oasis.

Samantha took in a long breath and slowly pushed it out. This had been an incredibly hard week, and the worst was yet to come. Of that much she was certain. But at least she knew she had her family's support. And now that Chad was home—

The sudden rush of adrenaline caused her heart to beat faster and her skin to warm. The notion of what he wanted to undertake had no precedence, at least not on a national level. To be a part of it—to possibly add a page to history, change lives and laws, was a Herculean feat that left her in awe.

She shut her eyes and the image of Chad's face bloomed behind her lids. Her eyes flew open and her entire body tingled.

Chad?

Samantha laughed quietly to herself. Who was she kidding? Chad was the one who gave her that hot flush, that extra beat of her heart. He'd been able to evoke that kind of response from her since she first met him six years earlier. But then, Chad Rushmore seemed so sophisticated and worldly—out of her reach—compared to the sheltered life she'd lived with her mother in Atlanta. She never felt he'd be interested in the woman she was becoming. Strong, driven and politically committed. All still in the bud. So she hid her feelings from him, from the world, hiding behind her books, her studies, her causes, her family.

But now—now she was in full bloom. She knew who she was and what she wanted to do with her life. She had convictions, values and supporters. People recognized her on the street and sought her guidance and assistance any day of any week.

She was his equal now and felt confident in that role, and if the possibility of a relationship existed, now she would have something to bring to it. Her own strengths.

She always swore that all she wanted in a relationship was a man like her father, Justin, and Chad Rushmore was as close as it comes. Seeing him again, being in his presence, confirmed what she'd only imagined.

CHAPTER SIX

Samantha arrived early at her local offices in Georgetown. On a clear day she could glimpse the imposing structure of the Washington Monument, and the outline of the Capitol building. It all looked so pure and powerful, strong and white, symbolic of the freedoms for which men and women fought and sacrificed their lives.

She turned away from the farce that darkened her window and crossed the tiny office space to her cluttered desk, stacked with files, forms, and to-do correspondence. Her assistant and dear friend Mia left her a list of calls to be returned and invoices to be signed. Although it was Saturday, this was the day she accomplished the most. When the phones weren't ringing off the hook, clients weren't running in and out, and her small but efficient staff wasn't pulling her in every direction at once.

This was her time, her quiet time for reflection and reorganization.

Although she'd made a silent vow the night before to sleep later, as usual she was up before the sun, and she had completed her ritual two-mile jog by six.

Energized, showered and her mind crystal clear, she'd wound up at her office before eight.

Moving to the make-believe kitchen—which was no more than a microwave and a miniature refrigerator—tucked in the back of the three-room office, Samantha ran some water in a mug and popped it into the microwave. A cup of herbal tea was just the thing she needed.

With tea in hand, she methodically went through the pile of messages, discarded calls she would not make, and then sorted by order of importance the ones to be made that morning and those that could wait until Monday.

Completing her calls to two reporters, one to her GYN doctor to reschedule her missed appointment and the other to a man who wanted her help in a housing discrimination suit, Samantha then went through the bills.

Although many compared her to the young and fiery Angela Davis, and the now in-your-face Reverend Al, Samantha Montgomery prided herself on several things which gave her an edge over both. One, she began her illustrious career working within the system, not against it. Two, she possessed parents in respected, powerful positions. And three, she had her degree in law, a fact very few people knew—but it served her well.

Her father's dream was for her to one day partner with Chad and run the firm. Especially now that Khendra and Sean had relocated to New York to open their own offices. But that was his dream. At least the part about running the firm. She had no inclination to become trapped behind the bars—no pun intended—of political etiquette and intrigue. Pairing up with Chad, however, was an entirely different story.

Samantha smiled as she signed her name with a flourish on the last invoice in the pile and filled out the accompanying check for payment.

Chad. She glanced at the phone and then at the clock. It was almost ten. She barely hesitated as she pulled the phone toward her and dialed her parents' home.

Simone took the blue plastic basket of laundry and sorted through the clothes as she made the appropriate choices and dropped them into the machine. Adding detergent and fabric softener—because she was never on time with the softener—she switched the dial to HOT and START.

The sound of the rushing water and the low hum of the washer was comforting in a way as she moved through her two-bedroom apartment, dusting, mopping, discarding, and changing sheets and towels. It was nearly eleven, and the pangs of hunger threatened to overshadow her zest for domesticity. She recalled Chad's invitation of the previous night. Maybe she should have taken him up on his offer of lunch—or dinner.

She pressed her lips together, debating whether to call him or not. After all, she didn't want him to think she was too eager, or worse—desperate.

She weighed her options. The worst that could happen was that he would tell her he was busy. The best, that he wasn't and would love to see her.

The phone seemed to beckon her from its perch of honor on the kitchen wall. Twisting her mouth in the final stages of contemplation, she snatched the phone from the cradle and punched in her parents' phone number.

Dottie answered on the second ring.

"Montgomery residence."

"Mornin', Dottie. It's me, Simone."

"Hi, dahlin'. What can I do for you? Your mom and pop are still asleep—or at least they haven't been seen today." She chuckled merrily. "You'd think those two were teenagers." She laughed again and Simone smiled, hoping that one day she'd find not just the lust but the love her parents had.

"No, I wasn't calling for them." She cleared her throat. "Actually, I was, uh, wondering if Chad was around. But—don't trouble yourself," she began to ramble. "If he's still asleep, I can call later or tomorrow. Really, don't bother—"

"Whoa, hold your horses. Chad is out back, been

up for hours. As a matter of fact, he just this minute finished a call with Sam. Hold the line while I get him."

Before Simone could register her protest, Dottie had laid the phone down and was gone in search of Chad.

Now she felt like a bumbling idiot. What would she say? Why was she even calling? This was so infantile. She should just—

"Hello?"

"Hi . . . it's . . . Simone."

"Hey, Simone."

He sounded happy to hear from her, she thought. "Busy?"

"Not at the moment. But I will be soon. What's up?"

"I was getting hungry and I was wondering if . . . you still wanted to . . . go to lunch."

"Uh, you're about five minutes late. Sam just called and asked me to meet her at Cisco's."

There was an uneasy moment of silence.

Sam? "Oh, hey, no problem. Have fun. OK?"

"Sure. Maybe another time. We'll have to get together at some point and talk about launching this case. Hopefully, one day this week."

"Yeah . . . the case." Her head was spinning and she had a sinking sensation in the pit of her stomach. "Anyway, let me run. I'll talk to you."

"Take care, Simone. I'll call you."

She hung up without saying anything further and possibly making a bigger fool of herself.

Heavily, she sat down in the chair. Maybe it was nothing, she concluded—Sam and Chad. Just a friendly lunch for old time's sake. What else could it be?

Samantha arrived at Cisco's at exactly noon. Chad was sitting at the bar of the upscale restaurant with his back to her. She pulled in a breath and walked forward.

"Hi, waiting long?" she asked, placing her hand on his back.

Chad turned his head and smiled up at her. "Not at all. Just got here myself. You want to sit at the bar or get a table?"

She gazed quickly around at the sprinkling of people in the trendy bistro. "Table sounds good to me."

He rose from the bar stool and brushed innocently against her in the process. Samantha drew in a quick breath, slightly unnerved by his touch, and smiled tightly.

Casually, Chad put his arm around her waist and led her to the hostess who sat them.

"What are you in the mood for?" he asked, scanning the menu.

"The house salad is excellent. And I love the Tahini dressing they use."

"I'm still growing." He chuckled. "I think I'll go with the burger and some fries."

The waitress arrived shortly and took their orders.

Samantha folded her hands in her lap. "So, how does it feel being back home?"

His brows rose, then lowered. "Good but strange. Everything seems the same but different. I've been so accustomed to odd languages, customs and time frames—it takes some getting used to."

"Yeah, I can imagine. I know you must have learned a lot."

He nodded. "That I did. I mean, I went abroad with the intention of seeing how unfair the laws are outside of the U.S., only to discover that the real problems were right here at home—disguised as democracy."

Samantha rested her forearms on the table and leaned forward. "How do you plan to go about the class action suit?" Her eyes studied him intently.

"I want to begin with securing a list, from you actually, of all the cases that have come through your office and begin contacting the families. Then I want to work with Justin to review case files and arrest records as well as hospital records."

"Wow. That's quite a load."

"It can be done."

"I'll do anything I can to help. You know that."

He reached across the table and covered her hands with his. "I'm counting on you."

Their food arrived and they ate for a few moments in silence. Samantha was the first one to break it.

"So . . . besides hunting down the bad guys, what do you do these days for entertainment?"

He chuckled. "That's a good question. I haven't

been out socially in nearly four years." Images of his last night with Simone suddenly danced beneath his conscience.

"Maybe we can change that," she said with a bold smile.

Chad cocked his head to the side, a playful glint coming into his eyes. "Are you propositioning me, Ms. Montgomery?"

"Absolutely. All work and no play . . . you know the rest."

"I think I'd like that."

The warm glow in her heart set her face aglow. "I was hoping you'd say that." She almost giggled.

"What did you have in mind?"

"If I remember correctly, you love jazz. Hopefully, that hasn't changed."

"No way. It was one of the main things I longed for while I was away."

"Great. There's a fabulous local band, Magique, that's playing on Wednesday nights. My treat."

"Well, well, a woman for the millennium," he chuckled. "Sounds great."

"What if I pick you up about eight. That will give me enough time to finish up at the office and go home and change."

"You don't have to pick me up. I can meet you."

"My treat, remember? That means transportation is included."

"I was never one to turn down a good deal."

Samantha looked at him from beneath her lashes, stuck the fork in her salad and slowly slipped a mouthful between her lips.

"You've changed, Samantha," he said as if seeing her for the first time.

"I know," she said softly.

Simone stared at the typed words in the book she was reading. All the lines seemed to merge together, not making any sense. Gibberish. She tossed it aside and gazed up at the bedroom ceiling. Her house was spotless. Her laundry was finished. She didn't have to return to work until Monday and she didn't have a damned thing to do in the meantime.

She crossed her legs at the ankle, then folded her hands across her stomach. She was edgy, too full of energy. Her mind was racing. Driving usually helped when she felt this way. The concentration it took to maneuver the roads, the relaxation that came from seeing the landscape spread out in front of her worked to knock the kinks out.

She popped up from the bed, put on her sneakers, grabbed her car keys and headed out.

After driving for a good hour, she took stock of her surroundings and was surprised to find herself on the road to the bed and breakfast that she'd shared with Chad. She kept going. That was then. This is now. A memory. A good time. That's all it was. So why couldn't she just file it away and forget it?

If only it was that easy.

Taking the next exit, she headed back. She needed to talk, get her feelings out, the ones she'd tried to pretend didn't exist for the past four years. And the one person who understood her feelings, her fears and struggles was her sister, Samantha. Her eyes momentarily filled. She'd been so determined not to get caught up in that love trap thing that she'd probably ruined whatever chance there might have been. It had been a matter of priorities. Her career had been more important. She'd been a modern woman of the nineties. No strings. No commitments. So she'd never admitted to anyone, not even herself, how much that one night had meant to her.

And now, she'd gotten what she wished for—a relationship free of commitments and strings. And he was free as well. Free to be with her sister.

"Thanks for hanging with me this afternoon. It was great," Samantha said as they stood together outside of Cisco's. Her voice dropped a note. "I'm looking forward to Wednesday."

"So am I."

Samantha pulled in a breath. "Well, I guess I'll see you."

"Absolutely."

"How long are you going to be staying at Mom and Dad's?"

"I have to start apartment hunting as soon as possible. They keep insisting that I can stay as long as I want, but I can't do that. I need to have my own space. Where I can work and think.''

"I know what you mean. As much as I love them, I love being on my own.''

Chad slid his hands into his pockets. "Are you really on your own?''

"What do you mean?''

"Are you seeing anyone, living with someone, planning to?''

She smiled nervously. "No to all of the above.''

"By choice or circumstance?''

"A combination of both. I haven't come across anyone that I want to be with—like that.''

"Hmm.''

"What about you? Is there a lady in waiting?''

"Not that I know of.''

Silence momentarily hung between them like a sheer veil until Chad brushed it aside. "Maybe if you have some time you can help me apartment hunt.''

Her heart raced. "Sure. Let me know when you're ready.''

"I'll do that.'' Suddenly, he leaned forward and kissed her cheek, not a big brother kiss, but a man kissing a woman kind of kiss. A kiss promising intimacy to come. A kiss which set her entire body to tingling. He eased back. "Good seeing you, Sam. Get home safely.'' He turned and headed for his rented car.

For several moments, Samantha stood there as if

she'd been glued to the concrete, watching him move languidly down the street.

"It was good seeing you, too," she whispered and opened the door to her car. She couldn't wait to get home and call Simone.

CHAPTER SEVEN

Simone tossed her keys and purse on the hall table and aimlessly headed for the kitchen. The drive had done little to unfurl the tight coils of her tense insides. Rather it aggravated her condition.

She opened the fridge, searched through its contents and took out a glass bottle of fruit juice. What she really wanted was a cigarette. A quick, relaxing smoke. But she'd given them up about a year earlier after a severe bout of bronchitis.

Sitting at the kitchen table, she twisted the smooth glass bottle around in her hands, staring blankly into space, and finally her gaze landed on the flashing red light of her answering machine. Slowly, she got up and pressed PLAY.

"Hi, sis, it's me. I have so much to tell you. Call me when you get in," she said, and Simone could hear the high pitch of excitement in her sister's voice.

Simone pressed ERASE. She stared at the phone, debating. A part of her wanted to hear the details and share her sister's excitement. Another part of her dreaded what Samantha might say. Did he kiss her, touch her in that gentle way of his? Did he laugh at her corny jokes and did his eyes crinkle at the edges when he did?

She tugged in a breath. The truth was, she didn't want to know, but she had to.

Simone defiantly snatched up the phone and dialed Samantha's number.

"Hello . . ."

The voice sounded breathless. Simone flinched. Was Chad there? Were they . . . ?

"Hey, sis, sounds like you were running."

"Whew, sorry about that. I was outside when I heard the phone. I was hoping it was you."

"This is your lucky day."

Samantha chuckled, missing the sarcasm. She pranced into the kitchen and skulked around in the fridge for her container of vanilla soy milk. "Guess what?" she asked, following a long swallow of the creamy liquid.

Simone briefly shut her eyes. "What?"

"I had lunch with Chad today—at Cisco's."

"Really." A tense bubble of laughter burst and dribbled over her lips. It was apparent that Chad hadn't mentioned their brief conversation, so neither would she. "You make it sound like more than business."

"Well . . ." She let the word stretch to four syllables. Simone gripped the phone a bit tighter. "What does that mean?"

Samantha went on to explain about their upcoming "date" to the jazz club and Chad's subsequent request for her to help him find an apartment.

"Sounds like you two are going to be spending a lot of time together."

Samantha sighed. "I hope so, Monie," she said, using her pet name for her sister. "I like him and I think we could have something."

"You figured that all out after one lunch?"

Samantha frowned, startled by Simone's sharp tone. "What's bugging you?"

Simone caught herself. "Hey, I'm sorry. I guess I'm just tired and I have a headache brewing. A bit on edge." At least that part was true.

"Did you take anything?"

"No, not yet. But I will." Simone's tight expression softened. Although they were only separated by one year, with Sam being the youngest, early on Samantha had taken the opposite role as big sister and nurturer. Samantha was the type of person who couldn't stand to see anyone suffering or in pain. She somehow believed it her duty and obligation to take on the weight of everyone's ills and find a way to make them better. You had to love her.

"You go and rest. If it gets worse and you need me, just call. OK?"

"Thanks, but I'll be fine. I think I will lie down for a while."

"Good. I'll check on you tomorrow. Later."

"Hey, uh, when are you guys going to the club?"

"Wednesday. Why don't you bring Chris and come along?"

"Chris Walker has risen to the top of my not-to-do list at the moment." She'd been dating Chris for about three months, and although he was smart enough to have "Doctor" in front of his name, it had become abundantly clear, at least to her, that his intelligence was trapped between his legs. Whenever they were together all he ever wanted to do with any enthusiasm was to have sex. Any other activity he was always "too tired" to participate. That wore thin pretty quickly. Their relationship was going nowhere fast.

Samantha chuckled. "Girl, you and men. You shed them faster than I can keep up with. One of these days you're going to have to figure out what you want and stick with it."

"Sam, you don't know the half of it. But that's another story for another day. Anyway, I'll talk to you later."

"Bye."

Simone absently hung up the phone. *Humph. Figure out what I want and stick with it. I thought I had, once upon a time. Guess I was wrong.*

*   *   *

"How's it feel to be back in your own office?" Justin asked, leaning against the frame of the door.

Chad looked up from sorting the files on his desk, happy to see his mentor. He leaned back in his chocolate-brown leather chair and expansively linked his fingers behind his head. "Man, I am home," he stated, enunciating every word.

Justin chuckled and stepped inside. Casually, he gazed around, intermittently picking up and putting down objets d'art that Chad brought back with him from his travels. Statues from Ghana, talismans from Uganda, native cloths from Liberia and fetishes from the Sudan, among others.

Chad monitored Justin's apparent ease and lack of agenda, and knew from years of working with him that he had something on his mind. It was a tactic that worked like a charm with juries, and Chad, too, had mastered the technique—biding his time before making his move. The only unknown factor was *when* Justin would strike. Chad didn't have to wait long.

Justin crossed his arms and pursed his lips as though preparing for his closing argument.

"I have a few concerns I want to discuss with you."

"I figured as much."

The two men looked at each other with quiet amusement.

"You know I think of you as a son, Rush," Justin began, using the name he'd tagged him with since Chad's early days at the firm. "You're one of the sharpest attorneys I've come across in years. I can easily see you winding up in a political office, maybe in the House or on the federal bench.''

"Thank you, Justin. You know your opinion means a great deal to me.''

"However . . .''

"I knew there was a 'however' in there some-where.''

Justin took a seat opposite Chad, crossed his right ankle over his left knee and eased back. "And I'm sure you know that even though I will support you in this endeavor, I have some serious concerns on how this will impact on my family. Simone has always been the more levelheaded, thoughtful one of my children. But she can be willful and stubborn once she sets her mind to something. This run for the Assembly seat is a major step in her political career. And with the Republicans running the show and backing the police, what you propose could severely damage whatever chance she may have. These are very powerful people you'll be battling, and the word defeat is not in their vocabulary. They'll do whatever is necessary to protect the status quo. Don't expect them to just roll over.''

"So what are you saying?''

Justin held up his hand. "Hold on. Sam, on the other hand, will run out into the fray with guns blazing. She's hot-tempered and doesn't care who knows it. Many times she thinks with that big heart of hers and not her head. Did she mention to you the death threats she's been receiving?''

Chad's eyes widened in alarm. "N-no. She hasn't.''

Justin nodded. "I didn't think she would. She believes she can handle everything. This is not the kind of thing you ignore."

Chad leaned forward. "How did you find out?"

"Purely by accident. I was in her office one day when the mail arrived. I saw her face when she opened one of the letters. I made her show it to me. That's when she admitted it wasn't the first one."

"Has anything been done?"

"All the usual precautions. But it's pretty hard to get police protection when they're the very ones you're going after. They won't do anything until after the fact."

"Damn!"

"I hired a private bodyguard. But Sam cussed him out his first day on the job, and pretty much made his life hell. He lasted about a week."

Chad tried not to smile, but he could just imagine Sam working the poor guy over. But he quickly became somber when he reflected on the dark implications of all that Justin discussed. Death threats were serious business.

"What do you want me to do, Justin? Forget this whole thing?"

"No. Not at all. What I do want is to keep my daughters as far out of the picture as possible. I want them out of harm's way. I know that's not going to be easy, given their ethics and personalities." He took a deep breath. "But I don't want them hurt by this in any way. I don't want to see anything happen to them."

"I understand, Justin. But the reality is, Sam and Simone are grown women. If I told them tomorrow that I'd changed my mind, that the whole idea was crazy, they'd take it upon themselves to keep moving forward. You know how they are."

"Exactly. That's why I want you to work closely with me. Involve them as little as possible. Stall them with the big stuff. Keep them in the background."

Chad's brows rose with doubt. "That's not going to be easy."

"None of this is," Justin said. "And it's only the beginning."

CHAPTER EIGHT

"Mia, has there been any word on the condition of those other two young men who were with Fields?" Samantha quizzed as she reviewed the statements from Roderick's family. She was certain the police would try to somehow discredit Fields even if it was with something as inane as cheating on a spelling bee in grade school. She wanted to be prepared for every inevitability, including a leak of some minor juvenile offense to the press.

"No. Nothing new," Mia said, "but take a look at this."

Samantha peered over the top of her thin-framed designer glasses and caught the tight expression on Mia's face. "What is it?" She felt sure she knew the answer before she read the headlines: more tragedy. She picked up the paper. UNARMED MAN SHOT BY POLICE. *The Washington Post* article referred to another New York incident involving some undercover officers who harassed a black man during a buy-and-bust sting. When the victim didn't offer information about the location of a nearby drug den, but rebuffed them, a violent confrontation ensued and the victim, twenty-six-year-old Patrick Dorismond, a Haitian immigrant, was shot dead despite being unarmed.

"Another 'accident,' I suppose?" Samantha said with disgust, quickly digesting the details of the latest killing. She blew out an exasperated breath and pulled her glasses from her nose. "When is this going to stop?"

Mia shook her head sadly, her berry-toned face bearing an expression of grief and denial. She'd been Samantha's assistant since she'd graduated with honors in political science from Georgetown University, and had the opportunity to meet Samantha at a voter registration rally two years earlier. She'd been so inspired by the fire and vision of Samantha Montgomery that she convinced Sam to let her work for free for the first three months—anything so that she could learn. Reluctantly, Samantha had taken her on, and never regretted a day. Mia Opoku was not only the best research assistant anyone could find, but had become a dear friend.

"Maybe when the tides turn, things will change," Mia said without much conviction. "Or when it hits them in the pocket."

Samantha nodded in agreement. Financial remuneration was just the route that Chad intended to take. Reparations paid for police abuses were on the rise around the country. But the scattered legal victories had done little to stem the onslaught of police shootings. She tossed the paper aside and massaged the bridge of her nose.

Muffled conversation from her staff of six and the sounds of ringing phones played havoc in the background.

Some days, like today, she wished she could walk away from it all. Walk away from the ugliness, the notoriety, the rallies, the tension, and simply have a life of her own. A quiet, simple life where her biggest worry was paying the cable bill on time so she wouldn't miss her favorite movie. A subdued existence out of the limelight.

That, of course, was fantasy. She could no more give up her commitment, her quest, than she could give up breathing. It was an integral part of her life.

Samantha gazed up at Mia, who was looking at her pensively.

"You generally don't have 'that look' until Friday," Mia teased, attempting to push away the cloud that had suddenly appeared above her friend's head.

Samantha tried to laugh it off. "I'm not that transparent, am I?"

Mia nodded, lips pursed. "What else is on your mind besides the usual chaos and mayhem?"

Samantha pushed her locks away from her face and tucked them behind her ear. "Chad is back."

"And . . ."

"It was good seeing him." She paused. "More than good."

Mia folded her arms. "And . . ."

"And—well, I just . . . wonder what it would be like to have a real life. Settle down, home, white picket fence, family, kids, you know."

Mia needed to take a seat. This wasn't the Sam she knew talking.

"I like him. Always did," she shyly admitted. "And it looks like we're going to have the chance to work together." She went on to explain Chad's bold idea and all that it would entail. She looked deeply into Mia's eyes. "I know he thinks I'm witty, intelligent, with high morals, a fighter for justice and the downtrodden. But I want him to see me as Samantha Montgomery—*woman*. You know what I mean. But it's been so long since I've even thought of myself outside of my work, I wouldn't know where to begin, where to separate myself. When I called him for lunch, I knew I had it all together. But lying in bed last night, the doubts slipped in. Chad seems perfect for someone like my sister Simone, not me."

"Why do you say that?"

Samantha shrugged helplessly. "She's talented, smart, pretty, and she has a way with men that I've never mastered. It was the one thing I envied about her," she admitted. "Men flock to Simone without much effort on her part."

"So you've become your work?"

"I guess," she sighed. "I live too much in my head. In my job."

"Believe me, I love Simone, but the only difference between you and your stepsister is that she isn't afraid of her womanhood. She embraces it."

"And you're saying that I'm afraid?" she tossed back defensively.

"Thou protests too much," Mia said with an arched brow.

Samantha backed down by degrees, knowing that Mia was right. "OK, OK," she finally conceded. "So now what? What do I do?"

"Depends on how much you really want him."

Samantha's gaze drifted away for a moment. How much did she want Chad? Or was he like everything else in her life, a challenge?

"Well," Mia pushed out a breath and stood. "I have work to do and by the sound of what you told me, so do you."

Samantha blinked and focused on Mia. "You're right. I need to get busy. I'll start pulling files that we've had direct contact with and later today, you have one of the interns make copies. No." She shook her head. "You make the copies. Although I trust Nettie and Steve, they're still young and excitable. I don't want them running back to G.W.U. and Howard spreading the word about what we're putting together."

"Got it. The sooner you get them to me, the sooner I'll have them screened and back to you."

"Before lunch."

Mia gave a thumbs-up and headed for the door, then stopped. "You know if you ever want to talk— about whatever—I'll listen. Might not have much to offer in the way of advice," she teased, "but I'll listen to anything. No judgments."

Samantha laughed. "That's definitely good to know." Her expression grew more serious. "Thanks."

Mia waved and left.

Samantha turned her attention to the stack of reports and statements on her desk. She didn't really see any of it. *Afraid of being a woman.* The telling phrase echoed in her head. Emotionally shut down. Was she? And if so, what was she willing to do about it?

Chad pored over the transcripts and police reports that Justin's secretary had provided for him. Some were a matter of public record, others were cases that Justin, Sean or Khendra had worked on personally.

Sean and Khendra, he mused. Now they were a team. Very effective. Several years earlier they'd successfully won a multimillion-dollar lawsuit in a wrongful death shooting. That was a case splashed all over the New York papers. If he remembered right, the victim's brother, Quinten Parker, launched a foundation for troubled youth with the settlement.

He stroked his chin in thought. Outcomes like that are a start. But the results are contained. His goal was to have far-reaching results—long-term. Black folks would never see reparations from slavery. That was a beaten trail that would lead nowhere. But today, here and now, they had a chance to get payment for their suffering and loss, if they would band together for a single cause before there was no one, not one black man left standing.

"Knock, knock. Can I come in?"

Chad's gaze snapped up and landed on the long, slender form framed in his doorway. For an instant, he saw her silky hair fanned out around her head like a halo, her eyes shut, mouth moist, swollen and inviting, as her body moved beneath him. That was then. It was pretty clear that that chapter in their life was closed.

He cleared his throat and his thoughts. "Hey, this is a surprise." He stood slowly.

"Pleasant?"

He rounded the desk and crossed the room. "Absolutely." He hugged her briefly and stepped back. "Come in and get comfortable. What brings you here?" He went to the small refrigerator, opened the door and peered inside. "Something to drink?" he asked, his voice slightly muffled.

Simone strolled to the couch and sat, crossing her stockinged legs in one smooth motion. It was a very feminine, sexy gesture that was not lost on him.

"Anything cold," she answered, fighting to keep her eyes off his slouched body. "Did you see today's paper?"

"Yeah." He emerged with a chilled can of Coke and an iced tea. He handed the iced tea to Simone and sat on the far end of the couch, draping his arm

along its length. "Just more fuel for the fire, baby."
He took a long swallow of the Coke. "But I know you
didn't come all the way down here to ask me if I'd
read the paper."

Simone averted her gaze, giving him her striking
profile. "No, I didn't. Actually I came to talk to Justin.
But he's not in." *Liar, liar! Why don't you tell him the
real reason?*

"Oh, yeah. He'll be gone the rest of the day. Maybe
I can help you with something."

"No. Just father-daughter talk." She forced out a
laugh.

"How's the campaign going?"

"I'm going to headquarters when I leave here, actually. My staff is out doing polling in various areas of
our district, and I've been trying to concentrate on
strategy and my platform. Now with this class action
suit you want to pull together, I've been trying to see
how best to incorporate it into my agenda, to make
it pay dividends at the ballot box, while weighing what
I can do to help."

Chad reflected on Justin's request: *Keep them as far
away from it as possible.*

He placed a hand on her shoulder. "Listen, whatever you can do is fine with me. But I can handle it.
I don't want any of this to cloud your agenda or
jeopardize your chances for election. This is going
to be a very problematic call, Simone. It could cost
you big-time. I'll understand if you can't give it one
hundred percent. I want you to win. Having you in

office is a greater asset than rallying the troops to storm the barricades.''

Simone stared at him, listened to the words beneath the words. Did she hear sincerity, the ring of truth, or simply that he'd prefer to work with Samantha, build something with Samantha, and leave her alone? It was getting muddled.

"I see," she said finally. She flicked her brows. "So, I hear you and Sam are planning to hang out on Wednesday night." His expression remained controlled, she noticed.

"Yes. it's been a while since I've been on the D.C. scene. It should be fun." His gaze rolled questioningly over her tight expression. "Problem?"

"No," she said a bit too quickly, then rose. "Why should there be?"

"Just asking, Simone. Are you all right? You seem tense."

"Not at all. I just have a lot on my mind. Listen, I've got to get going. I have a meeting at three." She headed for the door.

Chad trailed her by several paces. "We never did get that chance to talk."

"No, we didn't." She kept her back to him, refusing to allow him to see the hurt in her eyes. "But that's old news and a long time ago."

Chad flinched, but held his tongue.

"Take care, Chad."

"You make it sound as if we won't see each other again."

She spun to face him. "You've obviously decided

on what you want to do, Chad. And that's cool with me. We're both adults.''

He frowned. "Wait a minute. We've always been honest with each other, Simone. Why do I feel that's not what's happening now? If you have something on your mind, say it."

Her mouth stretched into a tight, meaningless smile. "Have fun Wednesday." She turned away, then stopped, looked at him over her shoulder. "Don't hurt her, Chad. She's nothing like me. She'll want more than one night." With that she left, leaving him with the sting of her parting words and unresolved feelings they had yet to share.

CHAPTER NINE

Blue Light was packed and there was a line of people waiting for tables, most of whom would have to wait for the second set. Samantha and Chad had arrived early and secured great seats right up front.

Chad dipped a buffalo wing in the blue cheese dressing and savored the spicy flavor. "Hmmm," he hummed in reverie. "I can't remember the last time I had these."

Samantha laughed. "I can tell," she said, eyeing the half-empty bowl.

"That bad, huh?"

"Absolutely."

He wiped his mouth with a pale green paper napkin. "Making up for lost time. What can I tell you?"

"Hey, enjoy yourself."

He looked at her for a moment, took in the sparkle in her eyes and in her smile, the smoothness of her skin, the way her body fit so perfectly in her dress.

"You really look great," he said as if truly seeing her for the first time.

Her face heated, but she didn't look away. "Thanks." She'd worried for hours about what she would wear. Nothing too provocative and nothing too conservative. Finally, she'd settled on a simple peach silk sheath with spaghetti straps and just enough material to cover her from the swell of her breasts to above her knees. Her only accessories were her thin gold watch and a mesh shawl that matched her dress and looked as if it was sprinkled with diamond dust.

"Did you . . . date at all while you were away?" she asked, raising the glass of water to her lips.

"No. I didn't. I was too involved with my work."

"All the time? Even at night? Didn't you get lonely?"

"Sure I got lonely. And no, I wasn't busy all the time, but enough to keep me occupied. Besides, I didn't want to put myself in a position where I became involved with someone and knew I wouldn't be around long enough to take it any further."

Samantha thought about Mia's observation: *Afraid of being a woman.* She took a breath. "What about now?"

"What are you asking me, Sam?"

"Are you planning on staying in D.C. long enough to see if your involvement with anyone will work?"

"I plan to stay in D.C. I don't have any immediate plans for involvement, but things change—every day."

The band, Magique, launched into their first song and further conversation was curtailed—at least for the moment.

"Thanks for tonight, Sam. I had a great time. It was good being out again," Chad said as Samantha eased her car to a stop in front of her parents' home.

"Maybe we can do it again sometime."

"Whenever you're ready. I'm game."

They were quiet for a moment, caught in that questioning moment of "what next?"

"I, uh, would invite you in, but that's kind of ridiculous since you have a key."

They laughed.

"Thanks, but I'll head home. Have a busy day tomorrow. When do you think you'll be ready for us to get together and plan a strategy?"

"Uh, I'm going to try to do as much of it as I can. Believe me, I understand how busy everyone is. And—"

"My father talked to you, didn't he?"

"No. Well . . ."

"You don't have to cover for him. I know he said something. It wouldn't be like him not to."

"He's just concerned, Sam. And I don't blame him.

I should have thought it through before I tried to involve you and Simone. If I were Justin I would feel the same way.''

Samantha could feel herself seething. How dare he? She was a grown woman, capable of making her own decisions. When was he going to let her live her own life? She gripped the steering wheel.

"Take it easy, Sam," he soothed, covering her hands with his.

"That's not the point, Chad, and you know it."

"He told me about the threats. And I'm worried."

She pressed her lips together and stared out her window. "I can take care of myself."

"That doesn't stop your folks from worrying, Samantha . . . or me."

Slowly, she turned toward him, her eyes glimmering in the soft night light.

Chad gently cupped her chin. "I wouldn't want to be the cause of anything happening to you," he said softly. "I wouldn't be able to live with myself." His eyes held her and she wondered if he could hear the pounding of her heart, hear the one thought racing through her head: *kiss me, kiss me.*

Never in his life had he felt so torn. The urge to take her in his arms, feel the softness of her against him, nearly blocked out the fact that once upon a time he'd slept with her sister, carried that one night with him for four years. Did she know? Did it matter to her? And yet, here he was, inches away from her lips, wanting her with an intensity that rocked him.

He was afraid. Afraid of what that meant and where this simple kiss would take them.

And then all at once he tasted her, the shivering sweet sensation of her. He gave in to the tender pull of her mouth against his. Memory faded. It was only the here and now, with Samantha.

She let go, let the moment seize her, savored it, took and gave, and it was just as she thought it would be, only better.

An eternity passed, but it was only seconds, seconds that changed everything—and them.

CHAPTER TEN

Simone couldn't sleep. She was sure if she did, she'd dream things she didn't want to see. Samantha and Chad.

On more than one occasion during the course of the evening, she'd been halfway to her car en route to Blue Light. After all, she'd been invited. So what if she turned up without a date? That's the thought that stopped her in her tracks. She'd look like a fool. She'd look desperate. She'd look like she was spying. And if she went she'd be all those things.

She turned off the television with the remote and the room was enveloped in near darkness, except for the pale light from the sprinkling of stars and the half moon that gleamed outside her window.

She turned on her side. The digital clock stared back at her. One A.M. Did he take her home? Did she let him stay?

"This is crazy," she mumbled into the room. She was making herself nuts. Whatever was going to be would be and there wasn't a damned thing she could do about it. She had her chance. She had it the night at her parents' house. She had it that afternoon in his office. She chose not to take it.

She could have told him how she felt. She could have told Samantha long ago about her and Chad, even if it was about only that one night. That one glorious night. They'd always shared everything. And this one thing she'd kept to herself would come between them. If she let it.

Slowly, she sat up. She'd never been one to back away from anything, to pretend things were as they were not. She always confronted her issues head-on. Her father said that was one of her best virtues and key assets. But now, she felt lost—trapped really— between what was in her heart and what was in her head. Reason never wins out when it goes against the unbridled power of the heart. However, she knew that Samantha wanted to pursue a relationship with Chad. To tell her now about *their* past could ruin whatever chance their relationship may have. And for what? For a man who may or may not still care.

Leave it alone, her conscience whispered. *Let it go.* She knew in her heart it was the right thing to do. But could she?

* * *

Samantha knew it was late, nearly two by the time she settled down for bed. But she was too excited to sleep. Over and over again she relived that first kiss. And though she was no novice in the artifices of men and women, tonight was completely new, truly "the first time."

She wanted to call Simone, try to explain to her how glorious she felt, how alive. For so long, her work, her causes, had been what brought a smile to her face, and prompted her heart to race.

Men, so few and far between, had been mere distractions, not additions to her life. And none could leap the high bar she'd stuck in their path until now.

Simone would understand. She was certain that her worldly sister would know exactly how she felt, tell her what to do next. Simone and Chad were the ones who'd been close before he went away. "He's like a brother to me," she'd often said. "We talk about everything. We're on the same wavelength."

Yes, Simone would understand, share in her joy and calm her fears. But it was now after two A.M. She sighed, tried to calm that giddy feeling that danced in her tummy. It would have to wait until tomorrow.

"This is even more widespread than I thought," Chad said, lines of worry etched across his forehead. "I can't believe the number of abuses. And these are only your cases."

Justin's jaw clenched. "I know. It's the tip of the iceberg, Rush. I can't begin to imagine how many more cases there are in Sam's files, not to mention the ones that don't get reported. How do you plan to pull this all together?"

Chad rubbed his hand across his face. "The hardest part of all this is keeping it as quiet as possible for as long as possible. Secrecy will be the strongest weapon in our arsenal, along with the element of surprise. The last thing we need is to have the police or the government clamp down on us before we get started."

"That's my biggest concern as well."

"My first line of approach is to begin to contact these people directly. Have them come into the office, hear the plan and decide for themselves if they want to pursue it."

Justin slowly nodded. "Have you gotten Samantha's files yet?"

"No. She told me they should be completed by Friday."

"Remember what I said, Rush, about Sam and Simone."

"Believe me, I have."

Justin headed for the door. "If you need any extra help, let me know. I'll get one of the paralegals to help you."

"Thanks, Justin. I appreciate that."

"I want this to work just as much as you do. I only want to protect my girls from the fallout as much as possible."

*   *   *

Simone sat down at the circular conference table for her weekly staff meeting. The topic, of course, was the mini-uprisings across Washington surrounding the Roderick Fields case. To compound things further, one of the other victims who sustained the head injury wasn't expected to make it.

"Reporters have been calling since it happened, Ms. Montgomery," Pam, her chief of staff, stated. "They're all waiting for a comment from you, especially since the incident happened in the district you're running in."

Adam Parsons, her speechwriter and campaign manager, slid the statement he'd put together across the table to Simone. Adam and Simone had worked together since their early days of campaigning for the mayor of Atlanta years earlier. When Simone relocated to D.C., she ran into Adam at a housing demonstration. He was writing speeches for corporate honchos and was bored out of his mind, he'd admitted over drinks. "I want to get my teeth into the meat of things, Simone. Write about something that's going to make a difference, change things somehow."

She'd told him about her political aspirations, fueled by her mother and stepfather, and their fate together was sealed. He became her speechwriter, cheering squad and friend. Simone always believed that Adam felt more for her than adoration and camaraderie. She could tell by the way she would catch him looking at her sometimes, or the notes of encouragement, offers of lunch or a single daisy left on her desk when she was feeling overwhelmed or blue.

Samantha had nudged her repeatedly in Adam's direction over the years, but Simone wouldn't budge. She said she could never have a relationship with not only a staff member, but someone who worked for her.

Simone quickly scanned the two-page document and knew it would be fine before she reached the second paragraph. Adam Parsons hadn't written a word she'd regretted saying in all the years they'd worked together.

"Thanks, Adam," she said, only to him. She tucked the smooth pages into her burgundy leather portfolio. She turned her attention to the group. "We know there's only so much we can do about the situation. Our goal must remain steady and focused. We still have a campaign to run. Adam will incorporate all of these latest incidents into each and every one of my statements to the media."

Pam raised a finger to interrupt. "The latest polls are in and you're up by another six points!" Pam beamed.

The gathering at the table applauded and slapped palms on the table. Simone grinned and held up her hands. By degrees, the group simmered down.

"Another six percentage points is cool, but Vincent McCall isn't going to roll over and play dead. There is still some fight in him yet."

Her Republican adversary, Vincent McCall, had successfully fended off any and all opponents for the prior two election terms, with some very questionable hardball tactics. His reputation as a determined campaigner and solid debater was renowned and several of his opponents saw their election hopes dashed on the stages with him. He had a strong, die-hard conservative following. He had clout with major businesses throughout the district and the ear of many prominent legislators on Capitol Hill. There was no doubt in her mind that he would be a formidable opponent until the very last vote was counted. He would never throw in the towel.

However, he'd made one fatal error. In the wake of violence upon the African American community by the police, he'd sided publicly, on national television, with Police Commissioner Herbert Benz within hours of the shooting. He'd stated emphatically that he had unconditional faith in Benz, the police of D.C., and believed they were doing an outstanding job of ridding the district of drugs and crime. "Unfortunately," he was quoted in the *Post* as saying, "lives are lost in that process. But those are the casualties of war. And this is a full-out war against crime in no uncertain terms."

The toll of innocent victims in the drug war had risen up and slapped him in the face on more than one occasion, but he was too full of pride and his own right-wing rhetoric to back down, and an erosion of his support was beginning to show in the polls.

"Our main goal," Simone continued, "is to stay focused on our agenda and not become overly confident because of polls." She grinned broadly. "And keep those poll numbers rising." The group shared a laugh of agreement. Simone turned to Pam. "What's the game plan for the week?"

Pam cleared her throat and slipped on her glasses. Quickly, she dealt out sheets of paper as deftly as a Vegas casino dealer. The staff followed the list as she recited off each item in her precise Ivy League modulation.

Simone did a good job of pretending to listen, but her mind had veered off in another direction. She couldn't help but think about Chad and Samantha. Probably alone together. She knew how silly this obsession of hers was, but she couldn't seem to get herself together. What nagged her most, she believed, was that she and Chad never really had a chance to see what could have happened between them. Maybe it would have worked and maybe not. But now she'd never know.

"Well, that's it," Pam announced, closing her folder.

Simone snapped back to her surroundings. "Thanks, Pam," she mumbled. "Let's get to work, folks."

Adam glanced at her curiously, monitoring the distracted look in her warm eyes. Something was obviously bothering her. He'd never known Simone to sit through a staff meeting without uttering a word. While the staff filed out, Adam lingered behind. He closed the door after the last person left. She didn't even seem to realize he was there until he spoke.

"What's going on with you, Simone? You were paying about as much attention to this as someone listening to the wonders of garbage disposal.''

The corner of her mouth curved upward before she covered her face in embarrassment. ''That bad, huh?'' she mumbled from behind her fingers.

Adam nodded. ''Very.'' He pulled out a chair from beneath the table, turned it around and straddled it, bracing his arms along the top. ''What is it, Simone?'' he asked, resting his chin on his folded arms. ''You haven't been yourself in days—totally distracted. Where is your head these days?''

Simone glanced at him, saw the concern hovering in the light of his doe-brown eyes, the arch of his brows. Yes, she did need to talk with someone, to get her guilt and her jealousy off her chest.

''I never told you this before,'' she began so softly that Adam had to lean forward to hear her. ''But . . . Chad and I had an affair . . . once.''

Adam generally prided himself on his ability to keep his expression clear and unreadable. He hoped his poker-playing skills were razor-sharp at the moment.

''But then he went away and for some reason we didn't call or write each other. Now he's back and he's dating my stepsister,'' she rambled on, her words tumbling over themselves. ''And I don't know what to do. I, we, never told anyone what happened between us, and . . . oh shit.'' Frustrated, she threw her hands up in the air.

''And you're upset that Sam is seeing Chad because . . .'' He let the last word hang in the air.

Simone pushed out a breath and drew her brows tightly together. "Because we . . . never really had a chance to see what would become of us, if there was anything between us, and now . . . it's too late."

"What is it that you're really upset about, Simone, the fact that Sam is seeing Chad and you're not, or the fact that you really care about him and never told him?"

"Both!" she snapped, annoyed with herself and pissed with Adam for pointing out the underlying causes of her anguish.

"Why haven't you said anything to Samantha— before now? Because you know you can't say anything at this point."

Simone pursed her lips. "I guess at the time I just thought what happened that night was so adult and civilized. Two people who physically wanted each other, no expectations, no explanations." She sighed. "I didn't want it to be important enough to talk about. We made no demands on each other. It was what it was."

"Maybe it was *too* important, Simone. Ever think of that?"

"What do you mean?"

"That for all your modern philosophy, it touched a special place in you and you held onto it, not letting it go because it was all that you had. If there was someone else in your life, maybe this whole thing wouldn't matter so much. And maybe that's why you're clinging to the memory of that one night."

Simone stared at Adam in amazement. It was as if

he'd read her mind—no, her heart. "H-how did you know that?"

Momentarily he glanced away, but not before Simone glimpsed a flicker of hurt in his eyes.

"Been there, Simone. I know what it's like to have someone right within your reach, but you can't grasp them. Or when the opportunity comes to speak up and say what's on your mind, you take the politically correct way out. Yeah, I know all about it," he ended with a slight edge to his voice.

For a moment Simone wondered if he was talking about her—but she couldn't allow her ego to lead her down that trail.

"What did you do about it?" she asked gently.

"Kept busy." He chuckled. "It does help. Date other people, and keep my options open. Find a way to put the past in the proper place."

She sniffed. "I know you're right. It's just so screwed up and emotionally frustrating—especially since he and I . . . and now. . . . You know what I mean. Why am I telling you all this anyway?" She stood. "I must have totally ruined your impression of me." She kept her eyes on the desk while she stuffed papers into her folder. "I'm sorry. I didn't mean to go on like that."

"Hey, it's cool. We're friends, remember?"

"I just feel so foolish."

"Why, because you told me what happened?"

"Yes. Here I am acting like an airheaded teen suffering from puppy love, and I want to run for higher office. What would my voters think?" She laughed, that hollow laugh that comes from the pit of emptiness.

"You're human, Simone. Flesh and blood, someone with feelings. That's nothing to be ashamed of. It's not a bad thing. We all have 'em."

She put on her political face and straightened. "Not me," she announced. "Feelings are too much trouble. They get in the way of thinking. But thanks for listening, anyway." She grabbed her portfolio, tucked it under her arm and walked out, leaving the door standing partially open.

CHAPTER ELEVEN

"Ms. Montgomery, there's a call for you on line one," Mia said.

Samantha barely looked up from her notes and instinctively reached for the phone on her right.

"How can I help you?"

"Sam, it's me, Chad."

Upon hearing his distinctive voice, her whole body seemed to relax and a slow smile of pleasure moved sensuously across her mouth.

Mia grinned knowingly and slipped back out of the room.

"Is this business or pleasure, sir?"

"At the moment, it's business, but it doesn't have to stay that way."

"In that case, get the tough stuff out of the way first so that we can move on to more . . . pleasant things."

"Samantha Montgomery, if Vaughn and Justin could hear you," he teased.

"Ha! My father and stepmother could probably teach me a thing or two," she said, laughing.

"I won't touch that one."

"And on that note—what's on your mind?"

"I was hoping I could stop by your office later today and start reviewing some of your cases."

"We're ahead of you on that. Mia's already taken care of it. They're being entered into a separate database even as we speak."

His dark eyes widened in surprise and admiration. "Great. I'm impressed."

"Hey, this is no mom-and-pop operation around here, brother," she joked.

"So I see."

"Come by whenever you're ready."

"How's three?"

"No problem. I'll make sure you'll have whatever you need."

"Thanks, Sam. I've gone through Justin's cases and compiled a list."

"Bring them with you. We can add them to the computer file. That way everything will be in one location."

"Your staff won't mind?"

"Of course not. It's part of the job. Besides, we want this to work as much as you do."

"Then I'll be there."

"And what about afterward?" she hedged, leaning back in her seat.

"Are you busy this evening?"

"Not really."

"Then we'll play it by ear. How's that?"

"Fine. See you later."

Slowly, Chad returned the receiver to its base, ruminating over his conversation with Samantha. He blew out a breath. Yes, he was attracted to her. Yes, he found her desirable. A part of him wanted to keep it all impersonal, strictly business—understanding the repercussions. Yet, that male part of him, the part that had been lonely for so long, nearly begged for what Samantha was willing to offer. But was that enough to embark upon a relationship? He knew it wasn't. He had to be clear about what he was doing. He needed to be sure that his attraction was not born of desperation, gratitude or availability. Or the fact that the woman he'd thought he'd come home to was not interested.

Samantha was too genuine, too open and caring to be dragged into an abyss of indecision on his part. But maybe if he just gave himself a chance, he could let go of his doubts and move on with his life. It was apparent that Simone had.

* * *

Exhausted from a two-hour session with church and community leaders about funding for a recreation center in her area, Simone finally made it to her car and headed home. Halfway there she had a change of heart. At the stoplight she slipped on her headset, reached for her cell phone and pressed the one button programmed to her mother's office.

"Congresswoman Montgomery's office," the tart voice of Martha Howell answered. She always reminded Simone of someone who'd unexpectedly sucked on a lemon and was annoyed at being tricked. But once you got to know her, she was the sweetest woman on earth, and she loved her mother to death. Martha would do anything for Vaughn, even tell her family to call back at another time when she knew Vaughn was overwhelmed.

"Hi, Martha, it's Simone."

"Hello, darling. How are you?"

"Pretty good. Busy as all hell. But good. How about you?"

"The old knees aren't what they used to be, but no sense in complaining." She laughed lightly. "You want to speak to your mom?"

"Yes, if she's not busy."

"She just walked back into the office a few minutes ago. Let me put you through before she gets involved in something else."

"Thanks, Martha."

Within moments, Vaughn was on the line. "Hi, baby. You just caught me. I was on my way back out the door. What's going on?"

"Hey, if you're busy . . . it's OK. It can wait."

Vaughn knew that tone of need. "What can wait?" she asked quietly.

"Nothing. Really, it's not important."

"It was important enough for you to call, Simone. And whatever I need to do, it can wait until I get there." She paused a beat. "I'm listening."

Simone swallowed and took a deep breath, knowing that once the words were out she couldn't take them back. "Would it be OK if I come over?" she asked, her voice suddenly trembling with emotion.

"Simone, what is it? Are you ill? Has something happened?"

She gulped over the knot in her throat. "No, I'm not sick or anything. I . . . just need to talk."

"Sure, baby. Do you want to come here, or the house, or can I meet you somewhere? Whatever you want."

Simone smiled weakly and sniffed. "I could come there. I'm already in my car. It would only take me about fifteen minutes or so."

"I'll be here."

"Thanks, Ma."

"And, Simone . . ."

"Yes?"

"Whatever it is, we can work it out. OK?"

"OK," she said weakly. "See you in a bit."

*   *   *

"You never mentioned anything about . . . being involved with Chad," Vaughn said softly, her heart aching for the pain in her daughter's face.

Simone was partially curled up in an overstuffed leather lounge chair, her fist pressed to her lips. "At the time I just figured it was one of those things."

"But it wasn't?"

Simone shook her head sadly.

"But, honey, let's be honest. You gave this man no indication that you were interested."

Her eyes flashed. "He could have written me too, if he cared."

"Yes, he could. But that's a two-sided coin, Simone. Chad is a decent man. But he's a man, and he took his cues from you."

"So what am I supposed to do now?"

"This may sound tacky and cliché, but you made your bed and now you have to lie in it. Maybe things will work out with Chad and your sister, maybe not. But you're not going to be the cause of whatever happens one way or the other."

"What are you saying?"

"I'm saying to leave it alone. Leave them alone to work out whatever. If he decides to tell her about his relationship with you, then let him. I doubt if he will. But if . . . anything . . . has intimately gone on between them, the last thing you need to do is lay that in her lap."

"And I'm supposed to sit back and bite my tongue,

work with both of them on this case and not say a word, not feel anything?''

''You're entitled to your feelings, Simone. Unfortunately, you've learned the hard way about taking sexual relationships lightly. Feelings do become involved, especially if it's with someone for whom you have some sort of care and concern.''

''Do you think he cares about me at all, Ma?'' she asked weakly, her eyes filling.

''I'm sure he does, Simone. And if he's still the same sensitive Chad I remember, he's gone through his changes, too.''

Simone lowered her head. There really wasn't anything she could do about it. And the longer she brooded over it, the more depressed she would become. Eventually it would spill into other areas of her life as well. What other areas? she taunted herself. Work. That was her life, and look where it had gotten her. She sighed in resignation and pushed herself up from her feline position in the chair. ''Thanks, Ma. For listening.''

Vaughn's heart felt as if it twisted in her chest. ''Always. You know that.'' She crossed the room. ''You have a great future ahead of you,'' she soothed, cradling Simone against her. ''Give yourself some time, open your eyes and explore your options.''

Simone nodded numbly. That's what she'd have to do. And she'd smile and be pleasant every time she saw Sam and Chad together, and she'd move on. They'd never know.

CHAPTER TWELVE

Chad walked with Samantha to her front door, head bowed. "Looks like we have a pretty awesome task in front of us," he murmured, referring to the more than 200 cases in the file that was still growing.

"I know." She reached in her purse for her key. "Are you going to bring it to trial yourself, or will Justin?"

"He and I'll work together to process all of the necessary papers. He said he'd serve as second chair."

She stuck the key in the lock. "Can you . . . stay awhile, or do you need to call the car service and get home? I mean I know it's late and tomorrow is a workday . . ."

"No. I can stay . . . for a while."

Samantha tugged in a breath, turned and unlocked the door. Stepping inside, she flicked on the light and the very Afrocentric apartment was bathed in a soft glow. The delicate scent of vanilla hung lightly in the air.

Chad casually looked around, taking in the tasteful decor, the subtle touches that added a unique charm to the sculpted room, with its earthy colors, bronze and wood statuettes of African kings and queens, fabric wall hangings and straw mats, the rattan couch covered with a mudcloth throw. And Samantha, in all her natural loveliness, fit in perfectly.

"This is a great place, Sam."

"Thanks. Make yourself comfortable." She took her shoes, which she'd removed at the door, and put them in the hall closet. "Can I get you anything?" she asked from behind the closet door.

"No. I'm cool. Thanks." He scanned her shelves of books. The eclectic blend included everything from Hemingway, Baldwin, Dickens and Updike, to law reviews, romance novels, music magazines and auto repair reference books. He smiled. Sam was truly a complex young woman with myriad tastes. He liked that. The sound of John Coltrane's "My One and Only Love" drifted to him from the stereo. "When I finally settle into my own spot, I'd like to be able to pull it together like this."

Samantha tucked her feet beneath her on the couch. "I'll take that as a compliment."

"Absolutely." He crossed the room and sat opposite her on the matching love seat.

"Speaking of which, when do you want to start hunting?"

"I was hoping if you were free this weekend, we could at least tour some of the neighborhoods. I know things have changed since I lived here."

"That's true." She laughed lightly. "This weekend sounds fine. Saturday or Sunday?"

"How 'bout Sunday? We can do brunch first in Georgetown, then spend the afternoon riding around. And we'll use my car," he added pointedly.

"Fine. I usually try to sneak in the office on Saturday anyway. So it works for me."

"My One and Only Love" segued to "In a Sentimental Mood."

"Sure I can't get you anything?" Samantha asked again.

"Yeah, maybe a rum and Coke if you have it."

"Heavy on the rum or the Coke?" she teased.

"You decide."

Her pulse thumped, then settled. Uncurling her long body, she padded toward the china cabinet that contained bottles of Chardonnay, Black Label and Johnnie Walker. She prepared Chad's drink, then one for herself—easy on the rum.

She felt him behind her before he uttered a word. It was as if the air was suddenly cut off and a gentle warmth wrapped around her. The muscles in her stomach fluttered and she nearly sloshed the dark amber liquid on the sideboard as she added a stirrer to each drink.

"Can I help?"

The hot, whispered breath brushed along her exposed neck. The tiny hairs quivered to attention.

"Uh, you can take this," she said, turning right into him.

Gingerly, he took the glass from her fingers. "This one mine?"

"Umm-hmm," she mumbled, bobbing her head.

"Thanks." He returned in camera-perfect movements back to the love seat.

Shortly, Samantha made it back to her seat, her head spinning and her pulse beating out of control. Did she just imagine what almost happened—that look in his eyes, the sparks that flashed between them? Maybe so. Because from where she was sitting Chad acted as though nothing happened.

"If you ever decide to give up the public life you definitely could tend bar."

She smiled and the wobbly feeling slowly ebbed. "I watched my father during all the politicking, fundraising and elbow-rubbing sessions at the house. Monie and I would practice when Mom and Dad weren't home," she said with a chuckle of mischief.

"Ever get caught?"

"Nope. Thank goodness. Even at our age, we'd still be grounded."

Chad laughed. "I can believe that. Justin isn't one to let anything slide. That must be where you got it from." he added thoughtfully.

"Got what?"

"Not letting anything get past the radar. Zeroing in on the issue."

She flicked her brows. "Maybe. It's hard to say what's inherent and what you pick up along the way. For most of my life I grew up without my father's influence." Her gaze drifted away for a moment as she thought back to the years she didn't know who he was or why he wasn't in her life. It was a question her mother deftly dodged for nearly fifteen years, simply telling her that her father had abandoned them. Realizing it had all been one big lie almost destroyed her and severely fractured her relationship with her mother, Janice. It wasn't until the past year that she was able to have a civilized conversation with her mother without it erupting into a fit of anger.

Her father was not the unfeeling monster her mother made him out to be. He was a decent, caring man who'd missed her in his life as much as she'd missed him in hers.

"Your father loves you a lot," Chad said, cutting into her thoughts.

Sam blinked several times. Her smile wavered. "I know. I'm lucky." She curled a bit tighter on the couch and took a sip of her drink. "What about you, Chad? Are you close to your family?"

He pursed his lips, watching the ice change shape in his glass. "Not as close as I would like."

"Why is that?" It was hard for her to understand those who were lucky enough to have families but didn't cherish them, want to be a part of something bigger than themselves—that link that made them who they were.

"My mother, hmm, what can I say? Naomi Rushmore never saw herself as a mother. It was a burden. She saw herself as the desire of any man she came into contact with. Her own pleasures were more important than raising me and my brother, Anthony."

Samantha watched the pained expression move like a shadow across his face, and her heart went out to him. She had been a victim of parental selfishness and knew what the effects of that could be. In her case she tended to reach out, wanting or needing to embrace those in pain or suffering a loss.

"I think Tony needed her more than I did. So he went looking for affection in the street." He paused, reflecting.

"What happened?" she asked with caution after several moments of silence spread out between them.

Chad pulled in a long breath. "Got hooked up with a gang when he was about sixteen, got arrested more times than I can remember. The ugly part is, he was finally getting his life together. He went back to school at night, got his G.E.D." His voice cracked as he continued. "He was, uh, on his way to his first job interview." He smiled at the memory. "Man, he was so proud. 'I'm gonna be something, brother,' he told me. 'I'm gonna get this job and turn my life around. Take care of Linda and my kid.' "

His nostrils flared as he sucked in air. He took a long, pensive swallow of his drink. "Your past comes back to haunt you," he said, his voice strained. "Tony was standing on the corner waiting for the bus and a member of a rival gang shot him dead in the street over some old beef."

Samantha's hand flew to her mouth. "Oh, Chad, I'm sorry."

"It was a long time ago." He said the words with quiet detachment, but the pain of the memory was evident in his eyes.

"What happened to his girlfriend and the child?"

"Linda moved out of Atlanta shortly afterward with her parents. Got married about three years ago. We still stay in touch and she sends me pictures of my niece, Tanya."

They were quiet for a moment. Coltrane softly serenaded them in the background.

"Hey, I better get going. Now it is late." He chuckled lightly, rousing himself from his reverie. He put his glass on the end table and stood. Samantha made a move to get up. "No. Stay put. I can let myself out." He stood above her, then leaned down and gently brushed her lips with his before grazing his thumb across her mouth. "See you soon." He headed for the door.

"Chad."

He turned, a questioning expression on his face. "Yeah . . ."

Samantha got up and stood in front of him. She reached out and stroked his face, never letting her gaze lose his. "I . . . don't want you to go." There, she'd said it. She'd put her cards on the table.

"Sam . . ." He released a short breath. His brows drew together. "And if I stay, Samantha, then what? Are you sure you want to take it there? Because I'm not looking for a fling." Not this time, he thought,

Simone flashing through his head. "It has to mean something and not just for tonight."

It was everything she'd wanted him to say. In those few sentences he'd clearly told her the kind of man he was—the kind of man she was looking for.

A slow smile, soft as a breeze, moved across her mouth. "You're right. I do want it to mean more than one night. And it will. When *you're* ready."

His tight expression softened. The corner of his mouth quirked upward. "Samantha Montgomery," he said as he shook his head slowly, drawing her to him, "what am I going to do with you?"

She arched her neck. "We'll have to see, now won't we?" She kissed him lightly and withdrew. "Good night, Chad."

Without warning, he slid his arm around her waist, pulling her completely to him. His mouth captured hers, his teeth toyed with her full bottom lip, his tongue dueled lightly with hers. It would be so easy to take this further, to give in to the sensations that rioted through him, take what this beautiful woman was offering. But he was never one for easy, and neither was Samantha. They would play this out. They had to.

Slowly he eased back and her eyes like two flames burned into his.

"Good night, Sam."

This time he made it to the door and she didn't stop him.

CHAPTER THIRTEEN

"I had an interesting conversation with Simone," Vaughn whispered, snuggled in the protective embrace of Justin's arms.

"Hmm," he mumbled, fighting the first wave of sleep. He'd just made the most exquisite love with his wife and all he wanted was to drift off with the memory of it and the feel of her in his arms. "What did she say?" He rubbed his feet together beneath the covers, and Vaughn knew it would only be moments before he was out for the count.

"Did you have any idea that she'd had an affair with Chad?"

Justin's eyes flew open, then blinked rapidly. "Huh?"

"Before he went away."

He was fully awake now. "I knew they were close . . . but not that close. I had no idea it went that far. But . . ." He turned on his side, focusing on her in the dark. "I hear something else beneath your voice. There has to be more to it than that." He pushed himself up against the pillows. "What is it?"

Vaughn quickly recounted her conversation with Simone, leaving out very little.

"Damn," he muttered from between his teeth. "And Sam knows nothing about it?"

"Nope."

"Well, don't you think someone ought to tell her?"

"No, I don't."

"And would you mind telling me why in the hell not?"

Vaughn now sat up as well. "First of all, it's personal between Simone and Chad. I don't see how it can benefit Samantha in any way. If anything, it could ruin whatever chance that relationship might have."

Justin shook his head vigorously. "Is everyone crazy but me? Of course, she needs to know so that she can make an informed decision. That's her sister—stepsister—for Christ's sake."

"That's exactly my point. If Simone were anyone else, it would be different. If Sam and Chad work out, do you really want Sam to be constantly reminded that he'd had a relationship with her sister? I know I wouldn't."

"So Samantha is supposed to stumble around in

the dark until she trips over the information herself. Is that what you're saying?''

This wasn't going well. She'd debated telling her husband, but there was one thing they'd promised each other from the early days of their marriage: they would never keep secrets and would always share what was going on with the girls—women.

Vaughn gently cupped Justin's upper arm. "This is something they will have to work out, Justin. Their bond is strong enough to handle anything, even this. As much as we might want to jump in there and fix things, protect them, we can't—and you know it.''

"I know no such thing,'' he grumbled under his breath. "Someone's going to get hurt, I just know it.''

Vaughn smiled in the dark. He'd come around.

"Would you tell Sam if she were *your* daughter?'' There was an element in his voice that said the blood tie between father and daughter was something not to be ignored. This was his child, after all.

She couldn't have been more stunned if he'd smacked her. For a moment, she couldn't clear her thoughts quickly enough to respond. "Because I didn't push her out of my body, because my blood doesn't run through her veins, does it make my love for her any less valuable? I have never,'' she ground out, "treated Samantha any differently than I've treated Simone, and I would hope that you have done the same.''

"That's not what I'm asking, Vaughn. I'm not asking you to quantify your relationship with Sam. I know you love her. I'm asking you if she were your flesh-and-blood daughter, would you tell her?''

For a second longer than she felt comfortable, she was torn. And it scared her. ''No, I wouldn't.'' But even as she said the words, the doubts hovered in the back of her mind and something she never thought she'd feel in her marriage began to creep into her bed—distance.

''Ms. Montgomery,'' a reporter from *The Post* shouted over the din of the news conference. ''How do you plan to approach this new wave of police violence into your campaign?''

''As you all know, I have remained vocal and steadfast in my appeal for police reform in this city. My sister, Samantha Montgomery, is working with the families of the victims and I intend to support her in any way that I can. This effort must be a collective one, which will need the unification of all who hold a deep disdain for injustice of any kind, whether it is practiced by an individual or an institution.''

''Do you think it will hurt your chances for election to the Assembly if you pursue your current uncompromising strategy?'' he tossed back. ''Your opponent, Assemblyman McCall, upholds the actions of the police and believes that in order to crack down on drugs and murders in D.C., we must have strong police, operating without any kind of oversight committee or watchdog agency reining them in. He says that law and order must take precedence over any other concern if the streets are to be safe for this city's citizens. You don't seem to think so."

Adam watched Simone carefully. They'd gone over this a dozen times.

Simone straightened. "I'm willing to take my chances on the people of this city, not the politicians and big business. I firmly believe that I speak for them and I will continue to do so. I believe I represent their concerns. I must devote myself to my beliefs and energy to serving them, and I cannot worry about currying the favor of any opponent, platform or political party."

Adam stood up. "That's all the questions for now, ladies and gentlemen. Thank you all for coming." He escorted Simone away from the microphones and into the back room of her campaign headquarters. "You did great," he assured.

"It still boggles my mind to think that simply because I'm running for higher office, I'm expected to cave in on everything I believe simply to get votes. What would be the point?"

"That's the nature of this business, Simone."

"Unfortunately."

"Most politicians say what they think people want to hear. The money people, the ones who fund their campaigns. They compromise their values to fit the popular trends of the moment or forget their commitment to their constituents in order to capture a greater share of the limelight. That's the nature of the political beast."

"I pray I never become that weak and shallow. I'd

quit first. I'd walk away and return to private life and become an average citizen."

Adam wrapped his arm around her shoulder. "I can never see that happening. You have too much fire in you, Simone. That's what the people need. A strong, uncompromising voice. A person of integrity and vision. Your career in politics is just beginning and anything you dream can be accomplished in this political arena if you stick to your guns. If you follow your heart, your instincts."

"We'll see, come November."

"When are we meeting with Chad and your father?"

She glanced briefly at her watch. "I told them three o'clock at my father's offices."

"Will Samantha be there as well?" he asked gently.

She felt her body tighten and kept her gaze averted. "Sure," she said, forcing a false note of cheer into her weary voice.

Adam monitored the tight expression on her face. "Are you cool with all that?"

"All what?"

"Everything you told me the other day—about Sam and Chad."

"It is what it is. I can't afford to get sidetracked with a lot of personal intrigue. I have to remain focused. We have a job to do, and that's all I can concern myself with."

He nodded slowly. "Do you want to order in or can I get you from behind your desk for an hour?"

he asked, switching the subject and lightening the air around them.

She turned to him, looked up and smiled. "I think I could stand to get out of here for a while. Let's go out and see if we can find someplace nice where we can get a good meal."

"Your chariot awaits, Madame." He bowed gallantly like a devoted butler and Simone's hearty laughter filled the room.

Later, as Simone and Adam approached her father's office, she could hear the familiar voices coming from behind the partially closed door—Samantha, Chad, her father. She drew in a breath. This was business, she reminded herself. She wouldn't let her personal feelings cloud whatever was necessary to get the job done.

She tapped lightly and walked in, Adam behind her. For an instant, conversation ceased, then swirled again with greetings.

Justin stood and approached her with his customary kiss and hug. He shook Adam's hand. Chad stood as well and was introduced to Adam.

"Good to meet you," Chad acknowledged. "I know you must have your hands full writing for this fireball." He winked at Simone.

"Every day is a challenge," Adam responded, quickly sizing up Chad.

"Good to see you, Adam," Samantha said.

Adam moved out of Chad's space and brushed

Samantha's cheek with a light kiss. "I didn't see your name in the papers today, Sam. I was disappointed," he teased.

Samantha grinned. "Slow news day, I guess."

"Why don't we all grab a seat and get down to business," Justin suggested.

Samantha extended her hand to Simone and pulled her close. "I have so much to tell you," she whispered as she eased Simone into the available space next to her on the couch.

"Can't wait." Her gaze darted to Chad, then back to her sister. "We can talk later."

"At least one hundred of the victims or family members have already been contacted by phone," Chad began. "The plan has been explained to them in as much detail as possible and everyone was more than enthusiastic to move forward. We'll finish up the list and begin the preliminary interviews in about another week."

Everyone nodded in agreement.

"I'll be preparing the court papers," Justin added.

"What can we do?" Samantha asked.

"You've done a lot already, sweetheart. The key now is to pull this all together and make it happen."

"The press is going to pounce on this once it gets out. They'll be relentless," Adam interjected, thinking of the impact it would have on Simone and her campaign. "You must be prepared to deal with the onslaught. We can't be caught off guard with any surprises or ambushes. Make sure that you are prepped for every possible scenario.''

"We can handle it," Simone said, looking at each face in the room. "As far as I'm concerned, it's more ammunition for my platform. The tides are turning against McCall every day. We're gaining in the polls. His aggressive reactions to our challenges of his stances on key issues, along with these police shootings, are eating into his base of support. He never reacts well under pressure and that's killing him with the voters. We must keep pressing him on the police abuse issue, keep his feet to the fire."

"We'll be ready to mobilize any street actions or rallies should they become necessary, which I'm certain they will be," Samantha said. "I strongly feel that we must keep the focus on the people, their voice, and not let it deteriorate into some political agenda. It won't do us any good to get into a mudslinging match with him. If we get into the gutter with him or any of our opposition, we'll only get dirty and lose."

"This *is* politics," Simone said with a bit too much force. "I think it's fine to fight in the street, but in the final analysis it's about laws and those who will implement them."

The room became suddenly still. The sound of typewriters from down the corridor could be heard.

"We're all in this together, Simone," Chad said, disturbed by her tone and posture. "We all have the same agenda."

"Do we?"

"Simone!" Justin snapped.

"Dad," Samantha cut in, touching his arm. "Simone has the right to her opinion. She does have a lot at stake."

"You don't have to speak for me, Sam."

Samantha's neck snapped back. "I wasn't trying to. I was stating the obvious."

Adam's gaze darted back and forth between the two sisters as if suddenly some invisible line had been drawn in the dirt, one on either side. And he knew the reason why. The tension between them was building, rising to an uncomfortable level, and anything could cause an explosion of harsh words that could endanger everything, from the election to Chad's prize project.

"This can potentially be a very volatile situation for everyone," Adam said. "We're all stressed by the recent developments, the coverage in the press and the impact it's had on our time . . . and our sleep," he added, trying to bring the growing combustion between them down to a harmless level. "But it's doable. And we're all prepared to work at it from our own strengths, our own positions of expertise. Am I right?" He looked anxiously from one to the other as each nodded in agreement.

"I'm sorry," Simone mumbled softly. "I had a tough press conference this morning and I guess it's still with me." She gave a tight-lipped smile to Samantha. "Nothing against you, sis."

Samantha's incredulous expression at her sister's outburst slowly eased away from her face. "Adam's right." She turned to Chad. "How long do you think it will be before we can go public with this?"

Chad deferred to Justin.

"I'd say within the next six weeks. Once all of the statements are taken, an overall strategy formulated after a complete evaluation of the responses, and the papers signed by all parties involved, we'll be ready to bring it to court."

"All of the files are in the database at my office," Samantha noted. "We should be finished with all of the entries shortly."

"I'll be working out of your office," Chad said. "That will make things a little easier."

"No problem."

Simone stood. "I've really got to get back to my office. If there's nothing else . . ."

"I think that covers everything," Justin said.

"Good seeing everyone. Keep me posted if there's anything I need to do." She moved toward the door, then stopped at the sound of Samantha's voice.

"I'll call you tonight."

"Sure." She walked out.

"What in the hell was wrong with you back there?" Adam demanded to know as they drove back to Simone's offices.

She glared out the window with her back to him. Her silence said more in that instant than any quick turn of phrase ever could.

"Simone, this isn't like you to let personal issues get in the way of what counts."

Her head snapped in his direction, and her nostrils flared. "What do you know about what I'm like!" Her chest heaved in and out and she knew she'd lost the last vestiges of her self-control. The cords strained in her neck, puffed with blood fed by anger. This wasn't Adam's fault, it wasn't Samantha's fault. But damn it, she wanted to blame someone.

"I know more than you think I do, Simone," he said gently. "I know you're a decent human being who loves hard and plays hard. I know that this thing, whatever it is between Sam and Chad, has really affected you. More than you want to let on. And that's cool. But you can't let it creep in, take over your life and ruin your relationship with your sister. Hell, she doesn't even know what's happening. She hasn't a clue about this entire business. Did you see the look on her face, on everyone's face, when you went off in there? Damn, what were you thinking? What were you trying to prove?"

Simone lowered her head, shamed by what she knew was childish behavior. "I said I was sorry," she mumbled.

"It shouldn't have gotten to that point, Monie, and you know it."

A tight smile tugged at her lips at the sound of her pet name. It always had a way of softening her edges, easing her back through time to a safer, simpler place in herself.

They stopped for a light. "Maybe what you're going

to have to do is tell your sister how you feel. Level with her. Be honest. Trust in the love between you two.''

She shook her head rapidly. ''I can't do that.'' That was unthinkable.

''Well, you've got to do something. You obviously can't let this continue. We have months ahead of us of working together. You're going to see them together. And you can't lose it every time you do. Eventually, it's not only going to affect your relationship with Samantha, but with the rest of your family, and maybe your election. Think about it, Simone. I'm telling you as a friend . . . someone who cares about you.''

She turned to look at him, let the impact of his advice settle within her. He was right. She was going to have to do something, and soon. But that didn't make any of it any easier. No one would walk away from this uninjured, unscathed.

With Simone and Adam gone, and Samantha leaving shortly afterward, Justin and Chad were left alone. Both men took a deep breath and watched the other with closed faces, digesting what had just transpired.

''I think that went pretty well,'' Chad commented, slowly pacing the floor, absently looking at the plaques on Justin's walls.

Justin knew what he and Vaughn had discussed. She'd been adamant about revealing anything to Samantha. Maybe she was right. The only thing that concerned him was that he didn't want to see his daughter hurt, and if keeping this one secret would further that cause, then he would reluctantly go along with it. However, he never agreed not to speak with Chad.

"We need to talk."

Chad turned and his brow rose in question. "About?"

"You and Samantha . . . and Simone."

CHAPTER FOURTEEN

Samantha sat on the edge of her bed staring at the phone on the table. For the better part of the afternoon, she replayed the scene in her father's office and Simone's uncharacteristic outburst toward her. Perhaps it was what she'd said, a carry over from the news conference earlier in the day. But she knew her sister, almost as well as she knew herself. Something was wrong and she had the underlying feeling that it had something to do with her. But what?

In the past few weeks, she'd noticed the change in Simone's attitude, specifically toward her. Had she done something, said something that she was unaware of? But she and Simone had always been up front with each other. There wasn't anything they couldn't talk about.

Although they hadn't grown up together and actually had never met until they were in their early twenties, the bond between them was undeniable. Simone was her best friend, her confidant, and this unexplainable rift between them left her feeling alone and hollow. Something was not being said. Something was pulling them apart.

She reached for the phone. Whatever it was, they needed to talk about it, get it out in the open. She dialed Simone's number, her stomach in tight knots of anxiety.

Simone had just gotten out of the shower, feeling mildly refreshed. She was determined to have a worry-free night, just relaxing with a glass of white wine and some mindless movie. But then the doorbell rang. Who could this be?

Annoyed by the unexpected intrusion on her quiet time, she stomped off toward the door, her skin glistening from its recent baptism of warm water and scented bath oil.

"Who?" she called from behind the heavy wood barrier.

"It's Chad, Simone."

She squeezed her eyes shut and pulled her robe tightly around her. Her heart thumped against her chest. She drew in a breath and unlocked the door. Pulling it partially open, she peered out into Chad's ruggedly handsome face, which wore a pleasant, boy-ish smile. All teeth and dimples.

"Chad. I wasn't expecting you."

"I know. I'm sorry. I should have called you first. If you're busy, I guess I can come back . . ." He retreated a step as if preparing to leave. Testing the waters.

"No." She stepped away from the door and pulled it completely open. "You're here now. You might as well come in."

He stepped inside, catching the soft, clean scent of her.

The door shut behind him, sounding solid and substantial, and he heard the locks click in place. He turned. "Jasmine," he murmured, remembering her favorite scent, taking in the full measure of her barely hidden beneath the folds of her silk robe.

She wrapped her arms protectively around her waist. "You remembered."

"I don't think there's anything between us that I've forgotten, Simone."

She glanced away, then walked past him into the living room. "Have a seat." She continued down the corridor to her bedroom, shutting the door behind her. She was shaking all over. What was he doing here? She wasn't prepared for this. What could he possibly want? This was much too soon. She wasn't ready. Could she ever be ready for what might happen with the two of them in a room? Sighing heavily, she opened her closet, sorted through her clothes, and pulled out a well-worn but cottony soft, gray sweatsuit, then pulled her damp hair into a ponytail and fastened it with a rubber band. Glancing briefly in the mirror, she put on her best nonchalant expression and returned in a casual gait to the living room.

"So . . . what's up?" Her voice was noncommittal but friendly.

Surprised by her sudden reappearance, he turned toward the sound of her voice, and hundreds of images flashed through his head: their long lunches in the park, bike riding on Sunday afternoons, political talks long into the night, swapping jazz CDs, and his final blissful night with her before he went away. No, he'd forgotten none of it. Every wonderful moment was still there in his memory banks; nothing was dulled by time.

Chad drew in a breath. "We need to talk, Simone. And before you ask about what, it's about us."

"Humph, what us? That was a long time ago, Chad. One night. No strings, no promises, remember?"

"Don't b.s. me, Simone. I know you. I know it meant more to you than that. It did to me."

"Why didn't you ever write, ever call?" she challenged, wanting him to defend himself so she could attack, get the hurt out.

"Why didn't you?" he shot back.

She spun away, her back to him. "I . . . didn't want you to . . ."

"To what?"

"To think that it mattered, that it changed things."

He crossed the room to stand next to her. "But it

did change things. And we'd be fools not to admit that.''

"That was four years ago, Chad. Things have changed.''

He grasped her shoulder and gently turned her to face him. "Look at me.''

She couldn't. Her face, her eyes, would say things to him that were best left unsaid.

"Look at me, Monie,'' he said softly.

By degrees, her eyes rose to rest on his face. She could feel the knot build in her throat. Why resurrect all of this now? What was the purpose of bringing up the past?

"When I came back . . . all the time that I was gone, I thought of you.''

She tried to pull away but he wouldn't let her. His hands on her served as a lie detector, registering each and every submerged emotion.

"But I thought you didn't care, Simone. That I was just someone to be with at a vulnerable time. That maybe you were just giving me going-away goodies because you felt . . . I don't know . . . sorry for me or something.''

"It was nothing like that.''

"Then what was it?''

"You were the one who said no strings, Chad. I took you at your word. I thought I could be modern and adult about it. But . . .''

"But what? . . .''

She hesitated, knowing that what she said next could change the direction of everything between them. She thought of Samantha, knew how she felt about this man, because she'd felt . . . and still did feel the same way. She wouldn't jeopardize her sister's chance at being happy. Sam deserved a taste of joy in her life. Someone completely hers. If it didn't work out, it wouldn't be because of her.

"I was . . . adult about it," she said with finality. "That's all there is to it. I wish I could say that there was more but there isn't. You know this is the right thing to do. For both of us. I'm sorry."

"I see." He let her go.

The phone rang.

"Excuse me." She walked toward the phone on the end table. "Hello?"

"Hi, Monie, it's me. You busy?"

She glanced across at Chad. "Hi, Sam. No, I'm not busy."

Chad looked at her for a long moment, nodded his head in resigned acceptance and closed the door quietly behind him.

Simone held the phone down at her side, composing herself, taking several deep breaths. She squeezed her eyes shut as the tears leaked out from beneath her lashes. Still slightly wobbly, she took the phone to the couch and sat. "Hey, sis, what's this you've been dying to tell me?"

"Before I get to that I wanted to talk about you and me. Something's not right and I don't know what it is. What's wrong? Have I done something?"

"Oh, Sam, you haven't done anything. It's just me being bitchy is all. It's the campaign and everything.

I'm sorry. I'm sorry I've been such a grouch. I've had so much on my mind lately. I think I've been taking it out on everyone these days."

Samantha relaxed a bit. "You sure? Everything cool with your campaign?"

"Positive. And yes, everything's better than cool with the campaign." She laughed lightly. *Samantha, always the worrier.*

"Well, I feel better." She settled down under her sheet, ready for some girl talk. "I really like him, Monie, more than I thought," she began. "And the more I see him, spend time with him," she added in a dreamy voice, "the deeper it gets. He's everything I've ever wanted. You know."

Simone swallowed down the hard kernel of regret in her throat, still inhaling the masculine scent of Chad that had seeped into her pores. "Yeah, sweetie, I know."

Under the purple sky of early evening, Chad drove aimlessly around the capital city, watching the street lights awaken, forming an endless necklace of illumination along the avenue, as his thoughts darted back and forth between his conversation with Justin and his meeting with Simone. Justin was clear, firm in his resolution to protect his children. He loved his daughters and he would hold Chad personally responsible if he hurt either of them.

"I believe that Samantha needs to know the truth about what happened between you and Simone four years ago. Vaughn is totally against it. Maybe it's a woman thing that escapes me,'' he admitted. "But the one thing that doesn't escape me is that both of them care about you and most of all they care about each other. And I won't stand by and let some macho ethics come between them.''

"Justin, I think you know me better than that. If anything, I learned how to be a man from you.''

Justin's gaze landed on the sincerity of Chad's face.

"To be truthful, I think that's what they both see in me . . . you.''

"Don't be ridiculous.''

"I don't think I am. They idolize you and any man coming into their lives has a lot to live up to. You've been like a father to me all these years. And I would never betray that by hurting you, Vaughn or your daughters.''

Justin appraised him for a moment. "How do you feel about them?''

That was Justin, Chad thought, not unkindly, cut to the chase.

"I care about them. In different ways. Simone and I . . .'' He shrugged helplessly. "I don't know what it could have been had I stayed in the States. Maybe everything, maybe nothing. When I came back, I had every intention of trying to bridge the gap, but Simone doesn't want any part of it.''

"That's not the way she put it to her mother.''

"What do you mean?''

"That's all I'm going to say about it. My advice . . . You need to straighten this out before it gets out of hand. Be up front. Tell the truth. Be real. It's better to get any hurt and misunderstandings out of the way now, rather than when it's too late.''

With that on his mind, he'd gone to see Simone. He wanted to hear from her own lips how she felt, what she wanted. That's what he got, in no uncertain terms. As far as Simone was concerned, it was over, done, finished, a thing of the past.

So be it, he conceded, turning into the driveway of the Montgomery home. If that's what she wanted, that's what he'd give her.

The instant he walked through the door, Vaughn was there.

''I'm so glad you're back. Justin's in some late-night meetings and can't be reached. I was on my way to Samantha's.''

The fear in her voice was unmistakable. Barely concealed terror.

''What is it?''

''Sam called. She'd just finished talking with Simone and had gone out to take the garbage. She found another letter. Sam doesn't frighten easily, Chad, and she's scared.'' Her eyes were wide and glistening.

''What did the letter say? Did she read it to you?''

''You know Sam. She never gets into details. She'll give you the condensed *Reader's Digest* version, but she won't tell the whole story. Maybe she'll tell you. She'll only try to appease me and convince me everything is all right. I'm surprised she even called. That's why I know she's rattled this time.''

"Okay, I'll go. You stay put in case Justin comes home. He'll want to know. I'll call as soon as I get there," he tossed over his shoulder, already halfway out the door.

CHAPTER FIFTEEN

In that first moment when Chad saw Samantha's horrified face, he knew this was no routine threat from amateurs. This was of the real McCoy, heart-stopping variety, something put together by pros. Samantha was afraid. It registered in the stark look in her eyes, the slight tremor around the corners of her mouth when she attempted a weak smile.

"Sam . . ."

She fell into his embrace and he could feel the tense shudders ripple through her entire body. With his arm around her shoulders, holding her tightly, he assisted her back into the house, through the spotless living room to the couch.

Trembling, Samantha pulled her knees up to her

chest, locked her arms around them and rocked back and forth. Her face was completely ashen with terror. She tugged on her bottom lip with her teeth, tried to still her quaking hands, and stared at nothing.

"Sam," Chad gently coaxed. "Where's the letter, hon?"

Her eyes veered toward a folded piece of plain white stationery on the coffee table. He picked it up and unfolded it, careful to hold it only by the ends, as he read the carefully considered words. Each word spelled out its implied threat, warning of her impending death.

THIS IS YOUR LAST WARNING BITCH. WE WON'T START WITH YOU. WE'LL START WITH YOUR FAMILY FIRST WHILE YOU WATCH. BACK OFF. WE'RE WATCHING.

The note was a series of letters cut out from a variety of sources, old yellowed newspapers and magazines, and glued to the page.

"How many does this make, Samantha?" he asked calmly.

"Three," she mumbled, still rocking.

"You have to take this to the police."

Her eyes snapped at him in anger. "Who do you think is sending this stuff, Chad, Santa Claus? It is the police! They want me dead. They want my family dead."

"You don't know that. It could be supporters, law-and-order fanatics, not the department." He walked over to her side and placed his hand on her shoulder.

"Don't be naïve. It doesn't become you." Her red-rimmed eyes glared at him.

"Relax, Sam, I'm on your side, remember."

She twisted her lips. "Sorry."

"Forget it." He paused a moment, then sat beside her. "Where did you find it?"

She tugged in a breath and covered her stricken features with her hands. "I went to take out the garbage and I found it on the step. At first I thought it was something I dropped. But . . ."

"The others . . ." He lowered his voice to assure her that he took this all quite seriously.

"They were nothing like this. Mostly just blowing off hot air. 'Mind your business. Get out of D.C. We don't need your kind here.' Stuff like that."

"This isn't something you can ignore, Samantha."

Her head snapped up. "What would you have me do, head for the hills, give up everything I've worked for, desert all the people who have come to depend on me?"

"What I'm saying," he uttered in an even lower, soothing voice, "is that maybe you should keep a low profile. Visit a relative somewhere until this thing cools down a bit. Or leave your apartment for a while at least. Let me and Justin take things from here. Stay out of the papers. Don't give any more interviews."

"Forget it, Chad. it's not going to happen. I won't be frightened off. I won't run."

Her fire slowly returned. He could see it in the gradual straightening of her proud posture, the glint of determination that replaced the look of panic in her eyes. The first wave of fear was over, supplanted now with anger and defiance. He had to admire her resiliency. But at the same time she needed to be clear-headed. The last thing any of them needed was a martyr going down for the cause.

"All right. If you won't disappear into the wood-work, then we need to take a firm, proactive approach." Now he had her attention. "Have you ever made these notes public?"

She shook her head. That had never crossed her mind. Her first notion was to ignore them, to pretend they were sent by some nutcase. There were a lot of them out there. But this was different.

"Then I think it's time that you did."

A slow, tight smile pulled at her mouth. "That's more like it."

He got up and moved closer to her on the couch, turning her to face him. "You mean a great deal to a lot of people, Samantha. Especially your family. They would be devastated if anything happened to you." He swallowed. "And so would I."

"Would you?"

"Yes. I would." He stroked her cheek lightly. "Have you thought about going back home?"

"That's out," she stated bluntly. "Dad would be all over me every minute. He would nag me to death. I'd go crazy there in three days, climbing the ceiling."

Chad chuckled. "Yeah, you're probably right."

"The thing is, the threats have moved beyond me

to my family." Her voice wobbled. "They're the ones I'm concerned about. I don't want them involved in this. I don't want to see them hurt because of me."

"Once Justin knows about this, I'm sure he'll take the necessary precautions."

"What about, Simone?"

His stomach muscles suddenly tightened. "We'll present this to your family. Calmly and rationally. Let them each make a decision about what they want to do."

She frowned slightly in thought and nodded in agreement. "Then we take it to the press ... no matter what?"

"Yeah."

Relief rushed out in a soft breath. "Thanks for coming, Chad. I guess I really got Mom upset. I'll have to call her, let her know I'm okay. I-I don't usually let things get to me like that. I'm usually pretty cool about this kind of thing."

"There's something in all of us that's vulnerable, Sam. For you, it's your family."

"Where's your vulnerability?" she asked softly, her eyes zeroing in on his face. It was her way of taking the conversation away from her and her troubles.

He glanced away. "Sometimes I let my emotions create things that aren't there."

She looked at him curiously, saw the shadow of something lost move across his countenance. "Would you stay here with me tonight, Chad?"

Slowly he looked at her.

"You can sleep in the living room. Stay with me tonight. The couch pulls out. I'll stay in my room. I just don't want to be alone."

He glanced down at his hands, which were folded in his lap. "Sure. I'll need to be up and out early to get back to the house and change."

"Whatever. I'll be sure you get up. I run at five."

"Are you sure that's a good idea now?" he asked, his eyes narrowed.

"I'm not going to change my routine," she said with grit.

He knew it was useless to debate with her. "But I warn you," he said, wagging a finger in her direction, "I don't roll out of bed that early. I need my sack time."

She smiled wanly in acceptance. Not everyone was an exercise buff like she was. She had to keep that in mind when she had her infrequent overnight guests. And tonight, for sure, she was grateful in the knowledge that she wouldn't be in the spacious town house alone.

"Thanks for staying with me," she whispered softly, laying her head back against the couch with her eyes shut.

"There's nothing to thank me for, Sam. I should have been the one to offer," he said with soft sincerity. "I guess this whole evening got to me more than I thought. I want to be here. Believe that. If I'd left, I know it would have driven me crazy knowing you were here by yourself."

The comforting words of assurance drifted to her, letting the fear slowly drain from her body, allowing her heart to stop racing at full speed for the first time in hours. But for how long? How long?

CHAPTER SIXTEEN

"It's only going to get worse when this civil action becomes public," Justin growled, pacing restlessly back and forth across his bedroom floor. He ran his hands over his close-cropped hair.

Vaughn clasped and unclasped her fingers. "What are we going to do, Justin?"

"I'm going to call Janice. Sam can go and stay with her mother in Atlanta for a while."

"She'll never do it and you know that. It'll only turn into a shouting match, and she'll win."

"Thanks for the vote of confidence," he snapped. He turned to her, saw the pained look on her face and knew she was just as concerned as he was. "I'm sorry, babe." He sat beside her on the bed.

She rested her head on his chest. "At least she'll be all right tonight."

"What do you mean?"

"Chad is staying with her."

"Damn." He blew out an exasperated breath.

"What is it?"

"I talked to him today."

Vaughn sat up straight. It was her turn to become indignant. "About what, Justin? You promised me."

"I promised you I wouldn't say anything to Samantha and I didn't. I never said I wouldn't talk to Chad," he snapped back. "We had a good man-to-man chat."

She shook her head. "Well . . . what happened?"

He replayed their conversation for his wife, making it all sound quite innocent and safe. His assurances to her that Samantha would not learn of their exchange didn't totally win over Vaughn.

"Now what?"

"Now I hope he does the right thing."

"But what is the right thing, Justin? Do we really know? That's between them. We need to stay out of it. This is not our business."

"I wouldn't be a father if I simply stood by and did nothing. I won't have my hands tied behind my back when it comes to my family. Whatever I need to do to protect them is what I'll do. And if a few egos get bruised in the process, then the hell with it. And Samantha is just going to have to be upset because I'm calling Janice in the morning."

Vaughn looked him directly in the face, composing what she had to say. "Justin, our girls are grown, capable of making their own decisions. If we try to live their lives for them, they will only end up resenting us for meddling in their affairs. Advise them, yes. But if you intervene and try to change the outcome to suit your own wishes, something bad could come of it."

"What are you saying? Just let them be killed because of their youthful bravado. I know they're adults, but that doesn't mean that they always know what's right for them. I don't want to see either of them hurt because they leaped into this business half-cocked. They have no idea what they're confronting with this campaign of theirs. This whole business will not just end with the police. Imagine if their lawsuit is considered a national security risk, then all kinds of agencies could get involved here. The Justice Department, the CIA, even the NSA."

Vaughn sagged against him as if all of her power had been drained. "Stop, Justin, you're scaring me now. I don't want to see them get mixed up in something that can become totally out of control, putting them and everyone they know in danger. I don't want to even think about what could happen with this thing."

"I don't want to frighten you, dear," he replied. "I just want you to realize what can possibly result from their so-called fight for justice. This can easily become a hardball affair. When the federal government feels threatened, pushed into a corner, it will strike back, and hard."

"Is there a way we can convince them to stop their

suit before it reaches that point?'' she asked, a sense of alarm coloring her words.

"I don't know if I can," he said. "They've got too much vested into this. In fact, I believe the opposition already knows the game plan or Samantha wouldn't have gotten this last love note. It was nothing like the others. Somebody knows something. Nothing is secret anymore."

"Do you think somebody close to them is feeding information to the feds? A snitch, an informer from their staff. If that's the case, they're in big trouble."

Justin stood and walked to the window, looking out through the curtains. "I pray they don't bite off more than they can chew. This is the big league and these guys don't take prisoners. You know how the Beltway works."

"Yes, I know," she answered sadly. "If they can go after a president, senators and cabinet members, people with clout and some power in this town, they don't have a chance. They'll be crushed before they file their first brief. Both of us know that. They're taking a big chance, a really big chance, by following through with this."

He came back to her and knelt before her, his hands on both sides of her worried face. "Believe me when I promise you that I won't let anything happen to either one of our girls. You have my word on that."

She nodded and let a false glimmer of serenity come into her face, just before he leaned forward and kissed her tenderly on the forehead. His hands never left her cheeks while he repeated softly in her ear: "You have my word on that. Nothing will happen to them, either of them." They held each other close, their arms surrounding the other. If only it would be that easy to surround and protect their girls.

CHAPTER SEVENTEEN

Samantha lay with her hands folded across her stomach, fingers linked, her gaze focused on the fluttering curtains at her window. Beyond its frame a multitude of stars glimmered against a blanket of midnight blue velvet. In the distance, the faint echo of night sounds filtered through the trees, and the soft rustle from the light breeze was a perfect musical complement.

Serene. Tranquil. Everything peaceful and safe. Yet, beyond the façade, elements were at work to dismantle it all, bringing their wrath against her and her family.

She shivered violently, the sudden force of the chill jerking her body.

She moaned and closed her eyes, tried to sleep. She couldn't. Images of faceless people, the sounds of wails and sobs blocked out the stars and muffled the comforting rhythms of night.

A strangled cry bubbled up from her throat. What was she going to do? If these threats were real, which she now believed they were, what was she going to do? Sure, she'd sounded brave and defiant in front of Chad and for Vaughn. But the truth was, she was terrified, not so much for herself, but for her family. Before, the danger had always been something distant, abstract. She'd understood that in her line of work there would be crackpots and zealots who would oppose her, try to scare her away. So she'd accepted the other notes as part of the job and considered herself lucky there'd been so few. Those notes had arrived at her office, a place connected to her only by virtue of her work. Now the line had been crossed, her personal space invaded. Whoever it was may have been close enough to touch her, peek into her window, jiggle her lock.

She sprung up in bed as if stunned with a prod. Her gaze raced around the room, searching the dark corners, hoping to find—nothing. Short, staccato bursts of air pushed past her lips. "This is insane," she mumbled into the night.

"Sam? You okay?"

A sharp gasp caught and held in her throat. Blinking several times, she focused on the dark figure outlined in the doorway of her bedroom.

She cleared her throat. "Uh, yeah."

"Can I come in?"

"Sure." She swung her legs over the side of the bed, quickly wiped her eyes and pressed her palms down into the firm mattress, thankful for the dark.

"I thought I heard you crying." He sat down on the ottoman near her bed, trying to make out her expression from the starlight.

A shudder scurried up her spine. He saw her tremble.

"Must have been dreaming."

Chad reached out and lightly touched her bare arm. "You're shaking."

"I'm fine."

He turned on the bedside lamp. Soft light bathed the room and illuminated the taut expression on Samantha's face.

"Sam . . ."

She snapped her head away. She couldn't let him see the tears.

"Sam, it's OK."

"What's OK? To sit in your own house and be terrified of every sight and sound, every shadow. Imagine someone lurking in the dark. Then when you close your eyes it's not you they're after but your family."

She wrapped her arms around her waist and rocked back and forth, something Chad realized she did when she passed her anxiety threshold.

"What I meant was, it's OK to be afraid. It's only human, Sam. Anyone would be afraid in your place."

"I don't have the luxury of being afraid. Too many people depend on me. I can't fall apart."

"That's not what I'm saying. You've had a shock. A big one. Give yourself a chance to go through the emotions. Whatever they may be. Don't fight them because then they'll spring up on you when you least expect it and paralyze you." He waited a beat, let his words settle. "I'm here tonight," he added gently. "Be afraid. Rant, rave, scream, cry, whatever. I won't judge you. But don't bottle it up inside, Sam."

"It's . . . it's just so hard for me."

"What is?" He pulled the chair closer and took her hand.

She stared down at their joined hands, memorized the circular scar on the third knuckle of his right hand, the way the veins pulsed gently beneath the warm brown skin, the long fingers and tapered nails. Samantha catalogued it all, even as she formed the words to explain a part of herself she'd never shared before.

He stroked the underside of her wrist with his thumb and she struggled to concentrate.

"My mother," she began haltingly, "always drilled into my head that the only person you can depend on is yourself. People will betray you, even the ones who claim to care about you. If they see weakness they'll use it against you." She paused and looked toward the window. "So I grew up pretty much a loner, steering clear of friendships and commitments, doing everything on my own. But I always wanted to be a part of something, you know. I felt as if something was missing from my life."

She got up and walked toward the window.

"Everything changed for me when I found my father and came to Washington."

Chad watched her slender silhouette in the frame of the window, saw the subtle relaxation of her shoulders and the tight hold she had on her body.

"All of a sudden I was finally a part of something—a family. A family who devoted itself to helping others." She turned to face him. "That's what had been missing in my life—the void that I couldn't figure out how to fill. And it became my life, helping others—being a part of something greater than myself."

"But all that 'stuff' your mother put in your head is still there—under the surface." It wasn't a question.

She blew out a breath. "Yeah. More than I realized, I guess."

"Sam." He rose, crossed the room and stood in front of her. He slid his hands into the pockets of the sweatpants she'd loaned him to sleep in. "There are all kinds of things that make us who we are. You said as much yourself. The key is to find a balance that works."

Samantha looked into his eyes and saw the tenderness and understanding there. Never before had she revealed this part of herself to anyone. Not even Simone. She felt totally vulnerable, yet had a sense that Chad would not abuse it.

"Thanks," she whispered.

"For . . . ?"

"Being here, listening . . . being you."

Chad smiled softly.

She moved closer to him. She could feel the protection of his warmth surrounding her. Her gaze drifted slowly across the planes of his face and took in the smoldering dark eyes that had seen so much, the deep brown complexion enhanced by the rays of the African sun, the full mouth with the bottom lip more lush than the top, and the sharp cheekbones that defined his face.

Slowly, she lifted her chin as if drawn to his mouth by an inner magnet. At that moment, right or wrong, she needed to be held, touched, assured of her life and vitality. She needed to feel connected.

She touched her mouth to his, tentatively at first, a gentle exploration, then with more assurance as his lips responded to hers and his hands found her waist.

Samantha moved against him, felt the fullness of him swell between the juncture of her thighs, and a soft sigh flowed from her mouth into his.

Chad's hands traveled along the curve of her waist, up the column of her spine, to let his fingers tangle in her locks, enjoying the coarse texture of them.

The night breeze danced around them, filling the room with the scent of cherry blossoms, brushing their skin, teasing, taunting, weaving between their bodies.

He held her tighter, deciding to let go for the moment, give in and let it happen. Yes, he'd promised Justin he wouldn't hurt her, and he wouldn't. His thumbs brushed across her nipples and felt them harden beneath the lightweight fabric of her gown, and he remembered Simone's parting words—that Sam would need more than one night—and so did he.

Torn between mounting desire and reason, he reluctantly broke the contact, eased back and looked down into her wide, questioning eyes. "Sam," he whispered, his voice thick. He stroked her cheek. "I want you, believe me I do. More than you can imagine." His erection throbbed against the soft cotton pants, reminding him how much. Samantha's thoroughly kissed mouth trembled ever so slightly. "But not like this," he said with regret. "Not when you're feeling vulnerable and scared. Whatever happens between us, I want it to be free from artificial reasons." He wouldn't have a repeat of what happened between him and Simone. Not again, and especially with Samantha. Maybe he was being too cautious, but it was better that than mistakes he'd regret later.

She spun away from him and crossed the room in hard strides, moving as far away as space would allow.

"Are you saying that your feelings and mine are artificial, too?" she asked, her voice unable to contain the hurt, the rebuff.

"No, Samantha, and I think you know that." He walked up behind her. "I'm saying that if we make love, I want to be sure it's for the right reasons. Sure, tonight would be a great release, a few hours of comfort, but what about tomorrow?"

"Fine," she blew out on a breath. "I'm going to try to get some sleep." She walked toward the bed.

He lowered his head. "Good night," he whispered and walked toward the door.

"Chad . . ."

"Yes?" He slowly turned around, his hand on the knob.

Silence stretched the distance between them.

"Good night."

He nodded and closed the door behind him.

This was the second time he'd turned her down, Samantha thought miserably, her body still tingling. She lay on her side and pulled the sheet up to her chin. At first she admired his sense of gallantry, the old-fashioned streak in him. But this time was different. At least she thought it was. She knew he cared for her, found her attractive, desirable. She sighed heavily. It was more than what he'd said. Something deeper than the words on the surface. But she had no idea what it was.

Justin and Vaughn had talked until the sun peaked above the treetops. She was dead set against his calling his ex-wife, Janice. It would only upset Samantha all the more, she insisted. Her relationship with her natural mother was tenuous at best, and Vaughn believed this would not help.

Justin on the other hand felt just the opposite. It was about time that Janice did something positive for their daughter—take care of her when she needed it instead of only concentrating on her own selfish needs. He knew Vaughn would be pissed, but he'd made up his mind.

He flipped open the large leather phone book on his desk and dialed the Atlanta number.

Janice's husky voice picked up on the third ring. "Hello?"

He hadn't spoken to her in nearly six years, not since Samantha had come to D.C., and the distaste he felt then still lingered in his mouth.

"Janice, it's Justin."

Janice uncrossed her bare legs and sat up straighter in the bed. She reached for a cigarette and lit it. "Well . . . what can I do for you, Justin?" She inhaled deep and long.

"Samantha's in trouble and I want to send her down there to stay with you for a while."

"Trouble. She's pretty old to be getting sent away because she's pregnant." She chuckled nastily. "That's very archaic of you, dear."

"Typical response, Janice. Not that kind of trouble."

She took another drag on her cigarette. "What . . . kind of trouble? Something with that job of hers. Her name is in the paper every other day. I told her—"

"Would you just listen for a minute," he almost shouted, trying to control his rising temper. "She's been getting threatening letters . . ." He went on to explain what had been happening and his reasons for wanting Samantha to get away.

Janice's lips trembled. As much as she may have

regretted what happened between her and Samantha, the fact that she left her alone to live with her father, and that Sam had little if anything to say to her when she called, she still loved Samantha. Loved her with all her heart, no matter what Justin thought.

She pulled out her sword and attacked, the only thing she knew how to do anymore. "She should have stayed here," she slashed. "You got her head full of all that craziness about saving the world." Her voice rose in pitch. "And now look what's happened. She's been in nothing but one incident after the other since she's been in Washington. What kind of father are you? I swear, Justin, if anything happens to my baby, I'll make you regret it."

"Don't threaten me, Janice," he said from deep in his throat. "You can think what you want about me, you always have. That's not the issue. The issue is Samantha and her safety. I'm sure we both can agree on that."

She was silent, refusing to give him even that much.

"I want you to call her, tell her to come, insist that she come." He paused, the next words out of his mouth bitter as bile. "And . . . I'll back you up."

Her finely arched brows rose against her sandstone-colored skin. She heard something in Justin's voice she never thought she would: fear. She crushed her cigarette and lowered her saber. "Sam and I don't seem to do well over the phone." She nervously lit another cigarette and took a long drag, blowing a thick cloud of smoke into the air. "I can be on a flight in the morning. I'd rather do this in person."

For an instant he was stunned by her gesture. He considered her offer, more than he'd anticipated. "Fine, but I want to be there. Call my office with your flight information." He rattled off the number. "We'll talk there."

"Always have to be in control, don't you, Justin. But obviously something's gone wrong in your perfect world or you wouldn't be calling me."

"This isn't about me, Janice, it's about our daughter. Try to remember that."

The sword was unsheathed again. "Maybe I'll even get a chance to meet your wife while I'm in town." She laughed lightly. "I'll call you."

The dial tone hummed in his ear and he wondered what else would jump out of the Pandora's box that he'd opened.

CHAPTER EIGHTEEN

Vaughn was so furious she couldn't think straight, couldn't pay attention to the bickering back and forth between her staff members over a new bill being presented in Congress.

Justin had called her less than an hour ago and told her what he'd done. The only thing that kept her from going completely ballistic was that her secretary Martha was in the adjoining office with the door open.

Impatiently, she tapped her foot beneath the conference table and tried to concentrate. *Janice.* Damn it, how could Justin do something like that. But that wasn't the worst, that wasn't the thing that was searing her insides like a hot poker. It was what he'd said, what he'd tossed to her like a bone: She's *my* daughter and I know what's best for *my* child.

Her throat tightened and her eyes burned with hurt and fury. It had come to that. Never in her worst nightmare had she ever dreamed that Justin would say such a thing—to her.

Following his remark, he'd tried to apologize after her long silence electrified the air between them. It was too late. The damage was done. Now they would both live with the painful words that could never be taken back.

"What's going to be our approach, Vaughn?" Spencer Carrington, her house advisor, asked. His deeply lined, craggy face resembled the sculptures on Mt. Rushmore.

Conversation halted and all eyes turned to Vaughn.

She straightened and cleared her throat. "We have to maintain the hard line on health care. It was one of the issues that got me elected into office. I'm not going to back down simply because the Republicans are in the majority and against adding any additional government support to the health care system."

"We don't have the support on the Hill that we did at the beginning of your term," Spencer added.

Spencer Carrington had worked with her father, Elliot Hamilton, when he was elected to his seat on the bench. He'd been with the family for as long as she could remember in some capacity or the other, and knew the ins and outs of Washington like his own face in the mirror. She trusted him.

"That may be, but I won't change my position, not

even for votes. What we need to do is begin lobbying to change opinion on the Hill before the bill is presented.''

"Not to add more fuel to the fire," Sharlene Gannon, her chief of staff, interjected, "but there are at least a dozen messages on my desk from reporters of every ilk who want to interview you about the police protests, specifically your daughters' participation.''

"Release the last statement I gave on this issue, Sharlene. My position on undue force, profiling and shooting of unarmed men hasn't changed.'' She massaged her temples and momentarily shut her eyes against the pounding that had been building in momentum.

The room grew noticeably quiet and the members at the table looked surreptitiously from one to the other.

Slowly, Vaughn opened her eyes and looked around. ''What?''

Sharlene leaned a bit closer. ''There are rumors that Samantha received a note threatening her life and the family,'' she said quietly.

Vaughn visibly stiffened. She released a breath. ''I see.''

"Is it true?'' Spencer asked.

"No,'' she lied on instinct. The note only arrived the night before. As far as she could determine they'd called no one, not even the police. How would the press have found out unless the person who wrote it told? Intentionally. And until they found out who that someone was, she had no comment. "Rumors abound in Washington. It's what makes our lives so interesting.'' She put on her camera-ready face. ''Is there any other business for the morning?''

''No,'' was the consensus.

''Great.'' Vaughn stood.

''You have a noon appointment with Congressman Williams,'' Martha advised as Vaughn breezed out of the room and down the carpeted corridor to her office. ''And a two o'clock with the contingency from Richmond about their historical preservation issue,'' she continued, going down the itinerary for the day. ''Then there's the Budget Committee meeting at four. And I'm sure that will last well past six. It always does. Do you want me to order dinner, call home for you?'' She kept up with Vaughn's unbroken, quick pace.

''Order something about five, a grilled chicken salad and plenty of Coke.''

Martha laughed lightly, knowing that was one of Vaughn's vices—downing ice-cold cans of Coke like water. ''No problem.'' She jotted it down on her notepad. ''Are you all right?''

Vaughn snatched a glance at Martha as she reached her office. ''Of course. Why?''

The two women faced each other, the years between them a silent, unbreakable bond.

''If you want to talk . . .'' She let the statement hang there.

Vaughn pressed her lips together and nodded, then turned and entered her office. Slowly she closed the door behind her. She did need someone to talk to, someone to whom she could explain the riot of thoughts and feelings whirling through her.

She crossed the room and took the seat behind her desk, swiveling it so she could look out the bay window. Talk, yes, she'd love to talk, get it all out. But after the announcement a few moments ago, she was no longer certain who she could talk to about anything.

Simone listened in pensive silence as Samantha relayed to her the events of the previous evening, from the finding of the note, up to and including Chad's spending the night and all that entailed. Simone didn't know whether to be relieved or furious at Chad, before her emotions would segue to this latest threat and its broadening reach.

Samantha sat curled up on her couch, still in her robe. She'd called Simone shortly after Chad left to go home and change. Although Vaughn had contacted her the night before to update her on what had happened, she wanted to get the details from Samantha. She could still catch the barely there scent of Chad's presence.

"I'm just a mess today," Samantha confessed. "My head . . . is completely screwed up."

"Did you get any rest at all?" Simone asked.

"If I did, it sure doesn't feel like it." She laughed lightly.

"You just need to take it easy today. Why don't you go stay over at the folks'. Let Dottie look after you."

"That's out. I'm fine, really. Or at least I will be. I'm not going to have whoever this SOB is running me out of my house. He's already stolen a good night's sleep. That's all I intend for him to take."

"I hear ya, sis. But on the real side, this is nothing to play with."

Samantha sighed heavily. "Yeah, I know. Chad said we need to go public, put everyone on notice."

"I agree," Simone said without hesitation.

"I'll need to talk with my staff."

"Are you planning on going in today?"

"Yeah, this afternoon. I have so much work to do, I can't afford to stay out."

"I know what you mean. Speaking of which, I've got to run. I have meetings until late today." She rose from her seat, crossed the short space and kissed her sister's cheek. "You take care, understand. And be careful, Sam. We don't need any more heroes."

"Back at ya."

The doorbell rang.

"Expecting someone?"

"No." She got up to answer the door.

"Check first," Simone ordered.

Samantha peered through the peephole. "It's Chad."

Simone's stomach rose, then fell.

"Hi," Samantha said, stepping aside to let him in. "I didn't expect you back . . . so soon."

"I didn't want you here alone, Samantha" Simone stepped into his line of vision. "Simone. I didn't know

you were here. I should have known you would be.''
He smiled warmly.

"Just leaving." She picked up her briefcase and
squeezed her sister's shoulder. "I'll call you later.
Take care, Chad." She brushed past him and down
the three steps to the street.

Chad watched her hasty departure and Samantha
watched him.

CHAPTER NINETEEN

Pam was in Simone's office when she arrived.

"Pam?"

"Oh," she spun away from the desk, her hand to her chest. "You scared me. I didn't hear you come in." Her red-tinted lips wobbled into a smile. She moved away from the desk, holding on to a manila file folder. "I was just leaving some messages for you." She tucked a stray strand of auburn hair back into its customary ponytail.

Simone stepped farther into the office and tossed her briefcase on a side chair. "They all can wait, whatever they are," she said absently.

"Something wrong?" Pam tugged on the hem of her fitted waist-length gray jacket.

"Nothing out of the ordinary." She stepped behind her desk and sat down.

Pam stood above her, arms folded, her large breasts accentuated by the action. "Something is wrong. It's all over your face. What's up?"

Simone looked up. How much could she say? Sam did indicate that she intended to go public with the threats, she thought. It was only a matter of time before it was out in the open, and it wouldn't be fair to her staff to let them find out from the media. Pamela Osborne had been with her since she was elected to office. She'd worked on the winning campaign, volunteering much of her time. Not one of the Washington insiders, Pam had a modest background, coming not from a prestigious school of learning but one of the city universities in New York. She was a hard worker with innate political instincts, and Simone had come to rely heavily on her opinion. They'd shared not just office talk, but many leisure hours at several of the local cafes and night spots in and around the district. Over drinks, Pam had spoken of her life in New York, coming from a broken home and having to work her way through school, baby-sitting, working as a supermarket clerk and telephone sales rep while trying to maintain a tenuous relationship with her college sweetheart. A relationship that didn't stand the test of time. They'd double-dated, gone binge shopping to soothe their relationship woes, and toiled late into the night on political strategy to further Simone's career. She wasn't given the position as chief of staff as a gesture. She'd earned it. Sure, she could talk to Pam, and Adam needed to know as well.

"Has Adam come in yet?"

"Yes, I saw him earlier."

"Do me a favor and get him for me. Then the both of you come in. We need to talk."

Adam's expression was drawn into tight lines on his angular face. His thick brows seemed to move like ominous clouds above his dark brown eyes as he listened to Simone lay out the events of the previous night.

Pam rhythmically tapped her pen against her thigh as she listened, a habit she had when deep in thought, her hazel eyes shielded behind her glasses.

"So . . . there you have it, folks, in all its ugly splendor," Simone concluded.

"I think Chad and Samantha are on the money in bringing this to the press. Whoever it is needs to be put on notice," Adam stated.

Pam was silent, still tapping the pen.

"However, my main concern has to be you, Simone," he added. "If these threats have extended beyond Samantha to the rest of you, the government has to get involved. We can have a secret service agent with you twenty-four seven, and I'm sure your mother will do the same thing."

"She hates them," Simone tossed back, dismissing that option.

"How is this going to impact on the class action

suit that Samantha is in the midst of putting together with Chad and your father?'' Pamela finally asked. ''I would imagine they'd have to let it go, at least until this thing is settled.''

''Good question. But knowing my sister, I can't imagine that she would back off or back down. And I'm sure Chad has no intention of letting it go either.''

''My recommendation is that Chad and your father handle it from here.''

''I agree,'' Pam cut in a bit sharply. ''And you should curb your public appearances as well.''

Simone looked from one to the other in complete amazement. ''How long have the two of you known me? Years,'' she answered for the both of them. ''When have you ever known me to run scared? When? Never, that's when. And I don't intend to start now. So that's out.'' She pushed some papers around on her desk.

Adam and Pamela shared a look of submission.

''Any other suggestions?''

''Business as usual . . .'' Adam teased, a smile flickering around his mouth.

''Thank you . . . both.''

They stood in unison. ''I'll have your itinerary on your desk in a few minutes,'' Pamela said, heading for the door.

''And I have your remarks ready for the meeting this afternoon,'' Adam added, following Pamela out.

''Thanks, guys.''

Left alone now, she could take off the mask of bravado. She covered her face with her hands, resting them in almost prayer-like fashion across the bridge of her nose. Her eyes skimmed across the contents of her desk, remembering Pam's statement about leaving messages for her. Probably buried, she thought absently as the phone rang.

"Councilwoman Montgomery," she said wearily. "Yes, Senator Hayes," she greeted, slipping back into gear, and at least temporarily pushing this latest series of events to the back of her mind.

"You really don't have to play chauffeur and bodyguard," Samantha said as she slid into the passenger seat of Chad's Volvo.

"I know I don't," he answered, shutting her door and rounding the front of the car. He got in beside her. "I want to. OK?"

"Are you going to follow me all over, skulk around corners and talk into handheld microphones hidden in pen tops?"

"It's not funny, Sam."

"Well, someone has to lighten up." She folded her arms and tossed her head, swinging her locks away from her face.

Chad rocked his jaw back and forth as he pulled out of the driveway. He didn't know what to make of her. One minute she was soft and tender, the next totally inaccessible and hard. He pulled the car out into traffic and turned on the radio.

Samantha glared at him from the corner of her eye, last night not forgotten. Yeah, it was real considerate of him to show up at her doorstep and escort her around. But damn it, she didn't want to be in his presence. Didn't want to risk the possibility of him seeing beyond the thin veneer of emotional protection she'd wrapped around herself.

She was hurting. She felt like a fool. And here he was, still being the gentleman. She folded her arms a bit tighter and wiggled down into her seat.

"Sam . . ."

"Hmm." She stared straight ahead.

"About last night . . ."

"Forget it, Chad. I really don't want to talk about it. And if you're going to be around me and this is a topic that's going to be revisited, we're going to have a problem, because I don't want to talk about it," she rattled on. She turned to look out the passenger window when she felt the sting in her eyes.

"Sam, not talking about stuff is what causes problems."

She tugged on her bottom lip with her teeth and didn't respond.

"If you're not going to talk, will you at least listen?"

Silence.

"Fine." He screeched to a halt at the red light. "I like you, Sam, more than you think. But being away has done a lot to me."

She turned to look at him askance, her right brow raised.

"No, nothing like that."

"Hmm." She stared back out the window.

"It made me think about what's really important, and it's not our own personal wants, desires and issues. Being away made me realize, Sam, that you can't take anything for granted, nothing, because life is so tenuous and fragile. Everything must mean something, have a purpose. And when I traveled the world and looked at the injustices, the atrocities, the hunger and devastation, I saw how infinitely small I am in the big picture, when these people are struggling every day of their lives just to survive. I want to have a purpose, Sam. I want my life and what I do to mean something."

Now she was beginning to feel like a pouting, selfish little girl. But she was still hurt.

"Do you understand what I'm trying real hard to say, Samantha?"

She turned her head to look at him, her eyes darting from his face to the dashboard, her hands, then back to his face. "Yeah, I understand. I'm just being bitchy and sensitive." She blew out a breath. "I guess last night, I . . . just wanted to be wanted. I needed to be held and made love to. And the only person I wanted to be that way with . . . was you. But it was all about how I was feeling and what I wanted. I know that. I guess I figured you were feeling the same way." She paused, collecting her thoughts. "I admire you, everything about you, your determination, your convictions. And to be truthful," she looked directly at him. "I still want to make love with you, make that connection with you. Maybe it will happen, maybe it won't, but that's how I feel.''

"Then let's take it slow, Sam. Work through this. Really get to know each other. Besides, until the dust clears, you're stuck with me, lady.'' He grinned mischievously.

The corner of her mouth quirked into a half smile. "We all have our crosses to bear, Mr. Rushmore.''

"Touché.''

When they arrived at Samantha's storefront office, the staff was in full swing as usual. Phones were ringing off the hook, and her harried staffers were scurrying around like worker bees.

"Welcome to my world,'' Samantha murmured to Chad as she waved and greeted Nettie, Steve and Mia on her way to her cubbyhole office in the back.

"Mia, we need to talk,'' she tossed over her shoulder.

"Be there in a sec,'' she called back, covering the mouthpiece of the phone.

"Have a seat,'' Samantha said to Chad, indicating a vacant chair with a toss of her hand. She stood behind her desk, hands on hips. "So, how does this 007 thing work? You kind of just hang around or what?''

Chad eased down into the chair. "You got me. This is my first gig,'' he teased.

"Ouch. I might have to look after you."

"Would that be so bad?" he asked, a sudden sparkle in his eyes.

"Let's not take it there. You know what happened with Whitney and Kevin in *The Bodyguard*," she taunted.

"Yeah . . . I remember."

A gentle warmth, an assurance, settled between them and they relaxed in each other's company for the first time in hours. And it felt good.

"I know you have tons of work to do," Samantha finally said, shifting the conversation to a manageable territory. "We can get you set up with a computer and a phone and whatever else you need."

"Great. Can I get access to the database that's been put together?"

"Absolutely. I'll get you a code and it's done. Anything else you can think of?"

"Some coffee."

"Help yourself." She pointed to the makeshift kitchen and laughed. "Coffee is as good as you make it."

Mia stuck her head in the door. "Ready for me?"

"Yes. Come on in. Chad needs to be in on this anyway since it was his idea. Close the door."

Once everyone was settled, Samantha began and Chad was once again amazed by this other Samantha, not the femme fatale, or the wounded soul, or the defiant one, but a woman in control, clear-headed and with vision. A woman respected by her peers and feared by her enemies, intuitive and bright. Samantha Montgomery was a woman to be reckoned with.

". . . I want a statement prepared," Samantha concluded. "I'll give you all the particulars, Mia. And then call Fleming, our contact at the *Post* and give him an exclusive."

Mia nodded as she took notes. "I'll get right on it. Anything else?" She looked from Samantha to Chad.

"I think Sam's covered everything," Chad said. "I don't have anything to add except this . . . be careful. Be mindful of new faces, packages. Pay attention to everything around you. And old faces as well."

"I trust my staff."

"And you should. But in instances like this, no one is above suspicion. It's hard to swallow, but it's true."

Mia looked away.

"No offense, Mia," he said. "Just stating facts."

"None taken. I know where my bread is buttered." She looked to Samantha and grinned.

"Then that's it. Mia, Chad is going to need a code to get into the systems."

"No problem."

"How's the database coming?" he asked.

"Just about finished."

"Maybe I can help," he offered.

"The more fingers the better. Mine are beginning to cramp."

"I'm a quick study. Just show me how it's done."

"Well, if you two can keep each other busy and out of trouble, I have work to do," Samantha said.

Before they were halfway out the door, her phone

rang. She waved with one hand and picked up the phone with the other.

"Samantha Montgomery."

"Sam, it's Dad. We need to talk, sweetheart. I'm on my way over there."

CHAPTER TWENTY

"Knock, knock."

Simone wearily looked up from the stack of reports from the latest Harris. She let a tired smile relax her mouth and briefly squeezed her eyes shut to rid them of the numbers running in front of them.

"Hey, Adam. Come on in. I could use a break."

"Can I close the door?"

"Sure." She looked at him curiously as he crossed the carpeted floor and took a seat in the antique cherry wood armchair opposite her.

"How's it going?" He peeked above the tops of the paper piles, stretching his long legs out in front of him, and loosening his blue and red geometric tie.

"Just reviewing the latest poll numbers. Not bad,"

she conceded. "But we'll have to be a helluva lot better if we're going to solidly beat McCall in November."

"That's what I want to talk to you about." His expression grew more serious. "I know you're dead set against toning down your stance, but, Simone," he leaned forward, his voice urgent and imploring. "You need to really think about it."

"I have," she snapped without hesitation.

"Simone, this isn't some meet-you-at-three schoolyard threat. These are real people with some serious issues."

"What about our issues, Adam? Are they any less serious because someone says shut up?"

"No. Of course not." He paused a beat, assessing the turn his next words would take—dare he say them. "Simone . . . I care about you. More than just a rising politician, more than just a friend." He held up his hand when she opened her mouth to speak. "I know you have some unresolved issues with Chad, but I was hoping you'd think about . . . us. Me and you. Try it on, see how it feels." He blew out a breath. "I guess what I'm saying is, I've always cared about you, Simone, for as long as I've known you. It took the threat of possibly losing you to make me say what I've been thinking all along."

He stood and headed for the door. "Don't say anything. Not now. Think about it. We can talk over dinner. Say around 7:30?"

Wide-eyed, Simone nodded numbly in agreement as Adam closed the door quietly behind him.

The ringing phone snapped her out of her daze. "Yes, Denise?"

"Your sister is on two," her secretary announced.

"Thanks." She pressed the flashing light. "Sam, hi. What's—"

"You won't believe what he did!" she hissed into the phone, sounding like a pot ready to boil over.

"What who did?"

"Dad!"

Simone shook her head to clear it. "Dad? What did he do?"

"He called Janice, my mother. Can you believe that? He actually called her. And it gets worse. She's on her way. She'll be here tomorrow."

"Oh, sh—"

"Exactly. Tomorrow. I guess she thinks she can play mom and convince me to go back to Atlanta—where it's safe. Monie, I'm so pissed I could scream."

Simone heard something crash on the other end of the phone and instinctively flinched.

"Sam, calm down a minute and tell me what happened."

Samantha huffed and puffed for a minute in an effort to pull herself together. "He just left," she finally uttered, reining in her spiraling emotions. "And it's a good thing too, 'cause I was a hot minute from throwing him out personally."

Simone bit down on a smile. Now that would have been worth the price of admission. "Okay, so he just left. What did he say?"

"Well, you know Dad, the consummate diplomat.

But the minute he walked in here, I knew something was up . . ."

"Hi, sweetheart," Justin greeted as he effortlessly strode across the room to where his daughter sat. His smile was ebullient, his dark eyes shining. Cover-model together in his gun-metal gray wool gabardine suit and burgundy and gray pinstriped tie, Justin Montgomery could easily move from the courtroom to dinner without missing a beat. He was a bit more silver-haired at the temples these days, with a soft sprinkling of snow across his cap, Samantha noticed as she stood to receive his customary kiss, but it only made him that much more maturely attractive.

"Hi, Dad. Have a seat. You made it sound urgent on the phone. Everything OK?"

Justin slowly sat down. He clasped his hands across his knees, leaning forward. "I've thought hard about this latest threat, Samantha." Samantha stiffened, sensing trouble. "I want you to go back to Atlanta for a while until things calm down."

She shot up out of her seat, rattling the pencil cup on her desk. "No. Forget it."

"Sam, be reasonable."

"I've already decided—"

"I called your mother."

"You did what?"

"She agrees with me."

"I don't care what she thinks," she tossed back,

folding her arms and glaring at her father. "How could you do that? Why, is a better question?"

"Your mother has a right to know what's going on with you, Samantha. She may be a lot of things, but she's still your mother."

Samantha stalked across the room, fury twisting her insides. "I'm not going," she stated emphatically.

"Your mother will be here in the morning."

"What! Is this some sort of conspiracy?"

"She's concerned, Sam."

"Pleeeze." She turned cold, gray-green eyes on him. "Was her coming here your idea, too?"

"No, it was hers."

Shocked for a moment, she didn't respond.

Justin stood. "I know you're upset," he said gently. "And you have every right to be. But you're my daughter, and whatever I need to do to protect you, I will. And on that, there's no negotiation."

Samantha remained silent.

"She wants to see you, Sam."

Samantha looked away.

"Your mother will be at my office after I pick her up from the airport. I'll call you."

"Does Vaughn know you've done this?" she hurled at his back between clenched teeth.

He stopped short, struck by the venom in her voice. "I'll talk to her when I get home."

"Damn," Simone whispered at the end of the conversation.

"That's putting it lightly."

"Hey, maybe it won't be so bad. Let her say whatever she has to say and you do what you need to do, that's all." Simone knew how deeply Samantha resented her mother for what she'd done, the years of lies. They'd sat up long into the early hours of the morning talking about her feelings, the hurt and resentment Samantha felt toward Janice for having deprived her of her father all those years. And now the very person that she'd stood up for, turned her back on her mother for, is the one who betrayed her. Or so she felt.

"That's not even it," Samantha said, her voice weak and full of sadness. "It's Dad. What he did . . ."

"I know, Sam. But he's just looking out for you."

"You're taking his side," she accused.

"No. I'm not. I'm just trying to be open-minded. Like you should be."

"Forget it. It's obvious you don't understand either." She slammed down the phone.

Simone stared at the phone in her hand, listening for several moments to the dial tone humming in her ear. She thought about calling Samantha back, but decided against it. Little sis needed some cool-down time. She'd call her at home, later.

Chad spoke with Justin in the hallway of Samantha's storefront office.

"Justin, man, why? You knew Sam would flip about something like this. I don't know all the details about

Samantha and her mother, but what little I do know isn't good."

Justin clenched his jaw. "It was Janice's decision, Chad."

"But you made the call."

"Yes, I did. And given the chance, I'd do it again." He shifted his stance from his left to right leg. "Janice took something away from me I'll never recover—the years with my daughter. I have her back now, and as much as I detest what Janice did, I won't stoop to her level, and I won't play the revenge role. I only wish I was involved in Samantha's life all those years. But I wasn't. I don't intend to repeat Janice's mistakes. She's her mother. Right or wrong. She deserves to know what's going on with our daughter. What she does or doesn't do about it will be up to her."

Listening to Justin, hearing not only the hurt but the sincerity in his voice, he had no choice but to alter his opinion. He only wished that if and when he was called upon, he'd be man enough to make those hard, unpopular decisions as Justin had.

Chad clapped Justin's left shoulder. "How can I help?"

Justin angled his chin in the direction of Samantha's office down the corridor. "Be there for her. I know this is a lot all at once: the protests, the threats, this pending suit and now a visit by her mother. And knowing my hotheaded daughter there's no telling what she might get it in her head to do: rally together college students to form a barricade around the airport protesting Janice's arrival."

Chad smiled. "I could almost see her pulling something like that off."

"Hmm." Justin agreed. "The funny thing is, she has enough charisma and clout in this town to make it happen. But that's the public Samantha Montgomery. The one I'm concerned about is the one behind the headlines and the microphones." He heaved a sigh and stuck out his hand for the black man's shake of the day. "I've got to run. Keep an eye on her for me, will you."

"Absolutely. I'll call you," he said to Justin's receding back.

"Samantha, Samantha, Samantha," Chad mumbled, head bowed as he returned down the corridor. "What are we going to do with you?"

CHAPTER
TWENTY-ONE

"Vaughn . . ."

She turned from hanging her clothes in the closet, saw her husband of six years and turned away.

Justin stepped fully into the bedroom and closed the door, not risking the chance that Dottie may overhear what could turn into an ugly conversation.

"We need to talk."

"About what, Justin? It's pretty clear that my opinion doesn't matter when it comes to your daughter." She took her robe from the closet and shut the door with a definitive thud.

He felt her sting as sharply as a slap and he knew he deserved it.

"I'm sorry about this morning. My comments were uncalled for."

She kept her back to him, brushing her hair as she faced the vanity mirror.

"I know how much you love Samantha," he continued. "And I never meant to hurt you with my thoughtless remarks. I'm sorry, Vaughn."

She spun around, her eyes steeped in the anger that had been brewing all day. "It's more than an apology, Justin. It's what came from in your heart. You may be sorry you said it, but the truth is, it's what you felt." Her voice trembled ever so slightly. "And you're right, she is your daughter, as Simone is mine. But we made a promise to each other when we married that no matter what, we'd never let our roles as their parents interfere with or harm what we have as husband and wife. Maybe they were just words. But I believed them."

He slowly approached her. "I believe them, too," he said gently, aching inside at witnessing the hurt shimmering in her brown eyes and knowing that he put it there. "I know I can't take back what I said to you, but I need you to believe that it was only said in a flash of fear and frustration. It had nothing to do with my belief about how you feel for Sam, or your role in her life. I love you. More than life itself, and I would never do anything to intentionally hurt you." He dared to step closer and his heart twisted when he saw her entire body tighten in defense of his approach. He stopped, drew in a breath and slowly released it. "I spoke with Janice this morning." She flinched slightly, but he continued. "She decided to come here. Her plane arrives at nine tomorrow morning."

Vaughn's lips tightened into a hard line. She turned away, walked toward the bathroom and shut the door.

Moments later, the hard splash of rushing water could be heard.

"I don't want to discuss my father, Chad," Samantha stated as she sat pinned to the passenger side door of his car.

"At least try to see his way of thinking, Sam."

"Look, I'm damn near thirty years old. If I can't take care of myself by now, I never will. And the last person I need supervision from is my mother."

Chad made the turn onto Sixteenth Street. "I don't think the issue is about your ability to take care of yourself, Sam. The issue is that your parents care about you. They want you safe. Put yourself in their place. How would you feel if your child's life was threatened? There's no way you can make me believe you, of all people, would sit back and just say 'oh, well.' You'd turn hell into heaven to protect them. You do it for strangers, Sam."

She huffed out a breath, tossed him a quick look, then stared out the window. "I don't think you know how much I hate to be wrong," she said in a tiny voice.

"Is that what you're saying now?"

"I'll never admit it."

He held on to a smile. "Now that we have that cleared up."

"I really don't want to see her, you know."

He reached over and covered her fisted hand with his. "I know, babe. But I can guarantee that you'll feel better when you do."

"You don't know my mother," she said, her gaze focused onto a place he could not see. "She's . . . manipulative. She plays the weak and vulnerable female, but underneath there's a heart of stone. Anything my mother does is only to further her own self-interest. It took me years to figure that out. She didn't leave my father because he mistreated her, or didn't love her or me, like she made me believe all those years. She left because she wanted to be the center of attention. And when I was born, the limelight was no longer on her. Then my dad's law practice started taking off. So she left to punish him, and she wanted me to punish him, too."

"People can change, Sam. Maybe your mother has finally seen what she's done to her life and to yours."

"That's hard for me to believe, Chad," she said sadly. "As much as I may want to."

"Well, at least hear what she has to say and make your own decision. Which I know you will anyway," he added with a smile.

"That's pretty much what Monie said, and I hung up on her."

"I'm sure Simone understands."

She angled her head and looked at him. "You two

were pretty close before you went away from what I can remember."

"Yeah," he said quietly.

"How come you two . . . never . . . got together?"

She saw his jaw clench and recalled his look that followed Simone when she left her house earlier. Her stomach did a slow dip.

"It . . . wasn't that kind of relationship," he finally answered, partly in truth.

"Did you want it to be?" she pressed.

"That was four years ago, Sam. I wasn't sure what I wanted back then." Again a partial truth, he thought.

"What about now?"

He turned when they came to a stop at a red light and looked directly into her eyes. "I'm doing what I want . . . right here, right now," he said softly and in even tones. "I hope that answers any and all questions about my motives or intentions." His gaze gently held her and the rolling in her stomach eased.

She pressed her lips together and nodded slowly. "OK," she said on a whisper.

"You want to grab something to eat or head straight home?"

She grinned. "I feel like hanging out for a while. You up for it?"

"I think we deserve it. Blue Light?"

"I'm with the driver."

Simone sipped on her mango Margarita, tapping her foot to the beat of the live band. She and Adam had been at the club for nearly a half hour and he hadn't mentioned another word about his proclamation earlier in the day. She wasn't sure if she was relieved or disappointed. She dipped a celery stalk into the blue cheese dressing and took a crunchy bite.

Adam chuckled and Simone looked at him, mildly curious.

"You even chew celery sticks with class."

"I'm going to have to take that one as a compliment."

"Everything you do has your personal stamp on it, Simone."

She glanced away, uncharacteristically embarrassed.

"I'm not making you blush am I?" He smiled at her.

The temperature beneath her skin rose another notch. "Not in this dim light," she tossed back.

She put the half-eaten celery on her plate, wiped her mouth with the paper napkin and leaned closer on her forearms. "Adam, why did you say what you did in my office earlier today?"

"Because it's how I feel. Nothing's guaranteed in this life. Especially time. I don't want to waste any more of it playing a waiting game."

"Waiting game?"

"Yeah." He chuckled lightly. "Waiting to see if you would ever notice that I cared for you more than just as an employer and friend."

The heat went up again, but she didn't back away this time.

"I'd like us to see each other—outside of the office—outside of D.C. Maybe take a weekend at Virginia Beach, really get to know each other outside of work, issues and pressure."

"Mmm. Suppose you find out that's all I am, work issues and pressure?" Her right brow rose.

"Even on a bad day you can do better than that."

She looked away, reached for her drink to give her hands something to do, then stopped.

"It's been a long time for me . . . since I've seriously been involved with anyone. And to be truthful—before you ask—I can't count Chad as an 'anyone.' We never got that far." She took her plastic straw and absently stirred her drink.

"Then maybe you're long overdue. I know I am."

"I can't guarantee anything, Adam."

"Not looking for guarantees, Simone. Just the opportunity. What would be so bad about that?"

She looked at him for a long moment, studied the gentle slope of his brows, the generous curve of his mouth, the way the brown of his eyes deepened to the color of mink when he was making a point, the smoothness of his copper-toned skin with just a shadow of a beard that gave him that extra-rugged appeal that she liked. He was bright, ambitious, and they had plenty in common. She tugged in a deciding breath. What would be so bad? she asked herself. She couldn't think of one reason, and then Chad walked in with Samantha.

CHAPTER TWENTY-TWO

They caught each other's eye almost simultaneously, their reaction nearly identical: a flash of excitement, quickly replaced with the realization of their respective circumstances.

Drawing on all her home training, Simone waved merrily and put on her best smile, even as Samantha glided across the room linked to Chad's arm, as if there were no other place she should be.

Adam looked over his shoulder to see who'd attracted Simone's attention and effectively cut off the response he'd waited far too long to hear. There was no missing the look that passed between them. It was only an instant, but it said so much. And he wondered if Samantha realized that the man she was falling for was in love with her sister.

"Hey, folks," Simone greeted when the striking couple stopped at the table.

"Great minds think alike," Samantha joked.

Adam stood and shook Chad's hand. "Join us, man, might be a while for a table. The place is pretty packed tonight."

Chad looked to his date, brows raised in question.

"Sure," she shrugged nonchalantly, even though she would have preferred to have Chad to herself for a couple of hours. Besides, she owed Simone a big apology for hanging up on her earlier. Turning down Adam's invitation would seem like another slap in the face.

After seating Samantha, Chad confiscated a lone chair from the next table and took his place next to her, directly opposite Simone.

"You guys order yet?" Chad asked, scanning the dimness for a waitress. He could use a drink.

"Just appetizers and something to take the edge off," Simone answered, holding up her half-finished drink for confirmation.

"Then we have some catching up to do," Chad said, signaling for the waitress heading in their direction.

"What can I get everyone?" a twenty-something supermodel type asked.

"This round is on me," Chad offered magnanimously. "Refills for whatever they're having." He looked to Simone. "Margarita, right?"

She raised her glass and smiled in agreement.

The waitress quickly took the rest of the order and disappeared.

"How'd the rest of your day shape up, Simone?" Chad asked. "You said you had a lot of meetings."

Adam glanced at her curiously, wondering when they'd spoken, when he'd seen her.

"Pretty grueling, but nothing less than what I expected. Everyone wants something—immediately. What about you two? Any new developments?"

"If you mean any more threats, not today. Hopefully they've filled their quota for the time being," Samantha said.

"Have you decided what you're going to do—about tomorrow?" Simone asked with caution, not wanting another outburst from her sister.

A look that Simone couldn't quite pinpoint passed between Samantha and Chad.

Samantha took a breath. "I've been convinced by a very influential source to, at least, see her," she confessed.

Simone instantly knew that it was nothing she'd said that changed Sam's mind, and a twinge of jealousy settled in her stomach. Her mouth pinched as if she'd sucked a lemon. "Glad to hear it." She raised the glass to her mouth and drained the rest of her drink. "I'm sure it will be fine."

"What are we talking about, for those not in the know?" Adam quizzed, looking from one woman to the other.

Samantha explained, leaving out the ugly details.

"It might not be a bad idea for you to lay low for

a while, Sam," Adam said at the conclusion of her revelation.

"That's not an option," she stated clearly. "I'll listen to what she has to say and then she can go back to Atlanta. We're just about finished processing the names for the suit, and there's no way I'm leaving in the middle of it."

"What are the next steps in the game plan?" Adam asked, speaking to Chad.

"I'm hoping by next week to get the preliminary paperwork done and begin interviewing the complainants. Justin is dealing with the filing."

"Chad will be working out of my office, since all of the files are there," Samantha added.

"Why not Dad's office?" Simone wanted to know.

"Justin has too much going on over there with his regular clientele," Chad said, although he would have preferred Justin's office himself, especially since Justin was very clear about keeping his daughters as far removed from the process as possible. Unfortunately, his wants didn't work with the need.

"Do you have enough hands to help?" Simone asked. "I may be able to squeeze in some time."

"I'm sure we'll be all right. But thanks for the offer, sis. Besides, you have enough to do with your campaign."

The waitress returned with their drinks and took their orders for dinner. The band swung into their rendition of "Misty," and everyone tapped their feet to the familiar classic rhythm.

"How is the campaign coming, Simone?" Chad asked, taking a sip of his Jack Daniels on the rocks.

"Our poll numbers are up by the latest count. But starting next week I'll be back out on the trail, shaking hands and accepting wet kisses from babies," Simone said drolly.

"She makes it sound like she hates it, but the truth is this lady shines under the glare of potential voter eyes," Adam joked, lightly touching Simone's arm, hoping to get her to tear her eyes away from Chad and Samantha.

"My sister and my mother are the consummate politicians. I only wish I had their tact and diplomacy," Sam added.

"You do tend to say what's on your mind," Chad added, giving her a private look.

Simone loudly cleared her throat. "I'm starved. I hope this food arrives soon." She took another long swallow of her drink and began to feel the buzz, the almost-there feeling that would take one more drink to reach. "So what made you two decide to come out tonight, especially since there's so much to do?"

"It was your sister's idea," Chad offered.

"You didn't seem to mind," Simone returned, a decided edge to her voice. Another long swallow. Almost there.

"He's been working real hard. I thought a night out would do us both some good." Samantha looked at her sister, trying to gauge where the tension was coming from. Maybe it was the residual effects of their earlier conversation. But somehow she didn't think so. It was almost as if Simone resented their presence.

"All work and no play . . ." Simone let the comment hang there. She signaled for the waitress. "Another margarita, please. This round's on me," she added.

"I'm fine," Samantha said, barely having touched her wine spritzer.

"I'm cool," came from Chad.

"Nothing else for me, thanks," Adam said. "Maybe you should slow down, too," he quietly mentioned to Simone.

"I don't need you to tell me how much to drink," she snapped from between her teeth. Almost there.

Samantha glanced at Chad, then at Adam, who both kept their gazes averted. "Would you all excuse me for a minute? I'm going to find the ladies' room. Simone, come with me. You know how bad I am with directions," she joked, making her voice light.

Simone pushed back in the chair and stood, grabbing her purse from the table in one swift motion.

The men watched them walk away, then returned to their drinking and feigning interest in the band. Silence hung between them until Chad spoke up.

"How many has she had?"

"One too many, obviously."

"Is something wrong?"

"Maybe you should tell me," Adam said, staring Chad in the eye.

"What's that supposed to mean?"

Adam took a breath, weighing the right and wrong

of what he was about to say. "She told me about the two of you."

Chad's brows raised in surprise, then lowered. "I see." He stared into the amber of his drink, watching the ice melt.

"She's not over you, and it's hard for her to see you with Sam."

Chad rocked his jaw back and forth before speaking. "Whatever is happening or not happening between me and Simone is her call. This is the way she wanted things."

"You really believe that?"

"I don't have much of a choice, do I, brother?"

"We all have choices."

Chad was quiet for a moment. "And where do you fit into all this?"

"I care about Simone—a great deal."

"I see," Chad said, nodding slowly. "And . . . ?"

"And I want to see her happy."

"So do I."

"Let me put it to you this way, brother. I want to give Simone and me a shot, and I don't want any surprises."

"Like what?"

"Like you deciding halfway through the game that you want to play on the other team." He took a sip of his drink and angled his body toward the stage, ending any further conversation, but his point had been made.

*   *   *

"What's up with you?" Samantha asked as she watched Simone apply a coat of berry lipstick.

"What do you mean?" She peered closer into the mirror, studying her reflection as if for the first time.

"What's with the subtle nasty comments?"

"I don't know what you're talking about." She dug in her purse for her compact.

"Is this about this morning? Because if it is, I'm sorry, Monie. Sorry about what I said. I shouldn't have taken my mess out on you. And I definitely shouldn't have hung up on you."

"Apology accepted," she said unenthusiastically.

"Simone. Look at me."

Simone spun around, her eyes hard. "What? I said I accepted your apology."

"It's more than that." She paused a beat. "What's going on with you and Chad?"

CHAPTER TWENTY-THREE

Vaughn feigned sleep when she heard Justin gingerly open and close the bedroom door. She had no intention of continuing their conversation.

Justin slipped between the cool sheets and lay on his back listening to Vaughn's breathing. They'd never gone to bed angry, and he wasn't thinking of starting now. He turned on his side, pressing his front to her back.

"Babe, I know you're upset. You have every right to be, but what's done is done." He slid his hands across her nylon-covered hip. The alluring, soft scent of her floated around them, drawing him to her like a magnet.

She shifted her body and eased away. "Vaughn,

I'm sorry. What more can I say? How long are you not going to talk to me? That's not who we are."

Suddenly, she flipped onto her back, then turned to him in the dark. He could feel the burn of her gaze.

"We're supposed to be a couple. A couple who talks and makes decisions together. But that's not what happened here, Justin. And that's your doing, not mine." She turned on to her side, her back to him.

"Vaughn, just listen to me for a minute. Maybe I acted too hastily. I should have told you what I wanted to do . . . I should have talked with you about what I wanted to do," he quickly amended. "But I didn't. And for that I'm sorry. And that thing about Sam being my daughter . . . you've got to know I didn't mean it to come across the way it sounded."

"But it did. And you did," she said.

He ran his hand higher up her hip, along the tender slope of her waist. "And I'm sorry. I swear I am. How long are you going to make me pay?" he asked in a pleading, little-boy voice.

Vaughn fought to keep from smiling. She couldn't let him off that easy. "Don't try sweet-talking me, Justin Montgomery. It's not going to work this time."

"So what am I going to have to do to make all this up to you?" he whispered, leaning down into her ear. He ran his tongue tauntingly along her lobe.

Her voice shivered ever so slightly. "More than that."

"Oh, yeah. Well, why don't you tell me what I need to do for my penance."

Slowly she turned over and looked up at the outline of his face in the darkness, the only illumination the sliver of moonlight that peeked in from between the curtains.

"Before you even think about 'getting on your knees' " she taunted, "I want it made clear that I'm going with you to the airport in the morning."

"Fine. I want you there. What else?"

"And no more decisions without us talking about it first."

"Agreed." His fingers eased up beneath the swell of her breasts. He heard her quick intake of breath.

"You're making . . . these . . . negotiations . . . very difficult to concentrate on," she said on a rush of air when his palm captured and gently cupped one breast, teasing the nipple to erect firmness between his fingertips.

"Nothing worth having comes easy," he whispered against her mouth, brushing his lips teasingly across hers. "Some things are very hard . . . indeed."

"I do believe . . . I'd have to agree with you . . . on that one," she said in a strained whisper as she took him in her hand and massaged the heated flesh.

The last hour of dinner was spent in an awkward silence, the obvious gaps in conversation filled with insignificant trivia.

Simone had walked out of the restroom, leaving

Samantha and her question hanging in the perfumed air. Chad and Adam remained at a stalemate; whatever move made by the other would determine who ultimately went home with the spoils.

Mercifully, the meal, all half-eaten but earnestly studied by the four diners, was finally over. Goodbyes and wishes for safe trips home were halfheartedly given as they made their way out and to their cars.

"What is going on with you tonight, Simone?" Adam asked the instant Chad and Samantha were out of earshot.

"What makes everyone think something's wrong with Simone? Little ol' Simone who always has it together," she mumbled, her words blurring together.

"You're going to have one helluva headache in the morning. And you're not driving. I'm taking you home."

"I don't need you to drive me home." She stumbled over an invisible crack in the street and Adam caught her around the waist.

"I'm taking you home. End of story."

"What about my car?" she mumbled, leaning her weight against him.

"I'll take care of it. We get you home and in bed and I'll come back for it."

She looked up at him, a crooked smile on her chestnut-brown face, her gaze slightly cloudy. "Never had anybody to just look after me, ya know. Nobody besides my folks. You're a nice man, Adam,'' she said, her compliment one long word. She rested her head against his shoulder as they made their way to his car.

"If you'd let me, I'd take care of you all the time." He kissed her forehead before opening the passenger-side door and helping her inside.

He got behind the wheel and started the car.

"Are you going to spend the night?" she asked, the inquisitive tone of a curious child lacing her voice.

He turned to look at her and her head was already back, her eyes closed.

"What did you and your sister talk about in the ladies' room?" Chad finally asked as they pulled up in front of Samantha's house.

They'd hardly shared two full sentences between them since they'd left the club, and it was a question she'd anticipated him asking.

"Why she was drinking so much, for one . . . you, for another."

Chad cut the engine. "The two aren't connected, I hope," he responded, keeping his tone light.

"Strangely enough, it seems as if they are." She angled her head toward him, monitoring his needless actions: checking the car keys and the CD player, and making a point of adjusting the rearview mirror. "Did you sleep with Simone?" she asked point-blank.

"Let's go inside, Sam." He opened his door.

She jumped out on her side. "Damn you, answer

me!'' she demanded, slamming her palm on the roof of the car, the frustration of the past few hours bubbling over.

He walked toward the house, utterly conflicted about what he should say. This was getting entirely too messy. "I'm not going to discuss my private life, such that it is, out in the street." His shoes crunched on something broken.

Samantha stormed up behind him, determined to get an answer once and for all.

"Wait!" Chad commanded, the force of his voice causing a shiver to run through her. He stepped closer. More crunching. He peered through the darkness to the layers of broken glass littering the entrance to her house. The curtain billowing out of the ground floor window halted them both. "Get back in the car."

Her heart started to pound. "Chad . . ."

"Go back, Sam, and get in the car," he ordered, enunciating every word. He walked up the three steps to the front door and saw that it was partially open. He pushed it open further with his foot, and total chaos spread out before him.

CHAPTER TWENTY-FOUR

"Looks like your garden variety B&E," the officer said indifferently. He gazed around. "Anything missing?"

Samantha curved tighter into Chad's embrace. "I don't think so," she said softly.

He made a note in his pad just as his partner walked in from outside. "A bunch of broken glass, but not much else," he commented. "I'd board that window up if I were you." He looked at the mess in the front room. "Really trashed the place, huh?"

Chad felt Samantha's body jerk as if she were about to leap out of his arms. He held her tighter. "Will there be anything else, *officers?*" he asked through clenched teeth.

The first officer lifted his beaked cap and ran his fingers through thick red hair. He gave Chad a hard look from ice blue eyes. "Call the precinct in the morning and get your file number, *sir*. If you discover anything missing make a list and bring it in."

"You're that Montgomery woman, aren't you," said officer number two. "Always in the paper."

"Ain't life funny, Jimmy," commented the first officer, heading for the door. "First ones to cry police brutality, down with the pigs, are the very ones who call us when they get in trouble." He hitched his pants and tipped his hat.

The second officer's face turned fire-engine red as he lowered his gaze and followed his partner out the door. " 'Night, folks. Don't forget to get your case number," he mumbled.

They watched the officers leave, and it took all of Chad's powers of restraint to keep from ripping the door off its hinges when he slammed it shut. He turned toward Samantha and was rocked to his core seeing the blank unfocused look in her eyes and her arms locked around her body as if she could single-handedly ward off whatever or whoever was out to hurt her.

Gingerly, he crossed the room and stepped up to her. He lifted her chin with the tip of his index finger. "Sam," he gently said. "Do you want to stay here tonight?"

She nodded numbly, looked around, shivered, then focused on something he could not see.

"Fine, let's get you settled and I'll try to clean up some of this mess."

"Don't call them," she urged in a sudden whisper.

"Who?"

"My family . . . I don't want them to know." Abruptly, she grabbed his shirt. "They can't know, Chad, promise me."

He cupped her cheek, his fingers tangling in her locks, and his heart seemed to stumble in his chest when he saw the terror swimming in her eyes. "Sam, baby, it's OK." Gently he pulled her against his chest and felt her entire body tremble. He stroked her back. "Whatever you want. All right." Her head bobbed up and down against his chest. "Come on, let's get you settled. We'll figure all the rest of this out in the morning." He started to guide her toward the stairs when she stopped cold.

"Tomorrow . . . My mother's coming tomorrow." She pressed her hands to her face. "Oh, God . . . I can't . . . she can't know. She can't."

"Just calm down, Sam." He pulled her hands away from her face and forced her to look into his eyes. "Listen to me. It's going to be all right. We'll work it out. If I have to stay up all night getting this place together I will. If you decide you want to tell your family, it's up to you, not me. But . . . I have to tell you, one way or the other they're bound to find out."

She blinked rapidly, pressing her lips together. Her entire body felt as if her skin were crawling, aware that something unseen was still out there, lurking, waiting. The fine hairs on her arms and the back of her neck stood up. She drew in a long breath. "You're right." A tear slid down her cheek. "They do need to know. They could be next."

"Come on." He draped his arm around her shoulder and led her upstairs.

It would be so easy to make love to her now, here, in her bedroom, the shadows of light and dark playing across her skin. Adam stepped closer to Simone's bed. She looked so soft and peaceful. *Vulnerable.* A combination of all the things he'd never witnessed before in her.

Simone stirred gently between the sheets, her eyelids fluttering. She turned on to her back. "Adam," he thought he heard her say. He moved closer.

Her eyes flickered open, closed, then slowly opened again. "Adam."

This time he knew she'd said his name. He sat on the side of her bed and brushed her hair away from her face.

"Didn't mean to fall asleep on you. Lousy hostess, huh?"

"Not to worry."

"My car?"

"Took care of that already. It's parked right out front next to mine," he added with a teasing smile.

"Hmm. That sounds kind of nice . . . the thought . . . you know."

"Yeah, I think I do." He swallowed and slowly stood. "I better get going."

Simone sat up in the bed, her hair a bit wild and unrestrained, her eyes bright and her skin glowing from the brief hour of sleep. She'd never looked more beautiful, more inviting, almost innocent, than she did at that moment, Adam thought. He knew he had to leave—then—or he wouldn't be able to.

"Why?" she asked so softly he wasn't sure if he'd heard her. Her gaze held steady as she waited for his response.

"Simone . . . I . . . You know how I feel about you. Don't—"

"—Ask you this if I don't mean it," she said, completing his sentence.

He slid his hands into his pockets to keep from touching her again. "Exactly."

"I don't do anything I don't mean, Adam. I think you know me well enough to know at least that much." She laughed derisively. "Things don't always turn out the way I expected, but I can always walk away knowing that I did it with my eyes wide open." She raised her chin as if to dare him to challenge her statement.

"I stay and then what, Simone?"

"That's what we'll figure out . . . together."

"This is a big turnaround from earlier this evening. That whole thing at the club." He knew he was pushing his luck, risking the chance that, yes, she'd agree, this wasn't as it seemed. But he had to know for certain. No games, no surprises in the fourth quarter.

She sat up further and the sheet slid down to her waist. Her blouse was partly unbuttoned. The laced edges of a pale-colored bra contrasted enticingly against her honey-brown flesh. Adam forced his gaze to rise and settle on her eyes.

"I never had a chance to answer you before . . . they came in," she said softly.

"And . . ."

"And I want to see what it could be like, Adam. I can't make it any simpler than that. Do I still think about Chad? Yes. Does it do something to me inside to know that he's with my sister? Yes. But you know what, that's life and life's a bitch. Simple as that. I can either spend the rest of mine kicking myself, or I can move on. And in between those four margaritas I decided to move on. And no, I'm not drunk, not even tipsy."

He took in all that she'd said. Made sure he wasn't only hearing what he wanted. He'd waited a long time to reach this point. The process had been a slow but relentless one. Inside he smiled.

"Mind if I use your shower?" he asked.

She tossed the sheet aside and stood. Her voice was low and inviting. "Let me show you where everything is."

CHAPTER TWENTY-FIVE

Samantha wrapped a towel around her body, still damp from her recent shower, and padded across her bedroom floor, keeping her door slightly ajar. The sound of Chad's movements below was infinitely reassuring.

Sitting in front of her dressing table mirror, she was stunned to see the strained look around her eyes, the fine lines, that she was certain had not been there weeks earlier. She pushed her locks back from her face, fastened them with a leather tie, and removed the ivory and wood earrings from her lobes. Gently, she applied a thin film of moisturizer to her face, mindful of the required upward strokes.

Her body felt weary and suddenly old, she realized

as she screwed the cap back onto the jar. All her muscles felt tight, coiled, unused. She wasn't sure if it was her fragile emotional state or her overworked mind playing havoc with her generally fit body.

She reached for her favorite vanilla massage oil and began at her feet, kneading each toe and the ball of each foot. Moving up, she rubbed the heavenly scented oil into the curved muscles of her legs and up her thighs, using her thumbs to press out the knots, loosen the muscles. She stood and released the towel that was tucked beneath her arms. It dropped into a pool of fluffy sea green at her feet. She poured a handful of oil into her palms and slowly ran her hands together before applying it to the tight rise of her behind, dip into the curve of her waist, across the taut terrain of her stomach, up to the high arch of her full breasts.

An unexpected sigh slipped from her lips, and her eyes squeezed shut as she tenderly rubbed the round globes in a slow circular motion. She nearly wept at the sudden pleasure of being touched, and felt the deep throb from between her thighs that caused her legs to momentarily weaken.

Her hand trailed downward, stroking, once again, her fluttering stomach. Fingers splayed when they reached the tangle of soft down—seeking . . .

He could have watched her forever—a majestic feminine beauty, illuminated by candle and moonlight. Her exquisite body glimmered in the light, the tight sinews of her form shimmering beneath her touch. Never before had he been so taken, so over-come with the sensuousness, the eroticism of touch, as he now experienced while watching Samantha.

Somehow, he felt the depth of her feelings, her need—not rushed, not demanded, but simply a desire born of knowing who you are, and not being afraid of that sexual soul. But rather, embracing it, welcoming it, succumbing to it.

He heard her soft whimpers, the steady escalation of her breathing, as she sought and found her plea-sure. Blind desire roared through him as her pants grew more rapid, her once slow movements picking up their pace. He wanted to be the one to bring her release, to fill the need deep within her, and perhaps in some way he did—when "Chad" rushed up from her throat and her body shuddered in the final throes of ecstasy.

For several moments he stood there, mesmerized at having witnessed something so intimate—so surreal. And something inside of him opened, softened, wel-comed the possibility of the experience. Standing there, watching her, connected with him in a way that a physical joining would never have achieved. Unknown to her, they traversed an invisible barrier and met on a higher plane.

Slowly he turned and eased back down the hall to the stairs, the feeling of having been enchanted following him.

Samantha gazed into the mirror, saw Chad's retreating form and wondered if he'd felt it, too.

* * *

They were both wet. Thin streams of perspiration ran along their hairlines, hung from their lashes, coated their naked bodies. The rush of hurried, harsh breathing began to ebb. Heartbeats thumped, skipped, stuttered into a regular rhythm. Their bodies still hummed, almost vibrated and Simone was acutely aware of the void her body now felt with Adam no longer filling it. She moved closer, needed desperately to reconnect, to feel that feeling again.

Lying there with Adam made her so aware of how lonely she'd actually been, how needy, but refusing to accept that those weak emotions could be a part of who she was. To acknowledge that about herself was something she'd been unprepared and unwilling to do—until now. Until Adam.

Funny, she thought, sighing when his arms wrapped tighter around her, all along a chance at happiness, at fulfillment, had been shining like a diamond in the rough, and she'd been too blind, too obsessed with the past to see it.

Adam lifted her damp, curling hair from her neck and placed a kiss there, sending a series of shudders through her body. Smiling at her response to him, he pulled her closer, their spoon-fashion repose giving him easy access to the wonders of her form. He shut his eyes, let the languid sensation of satisfaction flow through his veins. Whatever he needed to do to ensure that Simone would remain a permanent part of his life, he would do. Whatever . . .

* * *

Vaughn wasn't certain why she was so nervous. She'd barely been able to get her coffee down without her stomach rebelling. She'd changed outfits three times, put her hair up, down, then back up again. All during the night she'd tossed and turned, lingering between sleep and wake, until finally she slipped out of bed at five and went to the den to watch a mindless middle-of-the-night movie.

She peered at her reflection in the mirror. "What are you afraid of? Janice Montgomery is a woman, just like you." She lightly coated her lips with a hint of cinnamon lipstick. "You're a congresswoman for the United States, you decide policies, you dine with heads of state, the president calls you by your first name," she continued to chide herself. *What is it about this woman that has you questioning your worth?*

She knew the answer. It was simple. Janice Montgomery had been married to her husband. She'd shared his bed, his hopes, his fears. He loved her once, and she loved him back. They had a life together, shared dreams . . . and a child. On that expansive playing field she felt that she could equally compete. All except one area. She and Justin had no natural children together. It was a connection he shared with Janice alone. And neither time nor distance would ever alter that. Janice had something with him she could not duplicate. And it scared her. Even though Samantha was an adult, Janice and Justin were still her flesh-and-blood parents. And times such as these, when they were forced to come together for their child's benefit, drove that fact home.

"About ready, babe?" Justin stepped into the room, adjusting his tie.

Vaughn watched him in the mirror and her stomach seesawed and her heart pounded just as it always did when she saw him. She released a breath. "As ready as I'll ever be." She reached for her watch and fastened it onto her left wrist.

"Ready as you'll ever be? You're not walking the plank, baby. Just going to the airport—"

"To pick up your ex-wife, Samantha's mother," Vaughn said, cutting him off.

Justin walked up behind her and clasped her shoulders. "What is it, Vaughn?" he asked gently. "You think I didn't know you were awake half the night?"

She turned to him, frowning. "The least you could have done was ask me what was wrong."

The corner of his mouth tilted upward. "And what good would that have done? You would have told me it was nothing and for me to go back to sleep. Like you always do when something's on your mind and you haven't sorted it all out yet. You tell me when you're ready. Not a minute sooner." He gave her a puppy dog look. "I've come to live with it."

"Ooh, it just burns me when you go into your clever routine." She stood, and barely a breath separated them. "So you think you know me, huh?" she quizzed in her throaty voice.

He put his arm around her waist and pulled her

close. "Believe me, baby, figuring you out occupies all my free time and brain cells."

He laughed. She swatted his arm.

"So . . . ready to tell me now, or do you need more time to work it out?"

Vaughn turned out of his embrace and crossed to the farthest end of the room. She sat on the banquette beneath the bay window. "Why am I jealous of Janice?" she bluntly asked, staring at Justin dead-on, hands folded neatly on her lap.

Justin's brows flicked. He stepped closer, head lowered in thought. When he stopped, he looked at her, concentrating on the intense expression on her face, and he knew she needed whatever truth he could offer.

"Because," he began on a quiet note, "somehow you believe that whatever Janice and I had is infinitely different, maybe better somehow, than our love, our marriage. That no matter how long you and I are together, the years that I know her will continue to add up as well. And that Samantha will always be the link that binds us no matter what." He came to her and bent down, taking her hands in his. "And you know what, if you think all those things, you'd be absolutely right."

Vaughn sat completely still, but her gaze moved away.

"Look at me, Vaughn," he coaxed gently. Reluctantly she did, hurt swimming in her eyes. "The most important thing, the thing that makes us special, is what we build, our love, our dreams. Neither of us can go back and make the past disappear. It's there for all time and we can either put it in perspective or let it overshadow our future. Every day that we're together pushes all the yesterdays further into the distance to make way for the future."

She shook her head as if snapping from a trance. "I know you're right. I . . . I'm just letting my imagination run away with me."

Justin pulled her to her feet, then lightly kissed her lips. "Just remember, doll, if things were so great between me and Janice, we'd still be together, wouldn't we?"

Vaughn rested her head against her husband's chest and gave into the comfort of his arms, steady heartbeat and reassuring words. All her good sense told her he was right, she had nothing to worry about, he was her husband, not Janice's. But . . . there was that other voice, the little one, the emotional one fueled by old wives' tales and too many talk shows: *time heals all wounds,* while *absence makes the heart grow fonder.*

CHAPTER TWENTY-SIX

Simone rolled over in bed, felt the cool, empty space and came fully awake. She blinked against the early morning sun and listened intently for any sounds of movement. Silence. Except for the sound of rain tapping against the window.

She shut her eyes and sucked in her bottom lip between her teeth. Gone. Why did she think last night would be any different from all the other nights she'd spent with a man? Like vampires—they vanished with the dawn of a new day, sucking the life out of her in the process.

Since she'd become involved in politics, running for office, she'd had to be extremely careful of who she allowed into her life, who she allowed herself to be intimate with. Other than Chris Walker, there'd been no one significant since Chad—until last night with Adam.

What was it about her that made men think it was OK to sleep with her, but no more was required?

"The hell with it." She sat up, tossed the tangled sheets aside and sniffed loudly. She snatched her robe from the armchair near the bed and pulled it around her nude body. *The hell with all of it.* Some people weren't cut out for all that relationship crap, she thought vehemently, tossing her clothes out of the closet and onto the bed. She tugged open her dresser drawer and blindly pulled out a handful of satin and lace lingerie. Her eyes filled.

She stomped off to the bathroom and turned the shower on full blast. In moments, the jasmine-scented room was filled with steam, and her reflection in the mirror soon misted over and disappeared. Disappeared. Tears of regret and humiliation slowly slid down her cheeks. She stepped beneath the pulsing spray, letting her tears mix, slide along her body and down the drain.

Samantha found him in the kitchen, staring intently into a mug of steamy coffee. The richness of it, the scent of fresh grounds with a hint of mocha floated through the kitchen and teased her nose. She leaned against the door frame and folded her arms, studying the man before her.

What was he thinking? she wondered. Did he think

any less of her this morning than he did last night? Briefly, she shut her eyes. The more time she spent with him, the deeper she cared, and the more she wanted him. There was no denying that fact. What she was feeling day by day was not a young girl's fantasy come true, but the wants and desires of a woman for a man. But she had no clear idea of how he truly felt about her.

Sighing, she opened her eyes and found him staring at her, with an expression in his gaze she'd never seen before: acceptance.

"Mornin'." He stood.

"Hi." She felt suddenly warm.

"How'd you sleep?"

She raised her chin a notch. "Fine. And you?"

He came toward her. "I've had better."

She looked beyond the kitchen into the living room. "You, uh, did a great job straightening up."

"Told you I'd take care of it." He placed his cup on the counter and came closer.

Samantha swallowed over the sudden knot in her throat.

"I try to be a man of my word."

He was right up on her now, close enough for her to see the fine hairs that lined his upper lip.

"Chad . . ."

"I thought I'd drive you to Justin's office. Hang around . . . meet your mother."

"You really don't . . ."

"I figured you'd need someone . . . later, to talk."

He shrugged, "Or not. But my plan was to be there, however it goes down. Is that OK with you?"

She nodded. "Thank you," she whispered.

He tenderly stroked her cheek, searched her face. "I'd better get dressed." He kissed her lightly, once, twice before leaving her there in the doorway.

Flight 862 from Atlanta had just landed when Justin and Vaughn entered the waiting area for arrivals. The door of the jetway opened and the passengers began filing out, searching over heads and in between bodies for the familiar faces of loved ones, or at least someone willing to carry their bags. An array of greetings in many languages bubbled like a fountain, building in volume and intensity.

Vaughn spotted her first. Though she'd never laid eyes on the ex-Mrs. Montgomery, she'd know that face, those eyes, anywhere. *Samantha.* They possessed the same alluring gray-green eyes, set against a near-flawless sandstone complexion, full, sensuous mouths and a head full of thick mink-brown hair. They even shared the same stunning body and dancer's legs, hers flashing from beneath her opened gun-metal gray trench coat. The differences between them were subtle but significant. There was a hard look to Janice's eyes, and tiny, tiny lines around her mouth that even her artfully applied makeup couldn't hide. And even though her stride was strong and provocative, she gave off an aura of world-weariness, of having been around the block one time too many, of under-standing the full measure of loneliness.

Vaughn took a quick breath and squeezed Justin's hand. "I think that's her."

He snatched a glance at his wife, wondering how she'd know Janice, then quickly scanned the disem-barking crowd, and his gaze connected with his past. In that instant, he knew the answer to his question—Samantha looked just like her. He'd forgotten how much, forced himself to forget, didn't want to remember.

Vaughn looked up at him, saw the memories swim across his face and touch his body, which grew sud-denly rigid.

"Hello, Justin."

She had one of those voices that fill the confines of smoky jazz clubs, hushed, heavy and sensual, but strong enough to penetrate the senses. She turned those eyes on Vaughn.

"You must be the congresswoman." She spoke the word as if it was dirty. She almost smiled. Cocking her head to the side she said, "Looking well, Justin. But I wouldn't expect anything less." She glanced from one to the other and smiled, flashing even white teeth and a dimple that could be endearing on some-one else. "Ready?" She possessively linked her arm through Justin's and turned to Vaughn as if they were the best of friends. "How are things in Washington? I'm sure what we read in the papers is nothing close to the truth."

Vaughn smiled smugly. "Sometimes you can't even believe what you see up close and personal."

Janice's eyes darkened for an instant, then her smile returned in full bloom. "Politicians *are* quick on their feet, aren't they? But you can hardly believe a word they say."

Justin saw the tight mask descend over Vaughn's face and knew she was a breath away from cutting Janice to shreds with her tongue. Though he'd love to see Janice's demise, this was neither the place nor the time.

He gently removed Janice's hand from his arm and slid his around Vaughn's waist. "The car is in the lot and I'm sure Sam will be waiting at my office." He lifted her overnight bag with his free hand and moved off with Vaughn, never looking back.

Pam heard the distinctive click of Simone's heels and wondered what she was doing at the office so early. It was barely eight and Simone rarely arrived before nine-thirty.

"I'll have to call you back," she whispered urgently into the phone. "Yes. Tonight. Fine. Me, too." She hung up and shoved some papers into a manila folder, stuck it in the bottom drawer of her desk and locked it.

Simone walked in, holding her dripping umbrella at arm's length. She barely acknowledged Pam's presence other than to tell her to hold all calls, headed to her adjoining office and shut the door.

Pam sat there for a moment, staring at the door, debating on whether she should go in or wait it out. But she had to know. She stood, straightened her suit jacket. After all, how could she be expected to effectively do her job if she wasn't aware of *everything*? She tapped lightly and stepped in.

Simone had her back turned. She stared out the window, seemingly unaware of Pam's presence.

"Simone," she called out softly.

Simone mumbled something unintelligible. Pam closed the door and slowly approached. "Are you all right?"

"Fine."

Pam came to stand beside her. "You don't sound fine. Everything . . . OK with Samantha?" Her stomach momentarily clenched with passing anxiety.

"I'm sure she's just dandy." Simone folded her arms.

"Simone . . . what is it? Maybe I can help." She reached out to touch her when Simone turned suddenly, her eyes dark and foreboding.

"The only person who can help me is me. At least when I figure it all out," she said in a tight voice. She pressed her trembling lips together as she sucked in air through her nose. She turned away, tugged in a long breath and reached someplace inside herself for a reserve of determination.

"Since it seems we're both here early, we may as well get this day started."

Pam watched the transformation in amazement. The darkness around Simone's eyes seemed to vanish, her posture straightened and a veil of total control descended over her. She'd never known a woman like Simone, someone who could, at a blink of an eye, rein in her emotions and focus on what was necessary. She never used her looks to gain attention. She used her mind and her connections. A lethal combination. And her sister Samantha was the same way. Powerful and attractive.

Her insides twisted for a moment. What did it feel like to be in the limelight, the public eye, to have that much clout, to have people trip over themselves to do as you asked—to have everything?

Pam adjusted her glasses. "If you want to go over your calendar first, I can bring it in."

"Sure. I want to tie up any loose ends this week since the hand shaking and elbow rubbing begins again next week."

They both heard the sounds of voices, doors opening and closing and the beep and hum of computers being powered up.

"Another day," Simone commented dryly.

"I'll get the calendar." Pam headed for the door.

"Thanks. Pam . . ."

She turned, her hand on the knob. "Yes?"

"Why *are* you here so early?"

"Uh, just wanted to get a head start."

Simone looked at her a moment, then nodded.

The windshield wipers swished rapidly across the pane, futilely attempting to keep the rain at bay.

Adam drove around the block several times, passing the city council office and prime parking spaces. But he knew that once he stopped he'd have to get out, walk into the office and eventually face Simone. A roll of thunder hammered the heavens. What could he possibly say to her?

CHAPTER
TWENTY-SEVEN

Chad held Samantha's hand as they walked down the corridor to Justin's office, and she soaked up every minute of the comfort it gave her.

Low voices could be heard coming from behind the partially opened door. She recognized her mother's voice instantly and felt her chest tighten. Then she heard Vaughn's distinctive alto and was both surprised and alarmed. It never occurred to her that Vaughn would want to be there, especially in what must be an uncomfortable situation. But knowing her stepmother, she shouldn't have expected anything less. If there was anything to be said about Vaughn, it was that she didn't stand around and wait for things to happen. She was right in there.

Chad knocked once, pushed the door open further and ushered Samantha inside. Before anyone could blink, Janice was out of her seat with her arms wrapped around a stiff Samantha, who hadn't gotten any further than the threshold.

"Baby, baby," she nearly wept, holding Samantha in a body-locking grip, her long fingers stroking and stroking Samantha's locks. "I've been worried sick about you. You have no idea. Oh, Sam. Are you all right?" She backed up and held her at arm's length for observation.

Samantha stared into eyes identical to her own, into the face that would surely be hers in years to come. Her voice was flat and expressionless.

"I'm fine. There was no reason for you to come here."

She brushed by her, kissed her father's cheek and repeated the greeting with Vaughn.

The muscles in Janice's throat tightened like twisted rope, but she said nothing, turning instead to Chad and flashing her smile.

"You must be Chad Rushmore." She thrust out her hand, which Chad briefly took. "My husband's told me wonderful things about you."

Chad's right brow arched sarcastically. "I didn't realize you'd remarried. Who's your husband that's been telling you these wonderful things?"

Chad watched her sanctimonious expression slowly collapse under the weight of his carefully placed barb, while the rest of the occupants of the room held their breath.

Janice laughed suddenly, a tinkling sound like a glass bell being struck. She clutched his arm in that familiar way that people who don't know each other, but pretend otherwise, often do. "Oh, you. You know perfectly well I mean Justin. Husband, ex-husband . . ." She shrugged in dismissal, then whirled away.

Chad closed the door. "Morning, everyone."

"Thanks for bringing Sam," Justin said.

"My pleasure." He passed Vaughn and pressed her shoulder in greeting. She looked up and winked, holding her grin in check.

"Before anyone says another word," Samantha began, "I'm not going anywhere. I'm staying right here in Washington. So there's no need for discussion." She turned to her mother. "The only reason I came is out of courtesy to my father," she said, glaring at Janice. "And because Chad convinced me. It has nothing to do with you." Then she addressed the room. "So if you're all here to gang up on me, forget it."

"Samantha, be reasonable," her mother snapped. "You're in danger here. And I may not agree with your father on a lot of things, but on this I do."

"Mother, after all this time, after everything you've done, do you really think I give a damn what you think—about anything?"

"Sam!" Justin cut in.

Samantha shot him with a look but backed down.

Vaughn stood. "I think Chad and I should wait outside." She picked up her coat from the back of the couch. "But before we do there's one thing I want to say." She looked at Samantha, then at each person in the room. "Samantha is a grown woman. One who knows her own mind. Yes, she's been threatened. I'm sure she's scared. We all are. But if every time we were frightened, and ran off, where would we be? At some point, you have to take a stand. Samantha is taking hers."

"This is none of your damned business," Janice shouted, ready for a showdown. "She's our child."

Vaughn crossed the room and walked right up to Janice, a slow, dangerous smile easing across her rich mouth. "When I married your ex-husband, she became *my* child, too. So this is my *damned* business." With that, she spun away and walked out. Chad followed shortly behind.

"Now maybe we can talk like a family," Janice said in a huff.

"Janice, we haven't been a family since you ran off with Samantha more than twenty years ago, so cut the crap," Justin said nastily. "I thought I was doing the right thing by calling you, letting you know what was happening with Samantha. Which was more than you ever did for me." Janice stiffened. "But the fact remains, it's Samantha's decision, whether I agree with it or not."

Janice turned pleading eyes on her daughter. "Sam?"

"It's a little late to show so much motherly concern. I'm sorry you came all this way for nothing."

Janice pulled herself together. "You're never going to forgive me, are you? You never understood."

"Understood?" Samantha questioned, her voice raising an octave. "You lied to me. You took me from my father, told me he abandoned us, that being a father and husband was too much for him, that he didn't love us anymore. And for what? So you could sleep around with any man with money?"

Janice's face quivered as she spoke. "It wasn't like that, Samantha. I swear to you it wasn't. I wanted the best for us. I thought I did. Your father . . . he was just starting out, struggling. We struggled for everything. I was tired of not having, of waiting . . . for his big break." She swallowed hard. "All my life, all I'd ever had was nothing. And all I could see was my life being repeated all over again with you. I didn't want that for you. Whether you believe it or not. I . . . love you Samantha. More than you'll ever know."

Tentatively she approached her daughter. "I was wrong. I know that now. Have known for a long time. I know I can never make it up to you." She looked at Justin. "To either of you. But I pray that one day you can find a way to forgive me. I would just die if something happened to you, Samantha. I hope you believe that. I . . . I'm so sorry . . . for everything." She turned away and walked out, her stride not so sure, her posture not so erect.

A heavy silence hung in the room, fell between father and daughter like a velvet drape at the end of the final act.

Samantha turned to her father, her eyes clouded with unshed tears.

"Go to her, Samantha," he said gently. "Make things right between you."

She hesitated, thought about all the years of lies and deceit, saw the look of sincere pain and regret on her mother's face. She glanced toward the door.

"I can't," she whispered. "I can't."

CHAPTER
TWENTY-EIGHT

Simone was preparing for her morning conference meeting with her staff to reconfirm the campaign strategy for the upcoming weeks and everyone's responsibilities. With the rise in civil unrest revolving around the Roderick Fields case, and several other less deadly incidents, her plan was to take the issue directly to the people. There was a television interview scheduled for a two o'clock taping to be aired during the six and eleven o'clock news. Tomorrow morning she had an hour-long interview on the Cathy Hughes show, WHUR, then it was on to *BET Tonight* with Tavis Smiley. Now, if only the weather would change, but that had not been the case for much of the week. The city was seeing its share of London weather, with unusually dismal gray skies and rain, showers, cloud-bursts, thunderstorms. Sometimes all on the same day.

To avoid any slipups, Simone had reviewed everything with Pam, who'd already made arrangements for transportation and meals. Picking up her leather portfolio, she flipped it open to the meticulously detailed itinerary for the next two days. She wondered how she would be able to juggle everything without Pamela Osborne. She was the most efficient and organized staffer she'd ever employed. Her powers of recall for minutiae and her research ability were phenomenal. There was not a scrap of information left to chance or a stone unturned when Pamela was involved. At some point she was going to have to take time and really thank her for all she'd done for her and the campaign. She'd hate to think of all those skills working against her for the other side. Maybe she'd take her to a nice dinner sometime within the next couple of weeks, like the old days—before everything became so crazy.

She clapped the covers of the soft leather closed and reached for her purse. Thank heavens her remarks and every manner of possible question had been addressed in the prep meetings last week. Especially since Adam had yet to show up. Which was just as well. She wasn't quite sure how she would react if she saw him now. Her insides knotted. What an incredible fool she'd been. Damn it, she'd committed the cardinal sin—sleeping with a member of her staff, a subordinate. And for what? Sexual loneliness, a moment of feeling whole? That's the only tag she could give it, all the acknowledgement she'd devote to it. Because to admit that it was something more, something deeper than a purely physical desire would elevate it to a level she was no longer prepared to handle. She thought she was. She was wrong. So very wrong.

Pam suddenly rushed into the office. "There's a reporter outside and a cameraman," she said a bit breathlessly. "He wants your comments on the break-in last night at your sister's house."

Simone's eyes cinched in confusion. "What? What break-in?"

"I have no idea." She shrugged helplessly. "He said he got the news from a police report."

Simone tried to think. She pressed her hand to her forehead. "Tell him . . ." She stopped in midsentence. "Let me make a call. Stall him for a minute." She reached for the phone and dialed her sister's office, then remembered that Samantha was meeting her mother. She hung up and punched in the numbers to Justin's office.

Justin's private line rang. He released Samantha and crossed to his desk. "Montgomery."

"Dad. What's going on with Sam? A reporter is here asking questions about some break-in last night at her house."

Justin's gaze darted to Samantha. "Hold on." He covered the mouthpiece. "A reporter wants to know what happened at your house last night. He's at Simone's office.'' His hard stare held her in place, alerting her to the seriousness of the situation.

Samantha briefly shut her eyes and whispered a harsh expletive. Blowing out a short breath, she took the phone from her father. Another fire to put out. Crisis after crisis. No letup, no respite.

"Simone, listen . . . tell the reporter to meet me at my office in a half hour. I'll tell him whatever he needs to know."

"Sam, what the hell happened? Are you all right?"

"I'm fine." She paced as she talked, her thoughts racing. Later had come sooner than she'd planned. "Listen, sis, just get him out of your office. I'll handle it."

"Fine. I'll meet you there."

"Simone—"

"Don't want to hear it. I'll be there." She hung up, then went out front to the waiting area where the reporter had camped out. Pam stood guard. Nettie and Steve peeked out from their cubicles. Simone relayed Samantha's message. "And I'll have a statement at that time as well." She spun away, with Pam on her heels.

"What's going on?" Pam hissed under her breath.

"That's what I intend to find out." She grabbed her purse and her portfolio.

"I'll go with you."

"No, you stay here and hold down the fort."

"What about your two o'clock interview?"

Damn, she'd forgotten. There was no way she could

speed in this driving rain, but the appointment was a must. "I'm taking my car. I'll be there. If there's any change, I'll call you." She breezed by her, then stopped and turned. "Thanks." She headed for the front door and stopped abruptly when Adam turned down the hall right in her path.

Her body became infused with the heat of anger and humiliation. She felt like cursing him out or, better yet, slapping the hell out of him, or as her grandmother used to say, slapping the taste out of his mouth. But she kept her composure, or at least tried to remain civil. Especially after what he had done. Her faithful Adam.

"Simone, I need to talk to you."

She stared at him for an incredibly long moment, cataloging all the years they'd known each other. She replayed all the conversations they'd shared, the hopes and dreams, the secrets told . . . and then last night. Her head cleared. Almost nothing hurts like the betrayal of a lover who is also your most intimate friend. Almost nothing.

"I won't be needing your services any longer," she said in a flat, steady voice. "Neither business *nor pleasure*." She tucked her hair behind her right ear, and raised her chin in challenge. "By the time I return I'll expect your things and you to be gone, and your letter of resignation on my desk." She walked by him. "Have a nice day, Adam."

Adam tried to block her from moving down the hall. "You can't dismiss me like some damn servant. We have to talk. You owe me that much."

"I don't owe you a damn thing, Judas, nothing," she snarled at him as she stepped around him. Their eyes locked for two beats, with her barely suppressed rage clearly visible in her glare.

"It's not like you think, nothing is. Please let me talk to you, please."

Defiantly, Simone whirled and stood inches from his face. "What lies can you possibly tell that would undo what has been already done? What . . . what?"

He was rendered mute by the force of her words, her fury, and he stammered, unable to find the words that could make things right, that could make things what they once were.

"I thought so, Judas." The distinctive click of her heels echoed down the hallway.

By the time Simone reached her car, she was drenched from the windblown rain and shaking all over. In her rush, she'd left her umbrella in the office. She could barely get the key in the ignition with her wet, trembling hands. Taking a moment to steady herself, she considered what she'd done. She knew it was a hasty decision, one made out of hurt and anger. But what choice did she have, what choice had he given her? None.

She turned the key and the car hummed to life. Upon reflection, she realized she'd done the same thing with Chad. Shut him out, shut him down. Didn't allow room for answers to the questions that burned inside her. And here again, she'd revisited her old ghosts—fear of rejection. And in doing so, she went, as always, on the defensive. Putting up the walls, the barricades to ward off any attempts at reaching her, perhaps saying things she didn't want to hear.

She pulled out of her parking space, steered slowly out of the lot and merged with traffic. Why was she so afraid? Her stomach was in knots. But deep inside she knew the answer, had always known. Yet she couldn't seem to shake it, live with it and move on. A part of who she was had become twisted, distorted, and all because of a past she could never hope to change. A past that compelled her to see everyone as a possible enemy, a potential Judas. Indeed, that past had left its indelible mark upon her psyche. And she knew if she ever hoped to be better, to have a life—a real one—it would mean getting it out in the open. The only person who could do that for her was her mother, and she was afraid, too, of what Vaughn would reveal.

Sighing, she pressed the CD button and the muted trumpet of Miles Davis blew a gentle breeze into the car. Samantha's office was in the heart of downtown D.C. She'd selected the neat storefront location, amid much family protest, because of its proximity to transportation, but mostly for its visibility. The office was couched in between the Great Redeemer Baptist Church and a check cashing business, across the street from Sojourner Truth High School and two blocks away from the police precinct, with the surrounding neighborhood being a predominantly poor, crime-ridden African American community. "I want to be among the people," she said the day she'd moved in. "I'm not interested in safety, I'm interested in connecting. How are these people going to feel I'm one of them when they have to come to my suburban office to talk with me?''

Conviction and focus, that was Samantha. Once she made up her mind, there was no turning her around. What was equally admirable was that Samantha's youth had been manipulated as well, yet she never seemed to let that override who she was, what she was about. It didn't seem to cloud her judgment, mar her relationships.

There was no letup with the torrential rain and it was hard to see through the windshield. Slowly Simone turned onto a wide side street, taking her favorite shortcut, hoping to avoid some of the afternoon traffic. Since the terrorist threats of last year, many of the main thoroughfares going toward Capitol Hill and the White House were blocked off and cars were diverted into several narrow side streets.

I can't afford to be late, she was thinking when her car was suddenly slammed in the rear. The top half of her body was rammed into the steering wheel by the impact, knocking the air from her lungs. Before she could think, she was hit again.

"What the hell?!" she yelled, whipping her head around to glance in the direction of the smash. This was no accident; this was intentional.

Instincts kicked in and she stepped on the accelerator, gunning the engine. *Wet streets . . . can't spin away from this idiot without risking a crash.* Terrified, she stole a glance into her rearview mirror only to see the dark blue tail of a car turn the corner behind her. It was closing ground fast, moving into position for another assault. She looked ahead at the thick traffic in the busy intersection ahead, certain death if she was pushed into that. She waited for the next impact, afraid to turn around, to look. She waited, waited, waited. But nothing happened.

Gingerly, she pulled the car onto the side of the road, taking deep, full breaths to calm herself. Both hands gripped the steering wheel as she looked nervously around, as if expecting someone or something to leap out of nowhere. The street was suddenly quiet. Even the intersection ahead was mysteriously free of cars. It was as if everything that had just happened was a nightmare, or at least some bizarre sort of optical illusion. With her shoulders and neck in severe pain, she finally glanced around to see where her attacker was. There was nothing but a few abandoned shells of houses and a defunct tire repair shop. She crossed her arms along the steering wheel and lowered her head on them. Once more, her body began to shake all over as if she'd been dipped in a bucket of ice.

She peeked up and looked through the windshield. *What the hell had just happened?*

CHAPTER TWENTY-NINE

The word had gotten out. By the time Simone pulled up in front of Samantha's local office, there were three television vans and about a dozen print reporters with photographers milling about. The rain had diminished to an annoying mist, but it hadn't deterred the press.

The instant she stepped out of her car they descended upon her like locusts. She ducked her head and kept walking. The aftereffects of her near-fatal car ride unwilling to release their grip on her mind.

"Ms. Montgomery, Ms. Montgomery . . . do you have any comment on the break-in at your sister's house? Do you believe it's related to her fight against the police? What comments do you have? Have you been threatened? How will this affect your campaign? . . . Ms. Montgomery . . . any comment?''

The questions came in a torrent, tumbling over each other like pebbles rolling down a hill, gathering debris and speed. She pushed past the cameras and microphones, pulled open the glass doors and went inside. Her chest throbbed and she could almost see the black and blue bruise spreading across her skin.

Mia greeted her. "They're waiting for you in the back office."

"Thanks," she whispered, barely able to breathe.

"How did they find out?" were the first words out of her mouth when she entered the room and shut the door behind her. "Never mind. They always do." She dropped her purse on a chair, determined to put on a good front. "Would someone mind telling me what's going on?" Her chest tightened. Vaughn was seated next to Justin, and Samantha stood near Chad.

"When we came home from the club last night, someone had gotten there before we did," Chad offered.

The "we came home" rang over and over in Simone's head. She pushed it aside and looked to her sister. "Sam?"

Samantha nodded. "Trashed the living room, but not much else. We called the police."

"And . . ."

"And they did what they usually do, took a look and gave us a number."

Simone pulled in a breath and her chest constricted. Her eyes squeezed shut in pain and she blindly found her way to an empty seat, all efforts at pretense forgotten.

Vaughn rushed to her side. "Simone, what's wrong?" She sat next to her and put her arm around her shoulder.

Simone swallowed. "Not to add more mystery to the mayhem but somebody just tried to kill me, or give me a pretty damned good scare." She tugged in a breath.

"What?" the room chorused.

Samantha knelt in front of her, took her face in her hands. "Monie, what happened? Are you all right?" She began examining her body.

Simone explained as much of the bizarre incident as she could between gasps for air. The pain was getting worse.

Justin jumped up. "Enough," he boomed. "No more. I want you two out of this thing once and for all. This is exactly what I was afraid of."

Samantha looked up from her spot on the floor. "This is exactly what they want, Dad, for us to pack up our marbles and go away. If we give in now, they've won."

"Would you rather wind up dead!"

The harsh reality of that possibility hit each one of them with a chilling slap, settling the room in a deafening silence.

"Right now, the thing to do is exactly what Chad and Samantha have planned," Vaughn finally said, inserting a measure of calm with her steady voice. "We go out there, face the media and put it on record what has happened, what's been happening."

"I have to agree," Simone said, gritting her teeth.

"That's the master plan," Justin said sarcastically. "Do you really think a media event is going to have whoever this is ducking for cover? Hell no! They'll just be more careful next time."

Mia stuck her head in the door. "They're really getting restless and a crowd of onlookers is building up outside."

Samantha stood. "We'll be right there." She looked from one to the other, letting her gaze settle on her father. "I know you want to protect me, Dad, protect us. And I love you for it. But this is something that must be done. I'm not going to back down. I told you that weeks ago when we got into this thing. I'm going to see it to the end, whatever that means."

As much as he wanted to snatch her up and stash her away where she couldn't be hurt, he admired her tenacity. He hated to admit it, but he knew she was right, they were all right. If he was in their place, he'd do the exact same thing. He looked at Vaughn, who returned his look with a determined one of her own, yet laced with an understanding of what he was going through.

Justin pulled in a long breath, then slowly nodded. "Let's do this." He turned to Simone. "And the instant that this thing is over you're going to the hospital."

"Fine." She didn't dare tell him she had an interview at two o'clock. If there was any justice in the world, maybe she'd be finished in time.

Mia opened the front doors and the Montgomery family stepped out into the late morning sunshine. Three police cars had pulled up and were stationed out front. None of the officers attempted to approach anyone in the swelling crowd of onlookers even as they were booed and hissed.

Samantha stepped up, and a dozen or more microphones were thrust in her face. The crowd silenced by degrees.

"I'll make this brief. During the past few months, I've received several threatening letters, all related to my work with police reform and brutality cases. Last week I received a letter not only threatening me, but my family as well. Last night, my home was broken into and trashed. And today, my sister, Councilwoman Montgomery, was attacked on the road by another car while en route to my office."

"Do you have any idea who's behind these alleged attacks?"

"No, I don't."

"Do you think it's the police?"

"I couldn't say."

"But why would the police attack the councilwoman?"

"I never said the police were involved," she quickly corrected, already seeing the spin on that in tomorrow's newspapers.

"Councilwoman Montgomery, could this have anything to do with your campaign against Vincent McCall?"

Simone stepped closer to the crowd of journalists. "As you all know, I've been very outspoken about the police in this district. My opponent feels just the opposite. However, I would not presume to think that Vincent McCall would have anything to do with something of this nature. And I want to be very clear that today's incident will in no way deter me from my course of action." Her chest seized up as she tried to suck in air, and she swore she saw Adam in the back of the crowd.

"The reason for this gathering is to put whoever this is on notice and to make the community aware of what's going on," Samantha added.

"There's been talk that there is a class action suit in progress against the D.C. police department," a reporter from the back of the crowd stated. "Spear-headed by you and your family." Everyone turned. "Is there any truth in that and if so, how do you intend to pursue it?"

Samantha looked at Chad, then back to the crowd. She had to be careful here. "If and when the time comes we'll share whatever information we have. Thank you all for coming." She turned away and headed back inside, followed by the others and the shouts of more questions hurled at their backs.

As soon as they were inside Simone nearly collapsed. Chad grabbed her an instant before she fell.

"Bring the car around to the side!" He lifted her in his arms and hurried toward the side door.

"Yes, Pam, I'm fine. I swear. Yes, I saw the doctor. The chest wall is bruised from the impact and my neck is a little stiff. He gave me some painkillers. No, don't call off the interview. We've waited too long to get this. I'll have someone drop me off at the studio and you can have the car pick me up as planned. Yeah, I'm glad it wasn't worse, too. We'll discuss . . . Adam later. Okay, I'll call you." She shut down her cell phone and tucked it back in her purse.

"Ready?" Samantha gently asked.

"As I'll ever be." The smell of the hospital was beginning to get to her. She looked from one concerned face to another. "I'm fine," she reaffirmed.

"The doctor said you need to be in bed, Simone, especially when you take this medicine," Vaughn warned her daughter. "And your blood pressure is a little high. You could black out."

"It's just the stress from the accident, the doctor said. I'll be fine. I have a television interview that we've planned for months to secure, and I'm going. I'll take the medication when I get home." Her head was pounding.

"Well, you're not driving," Justin insisted.

"I'll take her," Chad offered.

"No, that's—"

"I'll take you." His tone and firm expression left no room for debate.

"Fine. Then we'd best get going. I don't want to be late."

Chad slid his arm around her waist . . . and it felt all too good.

CHAPTER THIRTY

When Samantha returned to her office, she was stunned to find her mother seated in the waiting area. Mia glanced up from her computer keys and shrugged apologetically. She didn't know all the details about the rift between the two of them, but she did know that Samantha harbored some very negative feelings about her mother. She felt as if her back was against the wall when Janice suddenly appeared and insisted that she'd wait for Samantha's return no matter how long it took. What could she do?

Samantha strutted to Mia's desk. "Any messages?" She glanced across the room at her mother.

"I left them in your office. Mostly calls from the

press. There were several from some of the clients on the 'list.' " She said the last word as if it were holy.

"Thanks." She lowered her voice. "How long has she been here?"

"About two hours. I told her I didn't know when you'd be back. She wouldn't leave. I'm really sorry."

"Don't worry about it. I need you to finish up the names on the database. Chad will be here later to review them. The court papers are going to be filed next week. We'll have to work like hell to get everything together by then, and I want to be sure not to inadvertently leave anyone out. We'll be putting in some long hours during the next few days."

"No problem. Whatever you need."

"Thanks." She sucked in a breath and walked toward her mother. "I thought we said all we needed to say at Dad's office."

Janice stood, matching her daughter in height. "No, Samantha, we didn't. And I couldn't go back to Atlanta knowing that. Please, can't you give me a few minutes?"

All of her earlier bravado was gone, Samantha noted. She gritted her teeth. This was her mother, the woman who gave her birth. If her father had found a way to forgive, if not forget, why couldn't she? "A few minutes, that's all." She led the way to her small office and closed the door. "Have a seat." She extended her hand in the direction of an empty chair.

Janice looked around, noting the shabby dignity of the space. This is not what she would have expected of her daughter, not what she would have wanted. She'd envisioned her in grandeur, with a wealthy man who would do anything for her. The life she'd wanted for herself. But this was Samantha's choice, and as difficult as it was for her to accept, she would have to reconcile with that if she ever expected to regain her daughter's love.

"Mind if I smoke?" Janice asked.

"Actually, I do. But if it will make you feel better, go right ahead." She sat behind her desk and wondered how Simone made out with her interview, what she and Chad may have said to each other.

Janice nervously lit her cigarette and blew a thin cloud of smoke into the air. Samantha turned up her nose, covered her mouth and coughed. Janice looked around for an ashtray. Finding none, she went to the makeshift kitchen and put the butt out with a splash of water from the sink.

"Thanks," Samantha mumbled, feeling smugly triumphant.

Janice turned to her daughter. "I know you don't want to hear this . . . but I'm sorry, Sam."

"You said that already." She folded her arms.

"I'm saying it again. I'm saying it in the hopes that you'll understand."

"What else is there for me to understand? You took me from my father, you lied to me for years about why, and now you want me to understand. I don't get it, Mother. What piece of the puzzle am I missing?"

"Samantha, I loved your father . . . and I still do—"

"Please." She held up her hand, her expression twisted into a frown.

"Listen. I never left your father because I didn't love him, or because he hurt me. I loved him too much. I saw how hard he worked, how hard he struggled and the look on his face when he would come to me and tell me there wasn't enough money for food *and* bills. I saw what it was doing to him, breaking him, and I knew what it was doing to me. I know what I did was foolish, selfish. But day by day my love was turning into resentment. And I couldn't let that happen. You and your father were the only perfect things in my life. And I saw it all coming apart. I didn't want to wait around and have his love turn on me because he couldn't take care of me.

"I was young. I was stupid. And if I could, I'd change it all to have the both of you back in my life, but I can't. All I can ask is that you try to forgive me . . . somehow."

Samantha stared at her in confusion. "That's . . . that's not what you said . . . this morning."

"How could I ever tell your father, that proud black man, what I just told you?" Her voice choked. "Don't you think I've done enough to him?"

"Why didn't you work? Why didn't you help if you were so concerned?" She had to grab for something, hurl something at her to keep the overwhelming emotion of wanting her mother from brimming to the top and spilling over.

Janice looked away. "We were married barely two

months when I became pregnant with you. I was sick from the beginning. The doctors didn't think I would be able to carry you to term. And we wanted you so desperately."

Samantha paced back and forth.

"I was on bed rest for my entire pregnancy. I . . . nearly died during delivery. After you were born, I never really recovered physically. Your father would not hear of me working and didn't want any strangers taking care of you. He did the best he could, gave everything he had, but things just kept getting worse, and I would see that look of defeat on your father's face at the end of the day, and I couldn't take it anymore."

She was crying openly now, tears running steadily down her cheeks. "So I left, filed for divorce, got on public assistance and made a life from there. Your father always thought it was about another man." She sniffed loudly. "That's what I wanted him to believe."

Samantha slowly shook her head in disbelief. "What do you expect me to do with all this? How am I supposed to feel?"

"I can't tell you what to do with your feelings, Sam. I only want you to deal with them with the truth in front of you." She crossed the room to stand in front of her daughter. "Be well, Samantha." She turned away and walked toward the door.

"Ma."

Janice stopped and looked over her shoulder.

"Thank you."

* * *

"I can wait for you," Chad offered when they'd pulled into the studio parking lot.

"I'll be fine." She'd spent the entire fifteen-minute drive with her eyes closed in the hope that they wouldn't have to talk. Up until now, it had worked.

"I don't think you should be left alone, Simone. What if you get dizzy again."

She turned to him. "I won't be alone. There's a studio full of people," she said a bit too sharply, then softened her tone, "I appreciate your concern, but I said I'm fine. Pam is sending a car to pick me up. It's a sit-down interview, no stress, no strain involved."

"Where's Adam? He should be here. Isn't he your press secretary?"

Simone inwardly flinched. "Adam doesn't work for me anymore." She opened her door and prepared to get out.

"Why, what happened?"

"Nothing I care to discuss."

Chad clenched his teeth. "Exactly what is it that you do care to discuss, Simone? Anything outside of politics? What about what's going on inside of you? Did Adam displease you in some way, too, so you dismissed him? Like you did me?"

She froze for a moment. The attack was on target. "Thanks for the ride, Chad. As for the advice, you can keep it, OK." She got out and slammed the door, headed for the entrance, not daring to look back.

He watched her leave and felt an overwhelming

urge to go after her, shake some sense into her. But he knew it would be pointless. He shook his head and pulled off. If that's the way she wanted it, he'd leave her the hell alone. He pulled out into traffic and headed back to Samantha's office. They had work to do, and he wouldn't cloud his thoughts with Simone and her issues that he couldn't get a handle on. But he couldn't help but wonder what happened between her and Adam Parsons.

CHAPTER
THIRTY-ONE

The black Lincoln Town Car pulled to a slow stop in front of Simone's house. She signed the voucher for payment and returned it to the driver, her body growing more rigid and achy by the minute from the physical aftereffects of the crash. *A nice hot bath.* Stiffly, she stepped from the car and ambled on leaden legs toward her front door, head bowed against the pounding rain that had picked up again during the past few hours. The heavyset hairstylist at the studio had done wonders with her damp tresses, but the unrelenting weather had taken control once again.

Normally, she would have jogged to the door, but this evening her body wouldn't let her. Wouldn't obey. *A nice hot bath and medication.*

A sharp breath caught in her throat when a shadow took on human form and stepped into her path from beneath the eaves.

"Simone," Adam said.

Her heart raced in triple time and she was uncertain if it was terror or anger that had its firm grip around her throat. "What are you doing here? If you've come to beg about your job, forget it." She swallowed and tried to slow down her galloping pulse. "Please move." Water dripped from him as if he'd been standing there for hours. For an instant she felt sorry for him.

He held her shoulder, both to restrain and reassure her. "I need you to listen to me. And you need to hear what I have to say."

"Fuck you, Adam! You don't know jack about what I need." She felt the hysteria building like the breath-stealing sensation that rises when the roller coaster reaches the top and begins that abrupt descent—and a chilling scream rips from the rider's throat. That's what she felt like doing, screaming at the top of her lungs until she was silenced.

"Simone, do you remember what we once said about never letting anybody or anything threaten our friendship?" He asked her this question in a soft, soothing voice usually reserved for cops trying to talk people down from tall buildings. "Do you remember what we said?"

She corralled her rampaging emotions for a few seconds, the stance of her body offering a brief truce that would only last for several sentences. He'd better talk and talk fast. This would be the last time her defenses would be down so low.

"We said our friendship, our everything, was built on trust, and just because we slept together is no reason to throw all of that out the window," Adam continued in that serene voice. "What did I do that was so bad? What part of us did I violate?"

"Don't talk to me about trust," she shot back. "I don't want to hear it. Not after you treated me like some cheap piece of ass you picked up for a quickie. You got what you wanted, scored big time, and walked out without leaving even a note. Why didn't you leave some money on the dresser?"

"How could you say something like that to me? How could you, Simone?"

"Because that's how you made me feel. Like a whore flatbacking in a hot-sheet motel. Do you know how I felt when I woke up and you weren't there? Do you have any idea how that feels?"

Adam was silent. He watched the suffering in her eyes, the vulnerability in the rushed cadence of her words, thinking how considerate he thought he had been by not disturbing her that morning. He let her sleep. Maybe he didn't want to face up to the emotional barrier they crossed by sleeping together. Intimacy. That was about trust. And, somehow, by doing what she considered the ultimate humiliation, he'd ruined that trust—kept himself at a safe emotional distance that he could manage, but at what cost? If he ever hoped to cross that emotional barrier, he'd have to learn to trust as well, no more than he was asking of her. He'd understood how frightened and vulnerable she was before that night, but he'd allowed himself to forget it, believing that their one night was a cure-all, able to make everything better, the past go away. Stupid.

"Well . . ." she demanded.

"I left because . . . I wasn't thinking . . . not because I didn't care. I went home to get ready for work, put everything in place—for you." he said. "If I thought my leaving . . ." He threw his hands up, shaking his head. ". . . I would have stayed." He cupped her face in his hands, his gaze pouring into hers. "Listen to me," he said in an urgent whisper. "Don't you think I know what you were saying about your feelings for me when we made love? Don't you think I understand what a tremendous gift you gave me last night?"

She was weakening, just a bit. "You didn't act like it. Why didn't you leave a note?"

"I was still high on what happened with us. I just wasn't thinking. It didn't cross my mind. I've waited, Simone, waited for us to get together. Believe me, I wouldn't do anything to put that in jeopardy. Nothing." He paused. "I love you, Simone."

Love. This was all too much for her to think about right now. Love. She touched him softly on the arm, then casually wiped the wetness from his forehead with a tissue retrieved from her pocket. They stood there, pushing beyond the chaos of the moment, recalling the splendor of that glorious night, before his departure, before this misunderstanding. But she couldn't deal with this right now—deal with love right now. Before Adam could react, she was gone through the rain and mist into the house.

The rain still pattered outside, even late into the evening. It was almost soothing now, continuous, the watery drumbeat a part of the dusk's natural rhythm. Flames flickered from white tapers on the mantel and tabletops in the semidarkened room, giving the cool evening an enchanted effect.

Samantha sat with her legs curled beneath her, Chad next to her with his arm draped casually around her shoulder. The tips of his fingers played with the strands of her hair. She took a sip of her chilled Chablis, staring into the flames. "Some day, huh?" she asked rhetorically.

Chad eased her closer. The unfolding of the day's events seemed to have been stripped from the script of a blockbuster movie. No dramatic device was left unused, from the break-in, the return of the estranged mother, a sinister car chase, the inevitable descent of the headline-hungry press, right down to the dark and gloomy night. If it weren't so painfully true, he would bust his gut laughing at the total absurdity of it all. Sheer melodrama. Unfortunately, it was all too true.

"Yeah, it was, wasn't it," he said finally. He kissed her forehead tenderly. "How are you holding up?"

She sighed. "I don't know what threw me the most today, the face-off with my mother or Simone nearly getting killed by some maniac." She shuddered.

"How was she when you dropped her off at the studio?"

"Quiet."

"Hmm. That's Sis all right. Holds everything close to the chest. I'll call her in the morning. I'm sure she must be exhausted."

"Did she . . . mention to you that Adam no longer worked for her?"

Samantha sat up, readjusting the curl of her legs. "When did that happen?"

"Don't know . . . have no idea about the details. Today, I guess. They were together just last night."

As if on cue, the ramifications of what his words really meant took hold and they looked at each other. Neither spoke anything out loud, but their thoughts were as plain as writing on the wall. Something had happened between Simone and Adam last night, and whatever occurred had somehow backfired in the morning.

"Damn," Samantha muttered. She hopped up from the couch and went to the phone. What happened? She had to know. Before Chad could say a word, she'd speed-dialed Simone's house. Her sister groggily answered on the second ring.

"Monie . . . it's me. You OK?"

"Yesss. Fine." She blinked, trying to clear her head. The painkillers and hot soak had kicked in with a vengeance. "W-what's wrong?"

"That's what I was calling to find out. Chad told me about Adam."

"Adam?" She tried to focus. How did Sam know

she'd slept with Adam, gave herself to Adam, let down her defenses with Adam—that Adam said he loved her? Would Samantha claim Adam as her own as well? "What about Adam?" she snapped, her thoughts in disarray.

Samantha kept her voice calm. "Chad said Adam doesn't work for you anymore. Is that true?"

Her head pounded. She tried to make sense of what Samantha was saying. All her thoughts kept tumbling over each other. Nothing made sense. Yes, she'd fired Adam . . . but she was wrong . . . wasn't she? She tried to sit up. She had to get him back. Tell him to come back. He'd been there earlier . . . he loved her. She'd left him on the porch. Maybe he was still there. Yes, on the porch, in the rain.

"Simone, do you need me to come over? Are you OK?"

She finally sat up. Her head spun wildly and her stomach lurched. She dropped the phone, stumbled to the bathroom and threw some cold water on her face. Her head slowly began to clear. Was she making sense? What in the world had she been saying to Samantha?

Gingerly she walked back to where she'd dropped the phone. "Hello, Sam . . ."

"What is going on?" Samantha's voice hinged on panic. She'd been a heartbeat away from darting out the door.

"Girl, this medicine is kicking my butt . . . thought I was hallucinating for a minute."

"You OK? I can be there in a minute."

"No, really, I'm fine. Just a little woozy. Can we talk . . . tomorrow?" She yawned loudly.

Samantha smiled, relief easing the knot in her stomach. "Sure. Are you up to going into the office tomorrow?"

"I'll call you. Maybe we can meet over here." Her lids were growing heavy again. She needed to lie back down.

"Sure. Chad is about ready to put the final touches on the deposition to file in court."

"Hmm . . ."

"You get some rest. We'll talk tomorrow."

" 'K."

"Night, sis." Samantha laughed lightly and hung up the phone.

Within moments, Simone's eyes were closed and the heavy veil of sleep descended over her. She never heard the downstairs door open, then gently close.

CHAPTER THIRTY-TWO

Chad went through the house, making sure that all the windows and doors were locked, then returned to the living room. He smiled, looking at Samantha dozing like a satisfied cat on the couch. He was tempted to leave her there, let her sleep, but knew she'd feel like she'd been beat up in the morning from sleeping in such an awkward position.

He knelt down in front of her and gently pushed her hair away from her face. She looked so innocent—so tempting. The other night flashed in his head, seeing her nude body glistening in the moonlight . . .

Her lashes fluttered and she looked at him through partially opened lids. Her mouth spread into a slow, soft smile. "Conked out on you, huh?" she said in that sexy voice filled with the smoky residue of sleep. She stroked his cheek lightly with the tip of a manicured nail.

A sudden, intense sensation shot through him like an overdose of adrenaline, and the steady pulse of his erection throbbed like a second heartbeat. His face heated. He couldn't get up. Not like this. "You were tired," he mumbled. He sat on the floor and brought his knees to his chest, wrapping his arms around them. *Think about trucks,* he silently repeated, using his magic mental trick to make his passion subside.

"What are we going to do, Chad?"

"About what?"

"Us." She looked at him intently. "I really want to know. I want to know if there's a chance for us, not some bull, but something substantial." She pulled herself into a sitting position. "You don't have to tell me what went on between you and Simone. Actually, I don't want to know. It's the past; it's ancient history. What I do want to know is: can you get past it? Can you move on? Is there something you need to do, so we can *be?* If there is, then I want you to do that. Whatever it means."

She stood, walked to the mantel, cupped her hand behind the flickering light and blew out the flame. Turning to him, she said, "I want to be with you . . . in every sense of the word. But I'm not going to be a substitute for anyone, not even my sister—especially my sister. I deserve more than that and so do you.

It's killing me you being here, night after night, right in the next room." She laughed, not unkindly. "Too much true confessions?" She ducked her head for a moment, then challenged him again. "It's on you, Chad. I know I'm worth it. You just need to figure it out. Good night," she whispered and walked slowly up the stairs.

Stunned by her ultimatum, Chad lay stretched out on the couch, hands clasped behind his head, staring intensely up at the ceiling. Samantha was right. Until he could correct what went wrong between him and Simone, he'd never be able to fully turn himself, his soul, his heart, over to anyone, no matter how powerful the physical attraction. What was it that still bound him and Simone together after all this time? What was the glue? Why couldn't he seem to forget that night, as she had, and get on with his life?

He knew he cared for Samantha, cared about her deeply—and could easily grow to love her—if he allowed her into his heart. *If.* He'd never been a man to do anything halfway. Nothing. Not in his professional life and certainly not in his personal life. And perhaps that's what plagued him about Simone. There was no closure, no resolution. They were incomplete. And that was what prohibited him from allowing Samantha to become a part of his world—his inability, at this time, to give all of himself. Samantha understood that, maybe even better than he did.

He'd work it out. For his sake, as well as Simone's. Samantha was right. She deserved better and he was determined to make sure she got it. She *was* worth it.

He threw his legs over the side of the couch and went upstairs to the shower.

Maybe she was dreaming, but it was a sweet dream. She felt as if she were cocooned in a cottony quilt, surrounded by warmth and protection. A warm hand moved slowly up along her thigh, gentle and soothing, across her hip, and came to rest on her waist. She breathed in deeply, but couldn't get her eyes to open. Didn't want to, the dream was so comforting. She wanted to burrow deeper into it.

Fingertips flicked across her nipples and a bolt of desire shot straight down between her legs. She heard a moan. It was hers. A tingle behind her neck, light as a night breeze. A feathery caress across her stomach. A hot tongue lingering at her breast. A slow massage of palms and fingers along the contours of her spine and thighs. That low moan again. Her eyelids were so heavy . . . pushing them open . . . dark . . . only the light from the lamp lights. A warmth, full and heavy, next to her. She moved toward it, drawn by its muscular pull.

"How did you get in?" Her voice was thick and slurred. The room became clearer. His image outlined against the backdrop of night.

Both of them merged in a quick, blurring burst of passion and desire. In the hazy realm of half sleep, the netherworld of consciousness and slumber, she felt the weight move above her, around her, inside her. She welcomed it, embraced it, and was filled by it. Ecstasy came to her in full force, in its complete dimension, just as she raised her head to recognize her seducer. He was not an incubus, but a man, flesh and blood.

"No questions, not now," the dreamy voice of Adam whispered in her ear, before he flicked a tongue along its rim. "I don't ever want you to wake up alone"—he moved deep and slow—"again."

Chad found Samantha in the kitchen, a towel draped around her neck, the remnants of sweat still evident around her hairline and down the bridge of her nose. A big wet spot filled the center of her chest, and he couldn't seem to tear his eyes away from the rise and fall of her breasts beneath the electric blue Lycra tank top.

"Mornin'," she said, a bit winded, and gulped down half a glass of orange juice without taking a breath. "Didn't want to wake you when I went on my run." She finished off the juice.

"Sam, you've got to remember things aren't like they used to be. Somebody's out there who wants to do you harm. Look at what happened the other night. Look what just happened to your sister. You don't want protection, but as long as I'm here, I'm all you got. So at least let me know when you're going out of the house."

She gave him a stiff military salute. "Yes, sir!"

He tried not to laugh. "This isn't funny, Sam. This is for real."

"Yes, sir!" She remained at attention.

"All right, all right, make jokes."

Samantha relaxed and put her hand on her hip, her lower body covered in the identical fabric as the top, giving her a long, sleek look. "Simone called me this morning."

"I must have really been out. I didn't hear a thing."

"Yeah, some great bodyguard you make."

"Hey, what do you expect for these prices. You fill my body up with wine and my head with all sorts of things I need to work out. Takes a lot out of a brother."

"Yeah, right," she said sarcastically. "Anyway, she sounded . . . happy."

He had a confused look on his face.

"You know . . . happy."

"Hey, great. She must be feeling better." He walked to the fridge and pulled the door open, conveniently blocking him from Samantha's view.

Samantha rested her hip against the counter. She wanted to push it, wanted to get a rise out of him, tell him that Adam was there, had been there all night from what she could tell. She didn't, but she told him about the arrangements instead.

"She said she won't be going into her office for the next few days. I told her we'd meet her at her house after we stop by my office and pick up everything we need."

"What about your father?" He closed the refrigerator door, his hands coming up empty.

"Called him. He said he couldn't get there before noon, but to get started."

"Fine. I better get dressed." He walked out of the room.

Samantha watched him and wondered how the rest of the day would pan out now that the seed of intimacy between Simone and Adam was planted. It would be interesting to watch. At some point, Chad was going to have to come to grips with what he planned to do about the two of them, and if a little push from her was necessary, then so be it.

She went to the front door, hoping that the paper had finally arrived. The delivery boy was late on the first decent day of weather they'd had all week. Go figure. She pulled open the door and was happy to find the paper rolled and in its usual spot on the bottom step. She went down to retrieve it and immediately snapped it open to the front page as she walked back inside.

The headline stopped her cold.

CHAPTER THIRTY-THREE

Like morning dew, the lingering effects of the unexpected late-night tryst with Adam still clung to her
well-tended body. Almost purring, she slid out of bed,
surprised that the aches and stiffness had diminished
considerably. The aroma of brewing coffee and the
muffled voices from the downstairs television filtered
teasingly upstairs. Simone smiled, catlike. *Lovemaking
certainly has its merits.*

He'd been so gentle with her last night, she
recalled, heading dreamily toward the bathroom,
treating her as if she were the finest piece of china,
and repeating over and over again how sorry he was,
how he would never do anything to hurt her, that he
loved her.

"Hmmm." She breathed in deeply, stepping beneath the waters. Love. It was a big word, a life-altering word. Did she love Adam, too? If she had to ask herself, maybe she didn't, but she believed she would—given the time. This ... this whole thing between them was so new. She was still getting adjusted to the idea. She let the water slide over her tender body, lathering the bruised skin with scented burberry soap.

True, they'd known each other for years, traveled in the same circles, and yes, he was good-looking, intelligent, fun to be with, determined, and an incredible lover. But love? She'd never allowed her mind to entertain the idea until now.

"Simone!"

She slid open the shower door and listened.

"Simone!"

"Yes," she shouted over the water.

"Hurry. You need to see this."

Wrapped in a white terry cloth robe, Simone sat with an expression of worry and outrage creasing her face.

Staring back at her and countless households across the district, her opponent, the incumbent Vincent McCall, was holding media court at his local D.C. office. He was glibly telling everyone present that Simone's car incident was no more than an elaborate publicity stunt to gain sympathy votes for a losing candidate, buttressed by her rabble-rousing sister's allegations of personal threats and alleged break-ins. "Councilwoman Montgomery's only platform has been to criticize the police of this district who are keeping *her* and *you* safe. I ask you: would you rather make a mistake and have just one of these criminals who sell drugs to your children, break into your homes, or shoot up your neighborhoods on the loose because the police were too intimidated by rhetoric to do their jobs? Or would you rather offend a few people for the benefit of many?"

Simone pointed the remote and made him disappear. "I should have known he'd pull something like this," she said with disgust.

"If I were still your press secretary, I'd prepare a statement."

She looked up at him and caught the smirk on his face. "Very funny." To be truthful, after last night, she'd completely forgotten she'd told him to beat it. Now she'd have to eat her words and face the staff with her misstep. She was a big girl. She could handle it.

"Consider yourself reinstated," she said, easily switching into business mode. "We can't let too much time go by and allow this to sink into folks' heads."

"Exactly."

The phone rang. Adam crossed to the end table and to Simone's amazement picked up *her* phone! But before she could react, he casually handed it to her, and she realized just how hard it was for her to trust.

"Thanks," she mumbled. "Hello?"

"Have you read today's paper?" Samantha demanded to know the instant she heard her sister's voice on the phone.

"No, but it can't be any worse than what's on television. Hold on a sec." She covered the mouthpiece. "It's Sam. She says the paper is littered with the same stuff. Would you mind checking to see if ours arrived yet?"

Adam nodded, ducked outside and quickly returned, his brow knitted in a frown as he scanned the contents of the personal attack. "We can't waste *any* time, Simone," he reemphasized, tossing the paper onto the couch, then following suit.

"Not too bad today," Simone was saying. "Slept pretty good, actually." She glanced across the room at Adam and grinned. "No, I'm not going in today. Probably not for a couple of days at least. Sure, come by here. See you then." She hung up and turned her attention to Adam, who seemed as comfortable lounging on her couch at six A.M. as if it were an everyday occurrence.

"Well . . . what words of wisdom are you going to have me espouse today?"

"I'm thinking," he said, stretching, then following it with a yawn. "Don't worry. I'll have something for you within the hour." He stood and looked back at her. "Samantha and Chad coming over?"

Simone nodded. "She said after one. You know I have the Cathy Hughes show to do this morning. Then I have to get to the BET studio by six."

"Then I better get busy. I'm sure we'll have much

more to talk about by the time they get here. We still haven't discussed your speech for the fund-raiser that the Women Against Violence are sponsoring for you next week at the Hilton.''

She shut her eyes and sighed heavily. "I'd totally put that out of my mind."

"That's why you have a staff, babe, to help you remember. I'll give Pam a call and bring her up to date.''

Simone frowned. "At this hour?"

He hesitated an instant. "Hey, knowing Pam, I'm sure she's up." He laughed lightly. "And if not, I'll just have to wake her." He headed for Simone's study.

Simone shook off the sudden, odd sensation, attributing it to all the stress, and went back upstairs to get ready for her interview.

Pamela was busy in Simone's kitchen putting together a plate of snacks. They'd been at it for hours and everyone was starved. The only real break had come when she'd accompanied Simone to tape her television interview for the talk show. Now it was near midnight and there didn't seem to be any letup in sight.

Wearily, she returned to the living room and set the tray on the coffee table that was already littered with empty coffee mugs and cans of soda, whatever was needed to give that extra lift. The crackers and sandwiches were gone in minutes.

"The main thing is to stand your ground, both of

you," Chad was saying to Simone and Samantha. "The first sign of weakness and they've got you."

"Perhaps, but at the moment it looks like *your* approach to be up-front about the attacks has back-fired," Adam said, his comment directed at Chad. "They're using it not only against Samantha, but Simone in particular."

Chad cut Adam a sharp look but held his tongue. This wasn't the forum to get into whatever their personal issues were.

"I agree with Chad," Samantha cut in, not appreciating Adam's accusatory tone.

"We all did," Simone added, her voice hoarse and tired. "What we need to concentrate on now is getting prepared to present this case, making sure everything is in place and that there is no chance it will be dismissed out of hand."

"And we need to keep your campaign in mind, Simone," Pam stated. "Bad press is something we can't afford, not while we're only a few points ahead of McCall."

"The statement we released to the press this morning should put out some of the fire," Adam said. "It's going to get ugly. He's getting desperate."

Chad walked across the room and sipped the remains of his Coke. "Justin and I have tied up every loose legal end we could foresee. What we don't need right now are any more accidents. Everyone needs to be extra careful about driving, coming in and out of buildings alone, and accepting packages. Whoever is behind this means business, and the closer we get to the court date, the higher the stakes. Especially once it hits the papers. You all understand that, don't you?''

Nods and mumbles of agreement responded to him.

''Good. Sam, you still have all the backup materials at your office. Make sure they stay in a safe place. In the event that there's any snafus I don't want to have to reinvent this whole process. Reconstructing the more than six hundred suits in this case would cripple us.''

''That's all been taken care of,'' she said, resting her head back against the cushions of the couch.

''Vaughn is arranging for added security for the fund-raiser,'' Chad continued, taking full control of the meeting. He was the only one who seemed to have any energy left. ''She'll be using some of her people. Mia, I know it's a monstrous task, but you need to contact each and every person on the list and make sure they're prepared for court, and have not and will not speak to the media.''

''I can get Nettie and Steve to help you with that,'' Samantha offered.

Mia nodded and added that to her lists of tasks.

Chad stood in the center of the room, tall, dark and decisive. He'd prepared for four years for the days ahead and he wouldn't allow any oversight to derail it. ''Anything else to add?'' He looked from one exhausted face to the next.

''No,'' was unanimous.

''Then we need to get out of here and let Simone get some rest.''

One by one they pulled themselves up from their various positions and prepared to leave.

"Excuse me if I don't see you all to the door," Simone said over a yawn.

"You get yourself to bed," Samantha counseled, bending to kiss Simone's cheek. "I'll call you in the morning." She left with her arm around Chad's waist, and for the first time, Simone didn't feel that twinge in her stomach.

Simone and Adam were finally alone.

Adam bent down and whispered in her ear. "I'm going to go home and get a few things. I'll be back if it's OK."

She smiled up at him. "I'll be waiting."

He kissed her lightly on the lips. "Not with the door unlocked this time," he said, reminding her of what could have been a disastrous mistake the night before.

"Take my spare set of keys. They're in the kitchen drawer near the back door."

He nodded. "See you in a few." He quickly went to get the keys and headed out.

Turning the key in the ignition on his black Acura Legend, he smiled thinking of the hours ahead. This was turning out better than he could have ever dreamed.

CHAPTER THIRTY-FOUR

Pamela sat on the side of her four-poster canopy bed, letting the final vestiges of adrenaline begin to trickle out of her pores. It was almost two A.M. Yet, she couldn't sleep. Her mind was weary, but her hyperactive body betrayed her, kept her revved up, would not let her rest.

She lay back against the cool, pearl gray satin sheets and the thick down-filled pillows, her short sheer nightgown of a misty sea green rising up to her hips. She drew up her knees, resting her hands on her flat stomach, and sighed heavily. With all that had happened in the past few months: stepping up the momentum of the campaign, the increase in media scrutiny on the entire Montgomery family, the long brutal hours and now this push for the class action suit, they'd had to forego their late-night-into-morning interludes. "Wait until everything calms down," he'd said. "There's too much at stake and we have to be on top of things every minute." She knew it was true. Everything hinged on staying focused. No slipups and then they'd be together and have everything she'd ever dreamed of.

Knowing all that, however, did not stem her need for him, did not quell the desire that throbbed so deeply within her it felt like another heartbeat. That unquenchable hunger for his touch.

She could have had any man she wanted. She'd had her pick from an endless parade of men, from politicians to security guards. Never had she allowed her less-than-stellar background to stand in the way of what she wanted—influence, affluence, and to be among the powerful. To take her place among the decision makers. It didn't matter that her parents hadn't gotten beyond the fifth grade in school, or that her sister had four children by four different men, or that her brother died of a drug overdose at sixteen. She'd put all that behind her. She'd come to Washington, worked her way through school, read voraciously of every fashion, decorating, style and etiquette magazine. She took Saturday classes in diction to erase her heavy southern accent, which was seen in some circles as a liability, the mark of the uncouth, the tongue of the classless hick. She went to the gym religiously to shed the hereditary extra pounds that always found their way around her hips and breasts.

And she made sure she was seen in all the right places, was invited to the right functions. She graduated from George Washington University with honors, proud of her double major in political science and economics. No, she was no dummy. No pushover. Except when it came to him. Him. For him, she became foolish, a prisoner of her heart, accepting bad behavior she would have never taken from anyone under any circumstances. And for the first time in her adult life, she felt powerless, powerless to shake this hold he had over her. What was worse, she had no desire to be free of him. She loved him. From the beginning. And he loved her. He'd whisper the words in her ear when he moved inside her, when he touched her so tenderly it brought tears to her eyes—he'd say it. "I love you, Pam." It was during moments like that when she felt she was the luckiest woman in the world.

She reached for the bedside phone. All she needed was to hear his voice, hear his assuring words so that she could sleep. His soothing words which would wrap around her like the comfort of a warm blanket.

Holding the phone to her breasts, she could almost feel his annoyance come through the wires if she were to call him now—after the promises they'd made.

No. She returned the receiver to its base. She could wait. It would be worth it. It always was.

Pam closed her eyes. The throb of passion continued to beat between her thighs. She moaned, turned onto her side and stared at the illuminated dial of the bedside clock.

After the fund-raiser, Simone's campaign would

shift into high gear, compounded with what she knew would be a grueling duel with the media and Simone's opposition once the information was released about the far-reaching ramifications of the suit. She anticipated the initial uproar which would accompany the news of their legal offensive. It would be a while before things settled down to a semblance of normalcy. But the instant there was a window of opportunity, she was going to convince him they needed to get away on a well-deserved vacation. Take a break. It seemed like forever since they'd been away together. Maybe a week in Hawaii, she thought, feeling her body slowly relax. Yes, Hawaii, just what they needed.

So much to do, she mused before drifting off to a dream-filled sleep.

Chad was seated on a kitchen stool at the island counter, his bare birch-brown arms bold against the sleeveless white ribbed undershirt and baggy gray sweats hanging low on his narrow hips.

Samantha watched the gentle ripple of muscle beneath the taut flesh of his arms and solid back as he raised and lowered a glass of orange juice. The back of his hair was squared off and perfectly even, exposing the roped muscle of his broad neck that spread to his wide shoulders.

"Morning," she said from her spot in the doorway.

He glanced at her over his shoulder. A warm smile greeted her. "Mornin'. Have a good run?"

She nodded but didn't move from her spot.

"I've been thinking, Sam—I can't stay here much longer. I really have to start looking for my own place."

Her stomach rose and fell at the thought of Chad leaving. Over the past weeks, she'd grown accustomed to his presence, the intoxicating scent of him, the husky timbre of his voice when he sang off key in the shower, his raucous laughter and his gentle yet strong touch. She didn't want to think about coming home not to him, but to emptiness. To a quiet set of dark rooms. To the sound of only herself moving about her empty home.

But he was right. He couldn't stay much longer— threats or not. She had to accept that. Empty.

Samantha mopped the sweat from her brow with a small baby blue hand towel, a perfect match for her running outfit of the day—baby blue biker shorts and a clinging Lycra half top. Her muscles still burned from the exertion of her run. Her body tingled with the flow of blood pumping through her veins. She felt excited, one long, sinewy mass of sensation. This was the way she always felt after a run. It was like foreplay—stimulating, awakening all the nerve centers in her body. And to come back home—her body still in the throes of exhilaration, her pores open, her thighs throbbing, her breasts feeling tight and full—to see Chad in all his black, virile maleness sitting in her kitchen was almost more than she could stand.

She pulled open the refrigerator and reached for her bottle of spring water. The water was icy cold, sliding down her throat in seamless gulps. Through her chest, down into her belly where the flame leaped and fanned through her insides, pouring across the fire over and over until the bottle was drained and the flame was reduced to tiny embers of warm light— until the next time.

Finally, she responded to his declaration. "I suppose you're right. We seem to have gotten distracted," she said, forcing a lightness into her voice.

He turned fully around on the stool. Her nipples suddenly stood erect as if they'd been tweaked by the tips of tender fingers. She didn't try to hide them, but she stood there, wanting him to see how aroused she was.

He stood up and stepped close to her as his tongue glided across his mouth, teasing and taunting all of the sensations to be found there. His full lips glistened with momentary wetness. Her breath rose to her chest, caught and hung in her throat, then slipped like a ghost across her lips.

"Distracted is a good description," he said, his voice slow, low and misty, almost dreamlike. "It'll be hard for me to leave."

"Leave this house—or me?" she softly challenged. A trickle of sweat ran slowly down her spine.

Chad stood, then deliberately moved toward her. His index finger extended and traced her damp hairline. He stepped closer, the hard peaks of her swollen nipples grazing erotically against the white ribs of his T-shirt. "What if I said both?"

"Then I'd tell you there was no reason for you to leave."

The bulky weight of his erection brushed against the damp invitation between her thighs, and the shocking thrill of it nearly caused her to gasp.

She could feel the race of his heart pounding against the walls of his chest. Its exaggerated rhythm matched the rapid beats of her own. She stood perfectly still. It was up to him. He would make the first move and then she would surrender to him, to his advances, to his caresses.

"Sam." His voice came from somewhere deep in his gut. "Being here." His eyes roamed across her face. "These weeks have been heaven and hell."

She ran a nail delicately across his bottom lip and savored the look of desire that momentarily clouded his eyes. Something stirred, uncoiled, down below his belt in his sweats.

He took her hand. "Do you know how much I want you? This much." He placed her hand on his heart, and she felt the racing beat of it. Then he took her hand and cupped it along the length of his sex where it throbbed in taut hardness beneath her fingertips. "Every day," he expelled on a long, hot breath that teased her lips like a feather.

She couldn't breathe. Words danced without meaning in her head, tumbling from her lips in a soft puff of moans and tender whimpers.

"I wanted to wait," he murmured, brushing soft titillating kisses along the supple column of her neck, while his free hand found the dip of her waist, his thumb caressing her ribs, then the sensitive underside of her breast. "But I can't."

She shuddered, her neck arching, her lower body pushing instinctively forward, searching for relief from the heat that seared her insides. And still she held him, gently kneading his smooth skin, stroking him. But she wanted to feel him, really feel him, feel what she knew would be that satin over hardened muscle of him. She must.

Bold, daring, willing, she grasped the elastic band of his sweats and eased it down over his hips, releasing him to do with as she wished. Free from the barrier of cloth, she ran her fingers teasingly along the elongated shaft of his sex, taunting its delicate head with her fingertips.

A shudder slammed him hard. A groan, a blend of sound somewhere between agony and ecstasy, crawled up from his throat. He gritted his teeth, bracing his back against the frame of the door, as wave upon wave of pleasure rolled through him.

Samantha felt the full extent of her feminine power and she was rewarded for her skillful ministrations with tiny drops of dew that christened the tips of her fingers.

"Sam . . ." he groaned, pulling her hand away from a certain end to this game of passion they played.

"I know," she whispered.

Chad pulled her fully against him, his ardor having crossed the boundaries of no return. His mouth covered hers completely, his tongue slipping into the hot, wet confines, giving and testing a sample of what was sure to come.

His expert hands roamed freely along her damp body, seeking out her most secret pleasure zones, moving with ease over her clothing, which had now become one with her, sealed to her skin. They pressed full-length against each other, holding on almost desperately while their hips met in a smoldering primal gyration that was beyond the measure of time. She mumbled softly into his neck about all the things she wished him to do to her, her arms still entwined around him like unruly tendrils of ivy over stone. The entire room suddenly became infused with their heat, the urgency of their need played out in a blur of emotion and craving against the golden beams of sunlight bathing them.

"No," she rasped into his ear, suddenly looking over his shoulder at a thinly sliced mango on the table. "Come."

His face wore a quizzical expression, then he understood where they were heading and allowed himself to be led down the long hallway toward the stairs to her bedroom. "Wait," he said and stepped out of his sweats. She pulled off her top as they mounted the stairs, and his T-shirt followed.

He watched the sensual curve of her back, the teasing peek at her breasts when she turned halfway toward him, moving up the staircase.

He stepped in front of her when they reached her bedroom door. He looked down at the soft swell of her honey-brown breasts, the dark areolas reaching out to be teased with his tongue, the dip of her stomach and the gentle dark rise that he longed to bury himself in. He pushed the door open and backed into the room, his arms locked around her waist.

Samantha eased him back on a corner of her bed, her eyes dark with all the wicked intent of a naughty Catholic schoolgirl, and knelt between his long bowed legs.

He leaned back on his arms and elbows, shutting his eyes tightly as she let her tongue trace wet curlicues on his inner thighs. Her head rolled and dipped from one tender spot to another, wringing the breath from him in short, shuddering gasps.

Chad nearly screamed when she suddenly stopped. His eyes flew open and he looked at her standing in front of him.

A slow, seductive smile curved her lush lips, swollen from his kisses. By degrees she pushed the baby-blue shorts off her hips and down her thighs, revealing her nakedness beneath, and stepped out of them.

Chad's heart shot against his chest. She was as beautiful in the full light of day as she was glistening in the moonlight as he'd watched her from her doorway. He swallowed hard and sat up, reaching for her, inhaling the womanly scent of her.

She shivered when his tongue dipped into the hollow of her navel and carved a trail down the sensitive center that fanned out to the downy soft tuft of hair that barely camouflaged the heart of her sex. He teased it with the tip of his tongue and her legs gave way. Holding her tighter around her hips, he drew out the sweet essence of her womanhood onto his lips.

Samantha's entire body trembled. The soft sounds of her whimpers were a symphony to his ears. He delved deeper and her fingers caught in his hair, her nails biting into his scalp.

"Ch-Chad." The sound of his name came as a strangled cry that escalated his own excitement.

"Let it go," he whispered, his breath like fire against her.

"I . . . Ch-Chad." She shuddered violently, pressing herself against his mouth as her body took over, leaving her mind. All sense of reason gave way and exploded into a starburst of inexplicable joy.

He held her, kept up the agonizing pleasure until she was certain she would lose her mind, and then she was on the bed. Chad was braced above her, his body between her parted thighs. Her head spun, her breathing out of control, her body singing, wanting something else, something more. And he gave it to her, slowly, little by little, until he filled her, not only with his body but with a sense of elation and completeness that she'd never before experienced.

The power of their union captured him, too. It stunned him in a way that could not be explained. He felt as if his soul had left his body and entered hers. They were as one unit, one soul, one body. Joined not of flesh, but of spirit. And the purity of it, the exquisiteness of it, filled his entire being, ravaged his mind, and he knew from this moment forward he, they, would never be the same.

Samantha raised her legs to drape them around his waist, and he sunk deeper into the volcanic heat of her, nearly crying out from the pleasure of it.

Chad's lips found hers, tenderly kissing them, teasing them as he moved with a maddening slowness, needing desperately to hold onto this moment, this time. But Samantha wanted him, wanted him like she'd never wanted anything. She wanted to know what that moment between them would be. She needed to experience it as much as she needed to breathe. She arched her hips, rotated them like a disk on a turntable and he did cry out, a deep guttural sound that sent an erotic chill down her spine. Again and again and again.

The pleasure mounted until they were no more than conduits of sensation. And then, all at once, his sex found and touched that secret place deep in the heart of her. A cry ripped from her throat. Her body trembled as if shot with a bolt of electric current, and her walls clutched him, gripped and released him, draining him as the final surge of pleasure roared through him and into her.

They lay still, unable to move, their breathing coming in quick, labored bursts, both still caught in the rapture of what had passed between them.

With trembling fingers, Chad brushed her damp locks away from her face, traced the arch of her brows, mesmerized by the glimmer in her eyes, the ethereal glow that radiated from her. "It . . . it's never been that way before," he confessed, his voice hoarse and ragged.

"I know," she said simply, grazing her thumb across his lips. "For me either."

Reluctantly he withdrew from her warmth and eased onto his side. She turned to face him.

"Still want to leave?" she asked him, her tone teasing and wanton.

"I'd be crazy to leave you. But I can't just move in."

Briefly she closed her eyes, then looked at him, studying his serious expression. "You really are the gentleman you present yourself to be, aren't you?"

"Did you really think I was something else? That it was all just for show?"

She shrugged. "I didn't know. I . . . I've never met anyone like you, Chad. Most men wouldn't have given a second thought to just jumping in the sack, no commitment, no promises."

The simple words struck a painful chord of the familiar. He turned away and sat up. "I try not to be like . . . everyone else."

Samantha watched the subtle metamorphosis, the retreat to some place she was shut out of. And she wasn't sure why, what she'd said or done. She reached out and touched his back and he flinched as if stung.

"What?" she asked, a sense of dark foreboding seeping into her pores.

He shook his head. "Nothing, babe. Everything's cool," he said, hating to lie to her. But he could never tell her about the untied threads that still haunted him, kept him from turning himself completely over to anyone. And until he did, it would always be this way—beautiful, mind-blowing and unattainable.

CHAPTER
THIRTY-FIVE

Simone took one last look at herself in the full-length mirror that hung on the back of her bedroom door. The ankle-length gown of black silk with a sheer mesh overslip, studded with tiny droplets of rhinestones that glittered like a constellation when she moved, slid gently over her curves.

She'd decided to wear her hair up off her neck and away from her face, her beauty accented by a band of rhinestones that matched the dress and the studs in her ears. As usual, she wore little makeup, just enough to highlight her eyes with a brush of black mascara, a sweep of blush for her cheeks and a thin coat of pecan-colored lipstick.

She stepped into her backless black heels and

picked up her beaded purse from the dresser. A last-minute inventory of her appearance assured her that nothing had been left to chance. Taking a deep breath, she stepped from her room and descended the stairs. Adam was waiting for her.

The seductive scent of her perfume drifted to him, alerting him to her approach. He turned from his seat on the couch and looked up. She was a vision of classic black elegance. Slowly he stood, watching her graceful descent. This was his woman, all his, and a wave of guilt engulfed him. He didn't deserve her, didn't deserve a gorgeous woman like Simone Montgomery. She was everything he could possibly want in a woman, everything he'd always imagined he would one day have. And now that he did, he—

"How do I look?" she gently asked, smothering his searing thoughts.

"Incredible, incredible," he said in a hushed voice.

She crossed the room to stand in front of him, reached up and straightened his black bow tie. "I'd almost forgotten how wonderful you look in a tux." She smiled. "Remember those galas in the early days?" she asked, stirring up memories of the past. "We were so eager to please then. Make the right contacts, be seen at the right places, even if we couldn't afford to be there." She laughed lightly at the recollection of their primordial beginnings.

"Networking is at the heart of everything. It's more important than what you know. It's all about *who* can do something for you. Get you what you want, help you get where you want to go. Bottom line."

She looked at him curiously for a moment, surprised at the sudden cynical tone in his voice. "I suppose that's true," she said haltingly. "But hopefully not for everyone." Her gaze trailed over his face, searching, for what she wasn't sure. "Hopefully, we do this thing of ours because it's what we believe in. That we hope to make a difference. Even if it's small."

He turned away, crossed to the coffee table and picked up his drink of Jack Daniels over ice. "Very altruistic, Simone. But the reality is none of us would be where we are without the right support, without the right amount of money and without saying the right thing—whatever that may be."

"Where is this coming from?"

He took a long swallow of his drink, shook his head and pushed out a long breath. "Not everyone has a silver spoon in their mouths, Simone. Some of us have to claw our way out of the ditches by any means necessary. Sometimes it's not pretty. Sometimes it goes against everything we hold sacred. But we do it anyway." He finished off his drink and had an overwhelming urge for another, but knew it was a lousy idea. He needed a clear head.

Simone frowned. "W-what are you saying, that I had it easy?" she asked incredulously. "That I somehow compromise my values to get ahead—get a vote?"

He held up his hands, knowing he'd gone too far. "Hey, forget it. I guess I was getting too philosophical for my own good. Tonight's your night, baby. Not the time to dwell on some craziness running through my head for a minute. It's just listening to all the rhetoric by McCall and people like him." He came to her and raised her chin up with the tip of his finger. "You have more integrity than anyone I know. I mean that. And I love you. I mean that, too." He took a breath. "Now, if we don't get going you're going to be late to your own fund-raising event." He tenderly kissed her lips, held her for a moment longer before slowly releasing her.

Simone hesitated, slightly off-balance by this see-saw ride she'd been tossed onto with Adam. But he was right. This was her night to shine, and she couldn't allow herself to be distracted by anyone or anything, not even Adam Parsons. Whatever it was that was really eating at him, they'd talk about later.

"You're right. Tonight is what's important. Has the car arrived?"

"About fifteen minutes ago."

She slipped her arm through the crook of his, kissed him lightly on the cheek and they headed out.

"Oh, how I remember my first major fund-raiser that my parents threw for me," Vaughn said wistfully as the car carrying her and Justin pulled up in front of the Hilton Hotel and lined up behind the other vehicles waiting to be parked. "I dreaded it."

"You'd never know it," Justin returned. "You were the epitome of cool," he teased.

"You made quite an impression yourself." She glanced at him from the corner of her eye and smiled mischievously, remembering his daring move of stepping out in front of her car when she was leaving the affair. "You nearly gave me a heart attack."

"Yeah, but the aftereffect was well worth it."

"Touché, counselor." She sighed. "At least we're not doing to Simone what my parents did with me. This was her decision to run for office. It wasn't thrust upon her."

Justin turned off the powerful engine of the midnight blue Jag. "True. But politics is in your blood, Vaughn. You have to admit that. You're a natural. There's no getting around the fact that Elliot Hamilton had his own vision of what he wanted for his daughter, but he wasn't too far off the mark, even if I can't agree with his methods."

"He nearly destroyed our relationship with his meddling and manipulating," she answered, feeling the old sensations of hurt begin to surface. Although her father had passed nearly three years earlier, the sting of what he'd attempted to do to her life still burned at times.

Justin leaned over and kissed her forehead. "But he didn't, babe. We survived in spite of him."

"I know, I know. And tonight is not the time to dwell on the past," she said, perking up. "I just hope the evening proceeds without a hitch and there are no more accidents. Those girls have been through enough in the past weeks."

"Security is tight. And your guy seems to know what he's doing," he added, referring to the pair of Secret Service agents assigned to her once the threats had hit the papers. "I'm sure everything will be fine, and Simone will shine like the star she is."

A valet tapped on Justin's side of the window. He exited the car and dropped the keys in the young man's hands. Rounding the front, he took his wife's hand and headed inside.

It was definitely a star-studded event, or at least a politically studded event. All the major Democratic players were in the main ballroom, milling about and making sure they were seen by those who counted. Glitter was everywhere, in lobes, on wrists and around delicate throats. Gowns that could easily take to the runway graced the multitude of womanly figures, and the men wore an assortment of traditional tuxedos to avant garde formal designer wear.

"Hmm, impressive," Vaughn said in a mock stage whisper.

"I'm sure all the publicity has brought out the curious as well as the true supporters."

"The more the merrier as long as they put their checks in the collection plate," Vaughn murmured.

Justin chuckled and guided her inside, where they were immediately swept up in greetings from their mutual acquaintances, then joined shortly after by Samantha and Chad, who'd just arrived.

"Great turnout," Samantha said over the sound of the band slipping into a rendition of "Satin Doll." All around the room, people were greeting each other, glad-handing, embracing old friends, discussing party politics and the upcoming elections. They were the usual activities seen at affairs like this.

Chad slid his arm around her waist. "Now all we need is the arrival of the guest of honor and the fun will begin. Did I tell you how beautiful you look tonight?" he whispered in her ear.

Her entire body flushed, thinking about what had happened between them. She'd worried for hours about what to wear and had finally decided on a short Dior cocktail gown. The strapless bodice in black velvet and the flounced skirt of gold lamé and tulle showcased her long legs to perfection. Obviously, by the gleam in Chad's eye, she'd made the right decision.

"No, you haven't," she responded in answer to his question, gazing up at him. "But you can whisper it in my ear all night long."

Justin caught the intimate exchange in a quick glance and wondered just how far their relationship had progressed. But from the glow radiating from his daughter, it wasn't hard to guess. He could only pray that it would work out for everyone, Simone included.

A flurry of activity among the press and photographers at the entrance to the hall pulled his and everyone's attention toward the door. Simone had arrived.

Vaughn could barely contain her motherly pride as she watched her stunning daughter work the crowd, giving everyone just the right amount of attention, not missing a beat, smiling and shaking hands with the skill of a seasoned politician. Lingering with each guest just long enough to make a lasting impression.

"She really is good at this," Vaughn mouthed to Justin as they observed Simone move gracefully through the room, totally unruffled by the flash of cameras and the multitude of questions directed at her.

"Of course, look at her teacher." He kissed her forehead and hugged her close to him. Finally, Simone made her way to them, with Adam close behind.

"Whew. That was like running the gauntlet," she said, not unkindly.

"You make it look easy," Adam assured. "Good evening, everyone," he said, nodding at the members of the Montgomery clan and Chad. They returned the greeting.

"Well, this is it, huh?" Simone commented, looking around in amazement at the turnout. "I really didn't expect this."

"People believe in you, sis," Samantha said, "and want to show their support."

"It's still a bit overwhelming. What a crowd! There has to be at least eight hundred people here. A lot of the old guard and quite a few new faces as well."

"At a starting rate of five hundred dollars a plate and up, I'd say you're going to make out very well," Adam calculated, his eyes sweeping over the throng gathered in the room.

"That's a lot of lobster," Simone joked.

"Speaking of which, why don't we get seated at our

table before the festivities begin," Justin suggested, looking up at the large banner above the podium with a huge portrait of Simone pointing like a true leader into the horizon. "I know everyone must be hungry."

All too soon the mistress of ceremonies for the evening, Madelyn Evers, the chairperson for the Women Against Violence, stepped up to the podium, tapped the mike twice and asked for quiet. The talking ceased and all attention was directed to the outspoken woman standing before them.

"First, I want to begin by thanking all of you for coming out in such great numbers to show your support for our candidate," she said in well-modulated tones, a voice smooth enough to host a radio show.

There was a loud flurry of applause.

Madelyn smiled, waited a moment for the audience to quiet and then she continued. "I feel honored that City Councilmember Montgomery—"

"Assemblymember Montgomery!" someone shouted from the back of the room. Applause erupted again.

"*Assemblymember* Montgomery . . ." Madelyn continued, humoring the crowd. "We are pleased that she has allowed us to honor her in such a fashion. We know what she has contributed to this community, to our community. As she has done with so many key issues, she has worked tirelessly and fearlessly in her fight against police brutality in the District of Columbia. It is her intention to make sure that not one more life, not one more young black man, is lost to this plague that infects our neighborhoods."

More applause.

"Believe me when I say I could stand here all night and go down the impressive list of her contributions to the residents of D.C., but that would take all night. Her influence is not just felt here in the District but on the Hill as well and throughout the country. I could go on and on but I won't. Instead, allow *Assemblymember* Montgomery to speak for herself. Please, join me in welcoming her."

Simone took the speech, written for her by Adam, from her purse and slowly rose to a round of deafening applause. Her family and friends noticed that she didn't rush to the podium but chose to let the roar of the applause from the faithful swell to almost ear-splitting proportions, then arc, diminish, and finally rise to an even higher pitch before dying out. Gracefully, she adjusted the mike, placed the speech on the lectern, and quietly began her recitation of the prepared text.

"Ladies and gentlemen, for so many of us, the problem of police brutality is not an old one," she intoned solemnly. "We've seen and felt its ugly, vicious presence in our communities for far too long. We saw it on television during the media's coverage of the bloody campaigns of the civil rights movement as high-pressure fire hoses and attack dogs were turned on black protestors only seeking justice. We saw it again when the police went after members of the Black Panther Party, often conducting midnight raids and ambushes that left many of the hunted dead or seriously wounded. We all saw in that infamous videotape of the savage beating by the LAPD of Rodney King, a case that thrust this issue directly into the national consciousness. The newspapers screamed out headlines not long ago about another case involving a Haitian immigrant who was sodomized by officers in a police station. Or yet another case where forty-one shots were fired by police at another unarmed black man as he entered his apartment building. What is going on here? Why has this problem reached such epidemic proportions?"

Someone yelled out in response, recalling a parishioner from the old sanctified churches: "Teach, sister, tell the truth." A few laughed at this reminder of what was at the core of most black communities, the black church and its bedrock faith in truth and righteousness. Going home. Back to the roots.

And Simone felt it too, the power of her ancestors, the strength of their conviction and commitment to gain justice and equal opportunity as well as full protection under the law. "Some would have you believe that this new wave of police brutality, this clash of wills between the police and our people, is confined to the inner city. That's a myth. We have gathered statistics that indicate a widespread incidence of humiliation, abuse and excessive force across the country."

A ripple of clapping interrupted her momentum for several seconds, but she quickly regained her stride. She waved one hand to silence the few stragglers who wanted to continue to show their admiration for her message.

"There is a cycle of violence and bigotry that threatens to undo all we fair-minded people in this country have worked so hard to achieve," she said, her face tight with concentration. "The police are there to serve us, all of us. If this is the type of behavior we're getting from them, is there any wonder why we now have a relationship of such conflict and tension? Why shouldn't we be suspicious of them? Why shouldn't we be slow to cooperate? Those who support this new hard line don't understand why our hearts race whenever we're told to pull over by police officers on a deserted highway road at night or why we're reluctant to call them even in situations where we're hurt or frightened. So many of these cases are not even considered pressworthy because their numbers have increased to the point where no one even raises an eyebrow anymore. Unless they're so extreme, unless someone dies."

More applause.

"What can we do about it?" she asked and paused.

"Plenty." A voice replied from a corner of the hall.

"That's right. We can do plenty. As of today, the rules of the game are changing. We are serving notice that this self-enclosed police culture must become more accessible to public scrutiny, and that means a more effective review process to weed out rogue cops. We're calling for extended investigative powers for Internal Affairs Departments independent of the precincts and greater cooperation for people filing civilian complaints. We need a more citizen-friendly police force all across this country and we will not stop until we see real and lasting changes.''

This time, the applause was thunderous. Her mother was glowing. This was the kind of talk, firm and resolute, that was heard from a candidate running for a national office. The crowd loved it.

"My opponent, Mr. McCall, is from the old school, the law and disorder school, and he does not see the need for any of this. He supports the authorities no matter what they do. We'll send a message to him on election day.''

The hall rocked from the sudden explosion of clapping, cheers and shouts of support. This time Simone did not stop it. She stood there, basking in the warm glow of the massive show of encouragement. She looked out into the crowd, spotting her family and friends. Her mother was wiping away tears from her eyes as she clapped wildly. It was a moment she would never forget, a moment that changed her.

"Thank you all for coming,'' she shouted over the din and regally left the stage.

"Incredible, baby,'' Justin said, embracing her, with her mother, sister, Chad and Pam, who'd arrived during the speech, following suit.

Adam stood aside, watching the outpouring of accolades for her inspirational speech. Those were *his* words she'd spoken, though heartfelt. He was the one who'd toiled over ever phrase, every nuance. He'd sat with her and coached her, ensuring that her declarations would receive the maximum effect. *His words.*

Would they have sounded just as convincing coming from someone else's mouth, or was it really Simone's charisma that brought the words to life?

Finally, she turned to him, a radiant smile beaming across her face. He adjusted what he knew was a hard expression, and flashed her a triumphant smile. He extended his arms and she gratefully walked into them. He kissed the top of her head. "Great job. You had them right in the palm of your hand."

"Couldn't have done it without you. I'll have to thank you later," she said so only he could hear.

He didn't comment and slowly released her. Pam came up behind her, a clipboard in her hand. "Several members of the press want to talk to you, Simone. And of course the Women Against Violence committee wants photographs." She put an arm around her shoulder and ushered her expertly away, cutting Adam a short look and a tight smile.

The band started up again, and with dinner finished, couples found their way to the dance floor, still caught in the afterglow of Simone's charged address. She gave brief statements to the eager press, posed for a round of photographs and graciously made her way back to her table.

Sitting down for the first time in what seemed like hours, she took a slow sip of her champagne and momentarily allowed herself to relax and enjoy the brief respite from the demands of the media and well-wishers. It had been a successful evening. She caught a quick glimpse of Samantha and Chad as they moved effortlessly, almost as one, across the floor, and she saw the radiance of happiness on her sister's face and the same look of joy on Chad's. And suddenly it was all right, as it should be. And a wave of peace, the peace she'd been searching for, settled within her.

The music segued to another tune, a slow one, and Simone let her gaze wander around the room, listening to the laughter, seeing the smiling faces. Yes, this was her night, what she'd groomed herself for, and she was going to enjoy every minute of it. This was about the future, no longer girlhood fantasies of the past. It was time to let go and move on.

"May I have this dance?" Chad asked, suddenly coming up behind her.

She turned, surprised, and looked up at him, her heart tumbling once, then settling in her chest.

"Sure." Slowly she rose, allowed herself to be led to the center of the dance floor and stepped into his arms.

For the first few minutes she closed her eyes and swayed to the music, allowing herself to enjoy the familiar comfort of his arms. The embrace of friendship and nothing more.

"I've been so wrong," she said against his chest.

He eased back a bit and looked down at her upturned face. "About what?"

"The way I've been acting, the way I've treated you since you've been home," she confessed.

"Hmm. You've finally noticed," he said lightly.

"What . . . happened between us was beautiful and right . . . at the time. And I realize that all these years what I was holding on to was an image, a dream, a fantasy. And because of that I didn't allow myself or you to move on. I trapped us up in a tight space inside my head, and was too stubborn to let go. I couldn't release the past."

"Why didn't you write?" he gently asked.

"I think a part of me was afraid that if I did, I might get more than I was willing to handle. This is my life," she said, looking around. "At least for now. And I must put every ounce of myself into it to make it work. Then when I do I'll be ready for what it was I *thought* I wanted with you."

Chad took a deep breath and slowly exhaled. "I think we've both grown up, Simone. Finally."

She leaned closer to him and shut her eyes. "Yes, we have." She paused for a moment, then spoke. "You love her, don't you?"

"Yes," he said simply.

She smiled.

There was a sudden ruckus in the crowd as bodies suddenly shifted and tilted to make way for someone pushing through. Justin appeared as the crowd parted, his face set in a mask of angry lines, his dark eyes intent. He leaned close to a startled-looking Simone. Her heart pounded. Chad gripped her arms.

Justin lowered his voice. "There's been a fire. It's serious. We need to leave as quickly and quietly as possible. The car is in the back of the building."

CHAPTER THIRTY-SIX

The acrid smell of burned wood, rubber and twisted metal greeted them before they exited their cars, stinging their eyes and noses. Swirling red lights dotted the night sky, cutting through the smoke in erratic rhythms like watchtower beams suddenly gone amok. Firemen were still on the scene, barking orders and hosing down the final smoldering embers, causing a cascade of thick black clouds and soot to be expelled into the air. Local residents lined the street in small herds, clothed in everything from bathrobes to night-club outfits. Yet their collective mood was the same: horror, shock and immense sadness.

Along the curb, a cluster of television news trucks with print and electronic reporters eager for a breaking late-night story relayed to their audiences the details of this latest of plagues inflicted upon the Montgomerys.

An overwhelming wave of despair rushed through Samantha, weakening her knees and sending the blood coursing to her head in thundering bursts. When she stepped, as in a dream, from the car, her hand flew to her mouth when she took in the full extent of the destruction. There was nothing left but the charred ribs of the building, shattered windows and the smoldering remnants of the foundation. Everything she'd worked for, built day by day for the last five years, was gone, destroyed, up in smoke.

One by one, whispers of incredulity passed through the tight family circle. They huddled together, comforting one another with their physical closeness and empty words of hope and support.

Samantha shook her head violently, tears springing to her eyes. Chad wrapped his arms around her, pulling her close. "Take it easy, Sam. It's going to be all right. Take it easy."

She turned into the hard lines of his body and buried her face in his chest, shaking uncontrollably as the terror of what could have been, had someone been trapped inside, settled over her.

"Come on, sweetheart, get back in the car. Justin and I need to talk to the fire chief." He was thinking of arson, if an accelerant—gas or the like—had been used to ignite the blaze. Whether it was a suspicious fire. He calmly guided her back toward Vaughn, who helped her back into the car.

Simone's heart ached for her sister. Never had she seen her so paralyzed, so weak, as she did at that moment. Yet she knew no words would assuage the acute feeling of loss Samantha was experiencing while standing before the collection of cinders and twisted metal that was once her headquarters. Someone was out to hurt them, to shut them down. And now their blind determination had reached a new, decidedly deadly level. She hugged her arms around her body. What was next?

Adam stepped up beside her, bracing the center of her spine with the palm of his hand. "The press are here en masse. They're going to want a statement. My advice is to tell them that you'll comment in the morning, when the damage is assessed and the preliminary fire report is issued."

Simone stared at the wreckage, nodded numbly and followed Adam to the limo.

Chad and Justin approached the fire chief, who was still giving direction to his crew. Three firefighters, with oxygen tanks strapped on their backs, tugged at an unruly coil of hose and another group passed out axes to probe the smoking structure for hidden embers and pockets of fire.

"I'm Justin Montgomery and this is my partner, Chad Rushmore."

The fire chief turned a sullen face toward Justin. "Looks like arson," he stated without preamble. "There will be an investigation beginning in the morning."

"Was anyone hurt?" Chad asked.

"No. We've been through every inch. Nothing."

The police began roping off the area in the distinctive yellow tape as the firemen began to pack up their equipment.

Crime scene, Chad thought.

"What did he say?" Adam asked as he approached, referring to the fire chief.

"Arson," Chad replied.

"There's nothing more we can do here tonight. We need to get everyone home, try to get some rest and sort this all out in the morning," Justin suggested.

The trio stoically returned to the limo, moving through the crowd which was now disbanding. Reporters watched them from across the street but did not move in their direction, respecting their right to maintain their silence until the official press conference.

"How bad?" Pamela asked when they entered, her words full of breathy concern.

Samantha spoke in a flat monotone. "The entire case was in that office. Everything. A total loss."

They regarded each other with weary eyes. No words were necessary as the chilling enormity of what "everything" meant took hold and rooted.

For the balance of the night, Samantha lay curled in the protective confines of Chad's arms, her back pressed against his front, as the terrible images of the fire played over and over in her head.

"What are we going to do, Chad?"

He stroked her hair. He'd been asking himself the very same question for the past few hours. They had less than seventy-two hours to present their oral arguments to the court. It had been through Justin's diligence and favors owed that they'd even secured a court date so soon. Cases as far-reaching as these could easily take months, sometimes years, to get on the calendar. But Justin had impressed upon the judge the urgency of the legal action and assured him that they were ready. He and Justin had worked tirelessly to prepare the documents, gather the supporting evidence and brief the witnesses—for when their court date arrived. Now he didn't know what they were going to do. And if they did figure out a solution, how could it be humanly possible to pull it off in the short time allotted them? Yet they couldn't back down, not now. Not after coming so far.

"We'll work it out," he finally answered, a deep weariness seeping into his bones. "The main thing is that no one was hurt. The rest . . ."

"The rest," she said morosely, "doesn't look good."

Seeking to reassure her without lying, he kissed the back of her hair and lightly stroked her cheek, knowing she was absolutely right.

That next morning, Adam eased out of his bed, not wanting to disturb Simone, after having finally convinced her it would be safer if she spent the night with him. Rubbing sleep from his eyes and face, he tiptoed quietly downstairs and put on a pot of water to boil for coffee. The images of the previous night still loomed large and so much remained to be done. This latest attack would severely cripple the class action case, especially with the case materials incinerated. Work of that magnitude could not be reconstructed in a few days. There was no question about that. How the media and the people of D.C. would respond was the next hurdle, and how it would impact Simone's ability to proceed with her election bid was another critical challenge. He knew this whole business was taking a toll on her, whether she admitted it or not. It had barely been three weeks since she was almost run off the road. The faint bruises and traces of black and blue coloring on her chest were clear reminders of how close a call that had been. How many more accidents, how many more veiled threats to her and to her family would it take before she buckled under and threw in the towel? It was now more than a battle of wills. It was a war of nerves and endurance. Her opponents were waiting to see what it would take to make her submit, to force her to betray her convictions and her constituents.

The phone rang, pulling him away out of the whirlwind of his thoughts. Who could this be? Quickly, he picked it up to keep from waking Simone.

"Hello?"

"It's Chad."

Adam frowned. Not now.

"Have you seen the morning paper?"

"No." Adam replied, but something in Chad's voice bothered him. Bothered him plenty.

"I think you should and after you do, we all need to talk and quickly." He hung up abruptly without giving Adam a chance to answer.

Adam secured the belt to his lightweight cotton robe and went outside on the front porch. His home-delivered copy of *The Washington Post* lay there in a neat roll on the stone steps. He stooped down to retrieve it and returned inside, his stomach clenching in an uncontrollable spasm of dread as he read the newspaper's banner headline: MONTGOMERY LAW FIRM SET TO LAUNCH MAJOR CLASS ACTION SUIT AGAINST D.C. POLICE DEPARTMENT.

CHAPTER THIRTY-SEVEN

After a flurry of round-robin phone calls, they'd all agreed to meet at Simone's local campaign offices to initiate a strategy of damage control and come to some sort of agreement about how to proceed. It was Simone's suggestion that they convene at her place. She had a small press conference at one that afternoon which she couldn't get out of, and still had to prepare for it. Most importantly, she did have security on site. She'd feel safe. A few weeks ago, this business of bodyguards would have been viewed as somewhat of an annoyance, an unneeded expense, but after this spate of mishaps, security was now paramount in all their lives. The meeting was set for ten A.M. Simone and Adam arrived first.

"We need to go over your comments for the press conference before the rest of them arrive," Adam stated, moments after they entered Simone's office. "As of this morning, I'm certain the entire direction of their questions will be different. They will want to focus on the fire, how it affected the family, and most of all the suit."

Simone slapped her purse on the desk and slipped off her forest green suit jacket revealing the silky mist green camisole beneath. She hung it on the back of her chair and gripped its top. "Damn it, Adam, who could have said something? The timing for the dissemination of that information was crucial. This premature release puts us on the defensive."

"My guess is that it was one of the witnesses. Who else could it be?" He turned his back and walked to the window. "My bigger concern at the moment is how all of this will affect your ability to campaign effectively. This wave of accidents, threats and now this fire has successfully taken everyone's mind off of the issues. And McCall and his camp are still insisting it's all a publicity stunt, which, of course, is untrue, but that kind of accusation severely clouds people's thinking and plants a seed of doubt."

"I know," she said quietly, shaking her head as she slowly paced the floor. "I looked at the overnights." Her gaze connected with his. "For the first time since this campaign started we're falling behind. I'm only ahead by a one-percent margin. All of these events are having a negative impact and I don't want to see us go into a slide."

He didn't comment. The deed was done.

She came up behind him and wrapped her arms around his waist, pressing her head against his back. "Poor Samantha," she said softly. "She's going to have to literally start all over again and rebuild. I'm sure there are documents in those computers that will never be recovered."

Adam arched his neck and looked further out across the horizon. "Whoever did it," he said quietly, "knew exactly who and what to hit." He turned, clasping her shoulders, a sudden urgency in his eyes and voice as a wave of untenable feelings swept through him with the reality of what could have been. "It might have been you, Simone," he said with such raw emotion it chilled her. "You could have been alone in your office, like you are so many nights— trapped. We could all be getting ready to talk about . . . something entirely different." He swallowed hard, and the acceptance of that dark possibility and all its ramifications suddenly registered, and magnified the scenario in her eyes.

"B-but we aren't," she said a bit weakly.

He gently brushed the silky straight hair away from the side of her face and tucked it behind her ear, revealing the tiny gold studs in her lobes. His thumb caressed her cheek. And when she looked up at him, with the same intensity she did after they made love, he could feel his insides shift, his thought patterns change. This was it. All of it. What *he'd* worked for. And he had no intention of losing it, to anyone or anything.

Suddenly, with an unusual fierceness, he kissed her, deeply, long and hard, pulling her body against the full length and weight of him. She permitted him to engulf her with his strong arms, their shelter offering her a welcome sense of protection and security. His lips covered hers and she broke away from his embrace for a second before coming back to another series of searing kisses which caused her to moan into the side of his neck.

Pam walked down the hallway, carrying her customary clipboard, moving at a brisk pace. Her eyes scanned offices on both sides of the corridor as she sought Adam for a few words about the manner in which to handle their response to the preliminary fire report that would be released later that afternoon. She slowed her gait when the sounds of passionate romance caught her ears. Her hand went nervously to her finely tailored gray business suit, tugging at the lapels.

With the stealth of a leopard stalking prey, she crept closer to the office with the open door, murmurs of soft talk and flickering shadows, hoping not to see what she knew would be there. She halted several steps from the entrance, swallowing hard, fighting for air.

"Adam," she expelled in a long hot breath of air as she stepped into the office to find Simone and Adam locked in a feverish kiss, their arms wrapped around each other as if their lives depended upon it. Her face grew flushed and finally contorted into a massive scowl while she attempted to blink away the unbearable vision before her.

The lovers heard someone enter and turned toward the open door. It was the anger and madness in her expression that caught them by surprise. They eased back from her slowly—reflexively.

"You bastard! How could you do this to me!" Pam shrieked.

Adam's eyes tightened in confusion. "What the hell are you talking about?"

She walked toward them, her eyes flashing with rage. "You told me you loved me," she said in a low, dangerous whisper. "You told me. Admit it," she suddenly screamed, making them both recoil. "Tell her," she ground out.

"I don't have anything to tell her, Pam. Whatever it is you thought we had is over. It's been over. You know that."

"Liar!" She turned on Simone. "Does he tell you that he loves you in a way that he never has any woman in his life? Does he say that he can't imagine living without you in his life?" She tossed her head back and laughed maniacally, then slowly sobered, her unfocused gaze singling out Simone. "If you knew what I know, you wouldn't want a damn thing to do with him."

Simone glanced at Adam and moved away from him. "What is she talking about, Adam?"

"Simone, believe me, I don't know what all of this is about. She's crazy."

"Crazy! You know what I'm talking about. Don't

even pretend you don't. Tell her how you've been working for the other side, how you've been feeding information to McCall's boys almost from the beginning of the race, how you let them know her daily schedule, how you're playing the stoolie for the Feds. Tell her, you snitch, tell her.''

"I'm calling security." Simone turned to walk toward the desk, placing it between Adam and her while she reached for the phone. As she dialed, he leaped at her and snatched it from her hands. She struggled briefly, but his strength proved too much for her.

"No, I can't let you call until you listen to me," he shouted, glaring at Pam, who was standing in the middle of the room with her arms folded across her chest.

"Ask him, Simone, how did the press know everything before they were officially told," Pam yelled. "Ask him."

"I don't know what she's talking about, Simone. I swear I don't. Pam, is this all because our little fling didn't go any damn where? Is this some sort of twisted payback? Who's the one really working on the other side? Tell us, Pam."

Her crazed stare darted back and forth between Simone and Adam. "We are. You and me." She nearly bent in half spewing her accusations at him. "You seduced me, then used me in your scheme to ruin Simone. I had no idea you'd go this far. Someone could have been killed the other night. You never thought of that, did you, Adam?"

Adam was furious and he quickly closed the distance between him and his accuser.

Simone screamed.

Chad and Samantha heard the scream the minute they alighted on Simone's office floor from the elevator. Chad took off, with Samantha hot on his heels, and burst into Simone's office an instant before Adam reached for Pam's throat.

CHAPTER THIRTY-EIGHT

Alerted by the chaos of the disturbance, a pair of building security men and a member of the Secret Service rushed into the office. They moved with startling speed to quell the action. Quickly assessing that Simone was not harmed, the security men proceeded to take Adam and a hysterical Pam into custody, while the agent radioed for backup.

A deadly calm settled over Simone as she watched the unbelievable unfold in front of her eyes. It appeared as someone else's nightmare. This was the man she'd slept with, thought about loving, someone she trusted. And Pam, she was her close friend as well as a trusted employee. She hired Pam to apprentice with her so Pam could learn the ropes through practical work experience. And now. . . . A shudder rippled through her and Samantha held her a bit tighter. The metallic click of the cuffs locking into place made her wince, but she felt no sympathy or compassion for either one of them. They tried to kill her, destroy her campaign, destroy the evidence for the suit. Why? Why? Nothing could adequately explain this betrayal to her. Nothing.

"Don't do this, Pamela!" Adam shouted as the security guard herded him toward the door, his hands cuffed behind his back. "Simone, listen to me. I didn't have anything to do with this."

She didn't want to hear it, couldn't hear it.

Adam struggled violently with the guard, who jerked his arms up to use the advantage of intense pain from the manacles to subdue him. He groaned and submitted to the guard's will. Pamela was also being brought to the door. For a long dramatic moment, they stood facing each other. Adam stared into her eyes, putting the anguish in his heart into his glare. He hoped to find the woman he once thought he knew, hoped to find any remnants of reason within her. Why couldn't he reach her? What had so hardened her heart and twisted her mind?

"Pamela, please, don't do this. Don't. I've done nothing to you to deserve this."

"We could have had everything," she mumbled distractedly to herself.

"What are you saying?" he asked almost too eagerly, his gaze darting for a moment in Simone's direction.

"I did it for you," she whimpered. "For us. I found a way. They said if I helped them we could have had all the money we wanted. We could have gone away together. All our dreams could have come true."

Chad gritted his teeth in disgust and started to lunge at her, snatch the truth out of her. Samantha saw his reaction and clutched his sleeve, rapidly shaking her head no. Adam appeared to be getting through to her. Any distraction now could ruin any hope of finding some measure of truth. Chad reluctantly backed down.

"Help who, Pam?" Adam demanded.

"McCall . . . and the others . . . from the government." Her body heaved and convulsed as sobs consumed her.

"All right. That's enough," the Secret Service agent said. "We'll sort all this out when we get you both down to the precinct. If what you're saying is true, young lady, you may want to retain the services of a lawyer. But all of that can be resolved downtown."

At the main entrance, the group was met by three D.C. police officers, who escorted them both out in the parking lot into two cruisers. Samantha and Chad stood with Simone near the doorway and grimly watched the police convoy stop at the intersection, wait for the light to turn green, then turn onto another thoroughfare.

Justin replaced the receiver on its base. He turned to face the shell-shocked occupants in his living room.

"Adam was just released. No charges filed. Pamela has been charged with conspiracy, and she's naming names."

"I still can't believe it," Simone said miserably. "Right under my nose."

Justin took a seat next to Vaughn. "As the saying goes, keep your enemies close."

"Right, but even more than that, she was out of her mind. Obsessed." And for a moment, she saw herself in Pam, a self that could have taken on a different shape had she continued with her own fixation about Chad and his relationship with Samantha. She shuddered at the possibility.

"What do you think they'll do about McCall?" Samantha asked.

"I'm sure the Board of Elections is launching an investigation even as we speak. He'll be taken care of."

"And the fire?"

"We may never know," interjected Vaughn. "But when Congress reconvenes, I will put a motion on the floor for an independent investigation of any government agency possibly involved in this, then we can determine if any of Pamela's allegations are true. With her working both sides of the fence, it will take awhile to sort things out. McCall had as much reason as the government to see that the files and the case never saw the light of day. I'm sure once the wheels are in motion, the rats will quickly abandon ship before they're caught. But at least they'll have been put on notice."

"Can I refill any glasses or anything?" Mia asked, playing hostess to the emotionally and physically exhausted group.

"No" was unanimous.

"What we still have to worry about is the case. How are we going to put the material together in time for the court date?" Samantha asked. "It's impossible. And it's my fault. It was my responsibility to take care of it. Why didn't I take the copies?" she berated herself, slapping her palm on the arm of the couch, then pressing her fist to her mouth.

Mia looked from one worried face to the other, confused by their distress. "You mean the records and all the data for the suit?" she asked in a soft voice.

"It's all gone," Simone said morosely. "Whoever set the fire made sure of that."

"At least the briefs are in the safe at my office," Justin noted. "Those will get us in and heard."

"But I have all the information," Mia said, still a bit confused by their mood.

Everyone looked at her at once. "What?"

"I have all the information, the lists, addresses, statements, all the notes." She turned to Samantha. "You know I like to work from home sometimes. I made a copy of the disks and took them home to finish."

Samantha's eyes lit up. Deliriously happy, she jumped up from her seat and wrapped Mia in a bear hug, raining kisses all over her face. "You're an angel, a lifesaver!'' she babbled. "Thank you, thank you, thank you.''

"Amen,'' Simone shouted. "Finally something to celebrate.''

With the first ray of sunshine in days, the group took a moment to revel in their victory.

And even as Simone joined in with the plans and relieved laughter, she felt the heavy weight of Adam's absence.

CHAPTER
THIRTY-NINE

The next two days leading up to their day in court was grueling at best. Journalists virtually camped out in front of Simone's, Samantha's and the senior Montgomerys's households. The phones rang incessantly. Chad and Justin sat up until the wee hours going over every inch of information they'd gathered. There wouldn't be any second chances.

In the midst of it all, Simone began looking for a new chief of staff . . . and a press secretary. She'd yet to hear from Adam. He hadn't returned any of the numerous messages she'd left on his machine, and he didn't answer the door when she'd gone to his house.

Could she blame him? If he'd reacted to her in

the same way that she did in the office that fateful morning, she would be doing the same thing. He'd asked her to believe him and she'd shut him out. Always willing to believe the worst. For the past few days she'd repeatedly asked herself why, why was it so easy for her to cast a shadow of doubt on anyone who came close to her? She'd done it with Chad and she'd done the same thing with Adam—shut him out, tuned him out. She knew where part of it stemmed from: her own youthful insecurities, her fears of emotional attachment that could be taken from her at any time without warning. As much as she'd loved her foster parents, the idea that they'd never sought to adopt her all those years had left its mark. Yes, there was a reason: they knew her natural mother, Vaughn, was out there, and her grandmother, Sheila, was paying them not to adopt in the hope that Simone and Vaughn would one day reunite. The reunion finally occurred but the emotional damage had been done. God, she wanted to get past it all. And she'd almost done it. Almost.

The limousine pulled to a stop in front of the district court building where a crowd was already gathered on the steps. Simone could see the photographers massing at the first sight of their car, their flashbulbs popping in erratic bursts that could be viewed even behind the tinted windows. She reached across to the opposite seat and took Samantha and Chad's hands. "This is it. What we've been working for."

"What happens here today is destined to change

the course of civil rights history in this country," Chad said slowly, solemnly. "None of it would have been possible without the help and support from the both of you."

Simone looked down for a moment, then at the couple in front of her. "There's just one thing I want to say before you go in there and kick butt." She paused. "Be happy . . . don't take anything for granted . . . and just enjoy every minute you have together. You never know when the next one will come."

Before either could respond, Simone stepped from the car, cut through the gauntlet of press and up the courthouse steps, followed by Chad and Samantha, who were immediately descended upon by the vultures.

Simone reached the top step and looked up. *Adam.* Her stomach tumbled and she suddenly felt like a pimply high school teen on her first date. She took the last step and stood in front of him.

He looked down at her for a long moment, and then his grim expression slowly softened and the deep lines appeared beneath his eyes. "I was hoping you wouldn't mind some company in court and maybe I could think of something really clever for you to say to the press while we sat there on those hard wooden benches."

Simone's throat constricted. "I-I'd like that . . . very much."

He cupped her chin. "I love you, Simone. And I would give anything to take back all that's happened, any role I've played. What happened with me and Pamela was a long time ago."

"We have all the time in the world to talk about it," she said. "And I'm ready to listen."

Justin was already seated when Chad and Samantha entered the courtroom. One entire corner of the room was reserved for press. Under normal circumstances, the bulk of those seats would be empty. They were not. This was no normal circumstance.

Justin stood as Chad approached the table and shook his hand. "You ready for this?"

"Ready as I'll ever be." He glanced over his shoulder and spotted Samantha seated next to her stepmother, Vaughn, three rows back.

"I love you," she mouthed.

"Me too," he returned, realizing he honestly did, with all his heart. She was planning to visit her mother after everything settled down and try to find a way to bridge the gap between them. He hoped that they could.

The court clerk came through the side door and commanded the members of the room to stand. "Judge Irving Stone, presiding."

"This is it," Justin whispered to Chad.

Chad nodded and drew in a breath of resolve, took one last sweeping view of the courtroom, this house of esteemed justice, and silently prayed that the words, the passion that he felt in his heart would reach out and touch everyone present.

Judge Stone had been on the bench for more than twenty years. He was known to be hard but fair. He looked out at the young man before him and across the courtroom to the attorney representing the D.C. police force. He cleared his throat and adjusted his half frames on his nose, his steady gaze honed onto Chad.

"Counselor," Judge Stone intoned.

Chad straightened. "Chad Rushmore for the people, your honor."

"Are we ready to begin, counselor?"

"We are, your honor," Chad replied in a strong, clear voice.

"You may begin."

Slowly Chad moved from behind the desk to stand at the podium set up in the center of the courtroom.

"Your honor, I stand before you today to ask you to become a part of history, a part of change, by strengthening one of the basic institutions of our American democracy: that of law enforcement. Our goal is not to indict this country's deeply felt commitment to a political system that guarantees the rights of every citizen regardless of race, religion or creed. Our goal is to bring to bear the might of the victim, seek a legal remedy which can serve as a catalyst for change, as a warning to those who are in the continuation of police misconduct against the very people they are sworn to protect.

"Too many of our citizens are losing their lives in this ongoing conflict between police and the African American community, and that cannot be tolerated.

Our critics insist we are seeking to further divide the races, to aggravate the tenuous relationship between those two parties, but that is quite far from the truth. We will produce substantial evidence to back our claims of widespread violations of the basic rights guaranteed to all of us by the Constitution and the Bill of Rights. We don't seek to stir up passions on both sides of this argument. We only want reform, we only want justice, we only want what is rightfully promised to each and every American. Today, we are taking our first big step toward achieving that aim and we only ask the court give us a full, honest hearing, with the hope that what we do here during this legal journey will spark a national dialogue on this most pressing of civil rights issues.''

Chad paused, feeling the weight of history upon his broad shoulders, as he glanced around the courtroom. Several people seated behind him were in tears or on the brink of some form of emotional display. Reporters wrote furiously in their notebooks. This was a big moment. The first step. And once they cleared this hurdle, they would take their case to the national level and ultimately come face to face with the law machine itself: the United States Justice Department. Once the significance of it all registered in him, he continued with his argument, calling for an end to the cycle of police and civilian suspicion for the sake of the country.

"We begin in this house today, your honor. But it won't stop here. It cannot."

Judge Stone stared at this daring young man for a

long, hard moment. He couldn't begin to imagine the struggle that lay ahead of him, but he had every belief that whatever it was he would take it on.

"Anything else, counselor?"

He turned behind him and looked at all the faces who'd come out to support him. Samantha, the incomparable woman he'd come to love beyond reason, the family who'd embraced him and the people who supported him. Yes, there was plenty, he thought, his chest filling with pride. One day at a time.

AD TK